Accidents will happen . . . but will they happen twice?

As I stepped out the rear door, trying not to grin at thoughts of lounging in my very own claw-foot tub, I bumped into the invisible man. Well, I suppose he wasn't really invisible, but he was so fair and so pale that he seemed almost translucent. I could almost have sworn that the postal uniform was walking on its own.

"So, it's you," he said.

"Sorry?"

"The new one. You are the new one."

I stared. "The new what, exactly?"

He blinked and raised his pigment-free eyebrows. "Maybe I shouldn't have said anything."

"About what?"

As he walked past me into the house, he said with a small, reassuring smile, "I'm sure everything will be fine this time. That other thing might have been an accident for sure."

This time I stared at his back and watched as the dark old-fashioned door closed behind him, leaving me more than a little creeped out. Our postman just drops off the mail. He doesn't walk right into the homes on his route.

Almost an accident?

Why did everyone in the Van Alst vicinity speak in riddles?

And what kind of accident?

THE
CHRISTIE
CURSE

VICTORIA ABBOTT

BERKLEY PRIME CRIME, NEW YORK

THE BERKLEY PUBLISHING GROUP
Published by the Penguin Group
Penguin Group (USA) Inc.
375 Hudson Street, New York, New York 10014, USA

USA / Canada / UK / Ireland / Australia / New Zealand / India / South Africa / China

Penguin Books Ltd., Registered Offices: 80 Strand, London WC2R 0RL, England
For more information about the Penguin Group, visit penguin.com.

THE CHRISTIE CURSE

A Berkley Prime Crime Book / published by arrangement with the author

Berkley Prime Crime Books are published by The Berkley Publishing Group.
BERKLEY® PRIME CRIME and the PRIME CRIME
logo are trademarks of Penguin Group (USA) Inc.

For information, address: The Berkley Publishing Group,
a division of Penguin Group (USA) Inc.,
375 Hudson Street, New York, New York 10014.

ISBN: 978-0-425-25528-5

PUBLISHING HISTORY
Berkley Prime Crime mass-market edition / March 2013

PRINTED IN THE UNITED STATES OF AMERICA

10 9 8 7 6 5 4 3 2 1

Cover illustration by Mary Ann Lasher.
Cover design by Olivia Andreas.

ALWAYS LEARNING   **PEARSON**

For Giulio Maffini, our miracle man. Welcome back!

ACKNOWLEDGMENTS

We are grateful to so many people who helped us in the course of this book. Some brought information, others inspiration, while many shared the kind of support and friendship you need to write a book.

Thanks to mystery readers and book collectors everywhere and to the booksellers and dealers who help them feed their habit. But special thanks are due to Jeff and Donna Coopman of The Usual Suspects, Don Longmuir (and family) of Scene of the Crime, Maggie Mason of Mary Mason Bookseller and Dee Suchall for insight and "intel."

Wendy Bartlett and her colleagues at the Cuyahoga County Public Library showed us the potential of a proper attic in the right mansion at the South Euclid Branch and inspired Jordan's garret.

We appreciate our lovely, supportive agent, Kim Lionetti at BookEnds, and at Berkley Prime Crime, our always urbane editor, Tom Colgan, the very helpful and capable Amanda Ng and our brave, mysterious copyeditor.

Thanks to our pal Erika Chase and our friends in the Ladies' Killing Circle, Mystery Lovers' Kitchen, Killer Characters, and

Crime Writers of Canada who have been so supportive in a tough year. With Linda Wiken, we share a love of collecting books that has been known to end up in the purchase of a bookstore.

Much gratitude is due to Kory Webber, Pat Connolly and Doug Martin for endless support and to Giulio Maffini for his amazing Lazarus routine.

We would also like to pat each other on the back because we are still alive, smiling and plotting away, ready to launch our first collaborative effort and knee-deep in the second, *The Sayers Swindle*. We have to admit, any errors are entirely ours.

Last but not least, where would we be without the great Agatha Christie? She taught generations of readers and writers to look at everything and everyone differently and gave the world her enduring legacy.

CHAPTER ONE

❖

IF I HADN'T been desperate for a job and a new place to live, I might have made a run for it as soon as I got a good look at that sour face. But I was feeling the pinch, and in a sea of want ads seeking waitstaff, topless dancers and telemarketers, this job description was clearly written for me.

RESEARCHER REQUIRED

Discreet, flexible and educated individual required to research documents and artifacts. Must be free to travel, and possess valid driver's license and reliable vehicle. The successful applicant must be willing to relocate to Harrison Falls, New York. Accommodation will be provided. Do not bother to reply unless you have an excellent grasp of the English language. Knowledge of Latin will be considered a distinct asset. Good personal hygiene and formal wardrobe required. Should be able to cope with irregular schedule. Must appreciate cats. No allergies please. Three

*references, official transcripts and other documentation to
be produced at interview.*

The inscription on my master's degree was barely dry,
much like the red ink on my student loans. My former
mooching boyfriend had maxed out my credit card before
I'd managed to catch on and dump him. The only thing
healthy was my run of bad luck. I could feel my PhD possibilities receding. There wasn't much call in our area for
an enthusiastic graduate in English with a minor in languages and a fondness for Jane Austen and the Brontës. I
had all the qualifications, and my family is nothing if not
discreet, for reasons that are nobody's business but our own.
Plus my references were solid. I was already back in Harrison Falls, and I figured I could always fake the cat thing.
There was no clue as to who was offering this position, but
I figured I had nowhere to go but up.

I MUST HAVE made the right impression because I was
instructed to present myself for an interview with Miss Vera
Van Alst at three in the afternoon, Thursday, May 17, a mere
two days after I'd sent my application to the PO box address.
Apparently, everyone in Harrison Falls knew exactly who
Vera Van Alst was. My own relatives were very happy to
fill me in about the Van Alst Shoe Company, now sadly
defunct, and the devastating impact of the failed business
on the community. The general opinion was that if there'd
been awards for arrogance and ineptitude, the Van Alsts
would have won them hands down.

Now Vera Van Alst was the only one left.

I pasted on my best interview smile, adjusted my posture
and headed for the imposing house from which she and the
Van Alst family had lorded it over the town of Harrison Falls
for a hundred years. I already knew it wasn't going to be easy.

The massive dark granite building had umpteen white-trimmed bay windows, a conservatory, crenellations and faux turrets. It gave new meaning to "imposing." As I approached, I was struck by the scent of fresh-cut grass, possibly my favorite aroma in the world. A middle-aged man with a straw hat was riding a tractor along the front lawn of the house. I smiled and waved. I got a curt nod in response. Oh well, I figured he would be kept busy keeping that vast property groomed.

The reception didn't get any better.

When the paneled oak door swung open, a gray-haired, pointy woman in a wheelchair looked up and eyed me as if I was something brown and gooey that had attached itself to one of her wheels. She hadn't bothered to introduce herself, but I knew from my research that she was Vera, the last of the Van Alst family, and possibly the most hated woman in Harrison Falls.

Once again, my smile had been a waste of energy, and by now it was starting to hurt my face.

"I was expecting a man." Beside the wheelchair a conceited-looking blue point Siamese cat glanced over its shoulder and licked its fur in disdain.

I kept my cool. "Understandable mistake."

Vera Van Alst showed her teeth and enunciated in a peculiar voice. "Jordan. That's a man's name."

How would I describe that voice? Like crunching gravel? A cascade of pebbles? It would take some getting used to, as would her attitude.

I said, "A man's name? Not in my family. I'm named after my mother." I didn't mention that my mother had been Jordan Kelly, as the Kelly name was probably enough to get me booted out the front door. As they say, you can choose your friends but you can't pick your relatives.

"Jordan Bingham? I don't know any Binghams. Humph, with that black Irish coloring, I would have figured you for a Brennan or a Ryan. But it doesn't matter because you are not at all what I had in mind."

My coloring? I figured there was nothing wrong with having pale skin, dark hair and blue eyes. I decided to ignore any ethnic slurs about my appearance, because I was *exactly* what she had in mind, and if she didn't know that, I did. You don't need testosterone to read Latin. Time to steer the conversation away from my heritage.

"My, what a beautiful cat," I lied.

Vera Van Alst seemed to soften slightly, and I took that opportunity to step further into the house. I noticed that there was a serious security system by the entrance. My potential employer did a one-eighty in her wheelchair and headed across the grand foyer. I had nothing to lose. I followed her as we turned left and rumbled down a long dim corridor, past looming portraits of what must have been dead and disapproving ancestors. There would be no possible esthetic reason for displaying them otherwise. Apparently, the cat also disapproved, judging by the flick of its tail as it preceded us down the hall.

This time, I inhaled the scent of furniture wax and old roses. We passed what I took to be a ballroom, a sitting room and a gallery of sorts before reaching what she called "the study" on the left. Miss Van Alst wheeled into the large room. Uncomfortable Victorian furniture hugged the twelve-foot-high walls. Much of the wall space held clustered portraits of even more disapproving ancestors. What had caused those expressions? Dental problems? Constipation? Whatever. In my humble opinion, that was one scary gene pool. The cat, seemingly reading my mind, flicked its tail yet again and sneered in agreement. It was a relief to glance at the tall Georgian windows, flanked by faded silk drapes, which had possibly once been red. Outside, the vast green lawns looked very appealing, but they were not why I was there.

"I have my references and other paperwork." I reached into my deep-orange vintage leather satchel.

Miss Van Alst replied, "Not that it will make the slightest difference to me. I am looking for a man to do this job."

I held out the documents in their crisp envelope. She waved them dismissively toward a spectacular desk behind her. Unless I missed my guess, it was Edwardian. Carlton House almost certainly. It would take at least fifteen grand to buy that baby today, and from my preinterview research, I was pretty sure Vera Van Alst's great-grandfather had purchased it when he furnished this massive pile of stone back in the late nineteenth century. I had inherited my uncle's ability to appraise valuables upon first sight, though I tended not to use this skill to the same ends. Someone in the family had to go straight.

On the walls around the room were shadowboxed memorabilia from the Van Alst Shoe Company. Old grainy photos of Van Alst men above tarnished brass plaques hinted about a proud past and thriving business. My uncles would practically spit on the ground and swear at the mention of the Van Alsts, but I really wasn't sure how the family fortunes had slipped. I thought better than to pry during my interview. Vera didn't seem like the type to swap family stories, so I snapped back to attention.

As I placed the envelope on the desk, the cat leapt up and settled on it, stretching out a back leg and continuing with the cleanup. The perfect job was growing warts, but it didn't matter, because I was in no position to be picky. A mental image of my future self in a paper hat cleaning a commercial deep fryer steeled my resolve to win her over. She swiveled slowly in the wheelchair. Her beady eyes narrowed. She said nothing. I was struck by the sharp contrast between her ratty appearance and the gorgeous, priceless and, yes, dusty antiques that surrounded her. I knew from experience that many people with the best minds care nothing for personal appearance. However, Vera Van Alst seemed to be doing her best to look her worst. Her bland, worn wardrobe aged her by decades. The holey elbows and frayed cuffs of her dull beige sweater didn't help. Judging by the style of the shoulders, I figured she'd had it since the mideighties. I waited. Nothing.

I decided to push my luck. "I think you'll find that I will do a better job than a man."

"Better than a man? How so?"

I took a deep breath and rattled on. "I graduated summa cum laude. I minored in languages. I worked in the rare book room at my college. I've held rare and wonderful writings in my hands. Wearing white cotton gloves, of course."

"Bah. You'll have to do better than that."

Of course, I couldn't give her any of the real reasons why I was suited for the job.

"I am educated, well spoken and have had considerable responsibility in my life. I have good instincts for finding things and information. And I want to work for you."

I didn't say it was because of the Carlton House desk or because I was desperately broke or that there was no way I could live with my uncles on a permanent basis or that I was terrified of yellow paper hats.

She stared at me without blinking. Finally, she broke the silence with, "You have two weeks. Don't disappoint me."

I hoped she didn't hear me exhale in relief. Clearly, she only respected strength.

"I'll need to know what the job will involve."

Vera Van Alst whipped around, and the creases surrounding her lips grew deeper. She wheeled toward the desk and picked up a file. "You may as well sit down." She pointed to a Victorian fainting couch upholstered in amethyst velour. I figured the color had started out as a regal purple.

I lowered myself carefully onto the faded fabric. The couch squeaked in protest. To tell the truth, I'd felt more in control standing up. Which she knew, without a doubt.

"I've heard whisperings of a manuscript that—"

The door flew open with a bang, scattering dust particles. A small, round, doughy-faced person pushed a tea cart into the room. She was dressed in black with a wide white apron and, at a guess, she was somewhere on the high side of seventy. Her hair was an unlikely shade of ebony and pulled back into a tight bun. Except for the bun, the hair might have been painted on her head. She stopped and placed her hands on her wide hips. "Tea is serve, signora."

Vera waved her away. "Not now, Fiammetta. We are right in the middle of something important."

"Yes, yes, yes. But now tea."

That seemed oddly dismissive. I felt a swell of admiration for this pushy apple doll.

"Tea can wait."

"No, no, no. Teatime. You must eat. Eat now."

"Fine. Then will you leave us alone? Jordan, this is Signora Panetone. Do not allow her to bully you."

I could hardly stop myself from drooling at not only the fine Georgian tea service and the antique tea trolley, but also the astounding contents. There were cucumber sandwiches, shortbread cookies, fruit, a cheese plate and a chocolate layer cake. I wondered who would be joining us. A committee of some sort? A football team? But apparently no one.

The small, round woman turned to me and said, "*Mangia*. Eat." She pointed a pudgy finger at me. "You. Eat!"

And she meant it.

Who was I to argue with authority? Of course, I was dying to know what manuscript was being whispered about. However, that would have to wait.

Fifteen minutes later (and three return visits with extra food), we finished up. Miss Van Alst had eaten like a bird. I had also eaten like a bird. A really big bird, say, a turkey vulture.

"If you're finished gorging yourself, perhaps we can get back to business."

I didn't fall into the trap of defending myself.

She said, "Take it away, Fiammetta. I never want to see food again."

"Yes, yes, yes. Dinner at eight."

"So," I said, digging deep for my alleged Irish charm, "whisperings?"

Vera Van Alst's face lit up. For the first time, her brown eyes sparkled. "There is a rumor of something very special. Just a rumor, but I must know. If it is true, I must have it. Hence you."

"And it would be?"

She took her time, savoring every word.

"You *do* know Agatha Christie's work, of course."

"Oh yes," I bluffed. Who on the planet hadn't heard of Agatha Christie? But the last mystery I'd read had been a Janet Evanovich. More my era. Good explosions.

"Naturally you recall her mysterious absence in December 1926."

"Naturally." Um.

Vera leaned forward and lowered her voice into a deeper layer of gravel. "She never spoke of it, you know."

"How intriguing. Although maybe not much of a stretch for a mystery writer."

"Now it seems that she wrote something during that time." Postcard? "Oh really?"

"It has surfaced."

"A book?"

"Of course not," she barked. "Not enough time for a book. Only eleven days."

"Short story?"

"No. But you do know that two previously unknown stories were found among her notebooks not long ago at Greenway, her home, in Devon."

I nodded to express "of course" without actually having to tell another whopper, although whopper telling is in my DNA.

But Miss Van Alst wasn't paying attention to me anyway.

She said, "I did my best to obtain those original manuscripts, but I was not successful." Her fists clenched and unclenched. Important, I guessed. "But I can't allow this one to get away."

I had to ask. "I understand. But what is it?"

"A play. They are saying she wrote a play. I must have it. I must. Do you understand? No matter what." Vera looked as though she could spring up from her wheelchair and perhaps float in the air.

I did understand. I know exactly how it is to want things that are just out of reach.

"What if it's not for sale?"

"Everything's for sale."

I thought she might be right about that. "There will be competition."

"Oh yes. Many people might kill for something like this."

The hair on my neck stood up.

Kill? "Okay. And what do the whispers say about its location? Who owns it? Do you have any leads?"

She raised her eyebrow and curled her lip, not a good look for her. "None at all. That's what I'm paying you for."

Well, what do you know. I seemed to have passed some kind of test.

OUR NEXT STOP was the Van Alst library. Not the wonderful old brick main library in downtown Harrison Falls that had been endowed by the Van Alst family in the early nineteenth century, but the in-house version. It appeared to be about a half-mile farther down that endless corridor in what was apparently called the east wing. I hurried to keep up with Vera Van Alst, who was a speed demon in that wheelchair. The cat could barely keep up. Even rushing after the speeding wheelchair, I couldn't help but notice more signs of disintegration of the house. A curling bit of wallpaper

here, a damaged bit of woodwork there and a faded rectangle every so often indicating a painting had been removed.
For repair? Or sale? For sure, no one in their right mind
would buy one of the framed Van Alst ancestors, no matter
who had painted them, but some of the oils in this wing
looked well worth a second glance.

It had been years since the Van Alst Shoe Factory closed.
The rumor was that the Van Alst funds were pretty well
gone, which might explain the fact that the only newish items
I'd spotted were the security system panels. Even the phone
in the library was a black rotary number.

On the other hand, this massive house and the manicured
acreage must cost a bomb to run. The other tale around town
was that Vera had received an insurance payoff after she'd
been badly injured in a car accident and that kept her going.
Was it true? Harrison Falls is a boiling cauldron of gossip
at the best of times, and gossip as we all know can't be
confused with fact. Was Vera selling off assets to keep
going? No way to know. Yet.

I decided that as long as she had the money to pay me,
all was well, because apparently, I was already on the job,
whatever that would turn out to mean. Unlike the rest of the
sprawling house, which was well past its glory days, the
library showed no sign of neglect or decay. An additional
security code was required to open the keypad that con-
trolled the door lock. Vera kept her back to me as she entered
her code. Inside, the room had its own climate control, and
the temperature was cool compared to many homes. Of
course, it was actually warmer than the rest of this damp
and chilly house. Why was I not surprised?

Vera Van Alst wheeled abruptly in her chair. "I want to
make it perfectly clear that there is never any food or drink,
and by 'never any,' I mean not a single crumb or a drop of
liquid in this environment. It doesn't matter what blatant
attempts Signora Panetone makes to entice you; one violation
of this policy and you are gone. Understood?"

"Absolutely."

"She will try."

"Noted. And I will resist. As I mentioned before, I have worked in a rare book room. I understand the dangers that food and drink present. I am no fan of rodents. You can count on me to respect your policy." For once, I was telling the truth.

She nodded.

"I can see you take excellent care of your collection," I said, determined to keep the conversation going in a positive direction. I admired people who looked after whatever it was they collected. I understood and appreciated that there were soft cotton gloves to be worn when handling books, although some would argue about this. "Is the climate control just for the library?"

"Fluctuations in temperature are very bad for books." She scowled at the thought of uncontrolled heat and cold inflicting damage.

"Of course." I nodded knowingly.

"Insects," she added darkly. "They can flourish if the temperature fluctuates."

Insects? My shiver was genuine. She spotted that and seemed to approve. I was mining my brain for what I remembered from the rare book room in my college library and the fears that haunted its guardians. "Acidity too," I said.

Vera Van Alst inhaled. "We are very careful."

"And I see you have no natural light here."

"Of course not," she said as if I had suggested hosing down the collection. "Think of the damage all that ultra-violet could do."

"Indeed. And I am sure that you needed the space those old windows would have chewed up."

Vera's forehead furrowed. "There's never enough space."

"Did you insulate when you closed them off?"

"Naturally. Although from the outside, it looks as though they are normal windows with drawn drapes."

I smiled approvingly. I might even get to like this job.

"We keep the relative humidity at fifty percent," Vera said, pointing in the direction of the dehumidifier.

I thought I appreciated books, but this was an altar to the book gods. It was hard not to be impressed. I didn't know what had the most impact: the rosewood shelving, the rolling library ladders, the mezzanine floor with the ornate spiral wrought-iron staircases at each end, the carved moldings, the scent of well-loved books, or the silky Aubusson rugs in a soft faded palette of rose, sage and aqua. More to the point, there must have been twenty thousand books there, each one obviously cherished by the collector. This place was Disney World for the book lover. I inhaled the intoxicating scent of old paper, polished leather and money well spent.

A small bronze statue of a naked man reading a book in a chair also caught my eye. I have always liked bronzes, perhaps because so many have passed through my uncle Mick's "antiques" shop.

I figured the rest of the Van Alst house could crumble around the pointed Van Alst ears and Vera would only retreat to the library. I was starting to understand how she felt. I hated to leave the room and the collection. It would have been a perfect experience if the cat hadn't orchestrated a sneak attack and raked its claws across my ankle.

MY OWN APARTMENT-TO-BE was part of the old servants' quarters, located on the highest level of the central part of the house. Signora Panetone led the way up the two flights of a dark narrow back staircase to the third floor. The staircase started between the kitchen and a rear door to the building. This was a far cry from the broad gleaming curved stairs in the front foyer. No question that this staircase led to the servants' quarters.

I was to use this entrance and park in the rear of the

building. I'd been given a key and my own security code for front and back entrances, plus a separate one for the library.

"Yes, yes, yes, no," the signora muttered, teetering slightly whenever she spoke. Nothing she said seemed to require a response.

I would be getting a very good workout hiking up and down those stairs. I might need to invest in some sensible shoes, although that would have been an extreme solution for me.

The attic apartment would never make a magazine cover, but it only took a minute to fall in love with the slanted walls and the sense of lives lived. As a bonus, the rooms were spotlessly clean, no doubt made so by Signora Panetone. The windows looked out on the manicured grounds. The ancient cabbage rose wallpaper was artfully faded. Needless to say, there was no keypad or security code needed to access my new digs.

I would have a small sitting room with well-worn and practical furniture: a striped love seat, a leather club chair with a lived-in look and a few brass lamps. I was pretty sure that Victorian rolltop secretary desk would be very collectible. I opened a drawer and admired the dovetailing before I checked out everything else. There were no books or personal effects anywhere and no coffee table either. I find a space without books and beloved items to be somewhat eerie, but I was imagining my own books here. If this situation worked out, I could bring in my bookcase. A bar fridge, microwave, small sink and open shelves were tucked into one alcove. The bedroom was spacious enough, with an oval braided rug covering the wide plank flooring, an ornate iron bedstead and a pretty green sprigged pattern on the well-worn fabric of the bedspread and curtains. Good thing the pattern was small and delicate, because the cabbage roses on the ancient wallpaper could flatten any competition. The freestanding dark wooden armoire could hold my wardrobe if I played my cards right. The rest of it could be stashed in the walnut dresser in the far corner.

The part I liked best was the bathroom. It must have been a bedroom originally because it was as large as the other two rooms. I felt instant lust for the claw-foot tub and the 1920s-style sink and mirror, even if the latter was slightly foggy. The plumbing worked, more or less. I figured I could ignore the bell in the living room. This was the twenty-first century after all. Servants didn't have to dash downstairs at the first ding to answer some ridiculous order regardless of the time of night. At least I had a home again. Well, for as long as I could stand Vera Van Alst and her project. And vice versa.

The Siamese purred past me, its tail sweeping against my leg just before it disappeared. I edged away, and it shot me an insulted glance before it jumped on the bed. I didn't trust it not to rake its claws across some sensitive spot. Cats were new to me. I'd never had a pet, although I'd cried and wailed for one as a child. The Kellys don't do pets. Doesn't suit the lifestyle.

And I wasn't planning to start with a furry creature that liked to leave scars.

Cat or no cat, I was thrilled and surprised at getting the job and amazed that I actually wanted it after meeting my new employer. But I did want it. I adore a challenge. And now I'd get paid for it. I found myself hoping that things would work out.

AS I STEPPED out the rear door, trying not to grin at thoughts of lounging in my very own claw-foot tub, I bumped into the invisible man. Well, I suppose he wasn't really invisible, but he was so fair and so pale that he seemed almost translucent. I could almost have sworn that the postal uniform was walking on its own.

"So, it's you," he said.

"Sorry?"

"The new one. You are the new one."

I stared. "The new what, exactly?"

He blinked and raised his pigment-free eyebrows. "Maybe I shouldn't have said anything."

"About what?"

As he walked past me into the house, he said with a small, reassuring smile, "I'm sure everything will be fine this time. That other thing might have been an accident for sure."

This time I stared at his back and watched as the dark old-fashioned door closed behind him, leaving me more than a little creeped out. Our postman just drops off the mail. He doesn't walk right into the homes on his route.

I've never seen him attempt to reassure anyone.

Might have been an accident?

Why did everyone in the Van Alst vicinity speak in riddles?

And what kind of accident?

CHAPTER TWO

❖

A FAMILIAR BUZZ in my pocket indicated a text from Tiffany Tibeault, my closest friend.

How's the job hunt?

I took the three seconds to answer. We always replied, no matter what, a steadfast rule since college. Reply and make it snappy or Tiffany will send out a search party.

Fill you in tonight . . . how's life in the Great White North?

Tiff had settled into a northern Alberta pipeline camp, making good use of her degree in nursing. The girl had guts. She was always up for a challenge and never one to wait and see what happens, Tiffany had leapt at an opportunity to erase her student loans with a stint in the frozen wasteland. The wages were amazing, and there was nothing, and I do mean nothing, to spend your money on. My shrewd friend would be sitting pretty in under a year.

Stellar ;) Chat tonight xo

When I'd entered my first day at college, I dreaded meeting Tiffany Tibeault. Since mid-August when dorm assignments arrived in the mail, I had been making myself miserable with one question: what kind of a person has a name like Tiffany? She would probably be the high-maintenance type, narcissistic, shallow and brimming with vapid conversation about nail polish. I was determined to hate her, but Tiffany was nothing of the sort. Her firm grip paired with her genuine smile put my month of fears to rest. A jeans-and-T-shirt girl studying nursing, Tiffany was the most gracious person ever to come out of the state of North Carolina, which is saying a whole lot. She also loved to brag that her Canadian roots gave her an uncanny ability to chug beer and drive in snowstorms, although not at the same time. We were thick as thieves before one box was even unpacked.

Life gave me a break and I spent my college years with this kindred spirit, who had no issues with my eccentric family and my resulting crises. She folded me neatly into her world, my first true "girl" friend. No doubt my social skills had been hindered by my entirely male, but not entirely law-abiding, upbringing.

I knew we'd video chat tonight and laugh ourselves senseless at both of our nontraditional work situations, and I knew she'd be incredibly jealous that *I* was getting to go to the Harrison Falls Public Library and with good reason.

Now, back to work. Of course, now that I had a job, I couldn't continue to pretend to know what I really had no idea about. You can fool some of the people some of the time, but something told me you couldn't fool Vera Van Alst for long.

First step: find out as much as possible about Agatha Christie before the next morning. If my cards hadn't been maxed out thanks to the ex, I might have blown a bundle at the bookstore, but instead, on the way home I hit up the most well-read person I know, the spectacularly hot librarian currently lighting up the Harrison Falls Public Library: Lance DeWitt. Luckily Lance was on duty.

"Hey, yeah, Jordan, everyone knows about Agatha Christie's disappearance."

Everybody *so* does not.

"It was a big deal then."

"Imagine if Stephenie Meyer vanished for eleven days."

"Eleven days? Did she really do that?"

"Not Stephenie Meyer or you would have known about it, but Agatha Christie did. She went completely MIA, and then she was found in a hotel at a famous spa. Poof. There was never any satisfactory explanation for what had happened. Remember this was before spin doctors and TMZ. People used to get their news from this thing called a newspaper. This story was splashed over front pages around the world."

"I am familiar with newspapers, Lance, but thank you for the teaching moment. So it was a big story?"

"Huge. Some people thought her husband had killed her. He had a mistress he wanted to marry, so he was pressuring Dame Agatha for a divorce at the time and she wasn't so keen on it. The whole world followed her disappearance."

"Eleven days."

Could a person write a play in eleven days? Sometimes it takes me two weeks to compose a text message.

"You want to know about it? We've got every book on the topic. Want me to select some for you?"

One thing you could say about Harrison Falls Public Library, the service was good. And easy on the eyes.

Five minutes later I staggered out to my car with far more than I'd ever wanted to know about the late great Agatha Christie. It was going to be a long night. Still, I was in a good mood because Lance had that effect on me. Always.

I noticed a police cruiser up ahead as I drove along Bird Street and as usual when that happens, I made a sharp, and unplanned, left turn to take a different route. Five blocks and three turns later, there he was again. I recognized the officer in the patrol car. I'd seen him around since I'd come home, and he seemed like a friendly and even harmless type, but in my family, we never want to attract the attention of the cops. Especially the type who can anticipate your left turns. Was I losing it or did Officer Whozit just smile and wave? That was more unnerving than spotting flashing roof lights in the rearview mirror.

I shivered and drove off, taking a few more unexpected turns as I went.

OVER FRANKS AND beans in my uncle Mick's kitchen, in back of his "antiques" shop, I defended my job choice. The early evening sunlight glinted off the gold chain nestled in Uncle Mick's ginger chest hair. It complemented the green apron that said "Kiss the Blarney Stone," with a downward-pointing arrow under the text. I feel safe to say that the besotted customers of Michael Kelly's Fine Antiques would never see the real Mick Kelly, and that was probably a good thing.

"You're a disgrace to the family, my girl," Uncle Mick said, plopping a second helping on my plate.

I shrugged. I love franks and beans. It is Uncle Mick's specialty (the secret ingredient is ketchup), and I didn't want to ruin dinner. "I need the money, and it's not like I'm becoming a cop or anything."

Uncle Mick turned pale. His freckles stood out in sharp relief against his white skin. His franks-and-beans spoon shook. "Becoming a cop? What are you trying to do, kill me? Don't even joke about something like that."

Across the crowded kitchen table, Uncle Lucky shook his head, which I usually interpret to mean "just ignore your Uncle Mick." Uncle Lucky is always on my side, but he's not the biggest talker.

"Those Van Alsts brought the whole town down and nearly ruined this family to boot and you're going to be taking money from them? Thank the good lord your mother never lived to see that."

"Even better that she missed out on knowing that your last Russian bride walked off with Grandma Kelly's rings."

"What do you mean, 'last'? There was only ever the one, and it's just a matter of time before Svetlana returns them. She's a decent girl at heart."

I hoped that Uncle Lucky didn't choke on that frank. I needed him alive and on my side.

"Look," I said, "I realize that everyone in Harrison Falls hates the Van Alsts and no doubt with good reason, but Vera must have been just a young woman when that factory shut down. She couldn't have been responsible. Anyway, she's in a wheelchair now, practically a senior citizen. And she is going to pay me well. This job means I can go back to school. *That's* what my mother would have wanted."

Of course, I had no way of knowing what my mother would have wanted as I didn't really remember her, but I had to talk as though I did, because my uncles are not above using her supposed wishes to discourage me from one course of action or another.

Don't get me wrong. I was grateful to my uncles for raising me and making sure I got an education up to the point where the money dried up in recent years, for a number of reasons we won't go into here. But they trained me to make unpopular decisions. If you're a Kelly in Harrison Falls, you need to be tough. And sometimes marginally reckless.

Uncle Mick opened the pantry door and reached for one of the bottles of Jameson eighteen-year-old whiskey. I wondered what truck they'd fallen off. But what I don't know won't hurt me.

"What's the job?"

"I'm supposed to find an unknown and unproduced Agatha Christie play. Any ideas where to start?"

Mick said, "Who owns it?"

"No idea."

"Who's selling it?"

"We're a bit light on details. It might be just a rumor."

Uncle Lucky raised his thick eyebrows. A distinguishing feature shared by all the uncles, the eyebrows were ginger and practically had personalities of their own. Lucky nodded toward Mick. I'd grown up listening to all my uncles trash the Van Alst family. I knew they'd have trouble with my choice, but they'd just have to get used to it.

I said, "She's an obsessed collector and she wants it. She has the money to pay for it and to pay me, so what's the problem? She's not taking advantage of me. Think of it as me taking advantage of *her*."

I wasn't actually planning to take advantage of Vera Van Alst, but this notion played well to my uncles.

Mick is always one to find a silver lining, particularly if the silver belongs to someone else. "I suppose it never hurts to have a man on the inside."

Lucky smiled.

"That's me," I said. "Our man on the inside."

Mick said, "I thought Agatha Christie wrote books. I get boxes of them in the shop when people clear out their bookcases."

"She's most famous for those, but she was a successful playwright too. To tell the truth, I have a lot of research to do. There are people who make a career out of her work."

Mick said, "You can only get so far reading."

We didn't always agree on that point.

I said, "I also have to talk to people in the know. People who might be aware of a manuscript like that if indeed it was for sale."

Lucky drummed his fingers on the checkered tablecloth.

I knew what he meant. Get to the point. I added, "If this play is for sale and it's just being whispered about, there must be a reason and one big one comes to mind."

Mick said, "Make that two."

Lucky nodded gravely.

"Right," I said. "Either someone's running a con or the thing is hot."

Uncle Mick poured himself two fingers of Jameson and said, "Lucky's right. Guess you should go see Sal."

I glanced at Lucky, who had said nothing of the kind.

Lucky shrugged. He's used to Mick pretending to read his mind.

Sal, I thought.

Oh no.

Although I've heard plenty about Salvatore Tascone, I hadn't actually seen Sal since my First Communion, but I knew he'd welcome me with open arms. Uncle Mick was right. There wasn't much going on in this part of the state that Sal didn't get wind of.

"Okay, I'll go see Sal. Does he have an office in town?"

Lucky nodded.

Uncle Mick lit a Cuban cigar and said, "I'll make the call. He owes me a favor. But you be careful, Jordan. You don't want to be in Sal's debt."

HOME IS WHERE the heart is. In my case, although I loved my uncles dearly, my heart was not in the bachelor apartment above Uncle Mick's garage, to the left of Michael Kelly's Fine Antiques and to the right of Uncle Lucky's digs. Sure, it was simple, clean and the price was right. No one would ever dare break in. All positives. Of course, no date would ever make it successfully past the uncle patrol, and I was young, single and still had hopes of a normal life. All to say, I was looking forward to getting out.

Even so, I knew my small space would be waiting for me if I ever needed it again. My uncles are nothing if not loyal, but I wanted to get moved into my new digs as soon as possible and get down to work.

Vera Van Alst wanted this elusive and possibly imaginary play *now*. Sure. But she was a collector. She'd want something else the minute she had it in her hands. And she was in no position to get out hunting for it herself. I had a chance to get on my feet without the collective Kelly breath on the back of my neck. I packed up my belongings quickly and efficiently, keeping in mind the two dark and narrow flights of stairs. Uncle Lucky helped me lug my books, computer and suitcase, and a small midcentury Lucite coffee table I had borrowed from the "antiques" shop.

After a cold and rainy spring, we finally had one of those perfect May evenings. I felt energized by the sun streaming in through the dormer windows. I'm not usually one to care about the view, but the glimpse of the spring garden was spectacular. The man in the straw hat was now kneeling on a pad and dead-heading the spring bulbs that had already bloomed, and carefully spreading what looked like cedar mulch around the beds. The scent of lilacs drifted on the air. I was in an excellent mood. I had that "summer is coming and anything is possible" feeling. By the time I wrestled my clothes, still on hangers, up the stairs, Uncle Lucky was hoofing it to his car. Vera Van Alst would have to be pretty sharp before she caught sight of him.

I found myself humming as I finished hanging my mostly vintage clothing in my old-fashioned armoire and settling the rest in the small walnut dresser in the alcove against the far wall. I was having fun already.

I settled half the Agatha Christie reference books by the bed and the rest on the Lucite table. I love the look of that table and the way it blends into any environment, including my new late-Victorian garret. I tried not to speculate as to how the perfect table had fallen into Mick's hands. The less I knew about its provenance the better.

Agatha's possible play? That was another story.

Next I curled up on the feather bed and got to work. Agatha Christie. Her name was synonymous with mystery. To tell the truth, my own tastes were contemporary and I wasn't sure I'd actually ever read an Agatha Christie book, although I felt I knew about them. My impressions were probably based on Miss Marple or Hercule Poirot movies or television programs on flickering VCR bootleg tapes from PBS, watched while I was a child. My uncles had loved the British vibe. Uncle Mick always leaned forward with a gleam in his eye. Probably gave them a good sense of authenticity for the "antiques" business. Of course, Hercule Poirot or Miss Maple might have been onto their tricks in a flash in real life. But I needed to know much more.

I dove into my project asking myself what was there about Agatha Christie that would lead a stranger to want to collect her unpublished work. Secretly, of course. Because it was obvious to me that Vera Van Alst was off the deep end over this play.

By midnight I had a stiff neck from reading in one position. That was a small price to pay because I now knew about the mysterious eleven days that had gripped the attention of the world, about Christie's stay at a spa in Harrogate, Yorkshire, under an assumed name, which was oddly enough the name of her husband's mistress. I liked that. I'd laughed out loud at the thought of Agatha Christie's fellow guests staring at her photo in the papers and discussing the disappearance as she sat right in front of them, dressed to the nines. I had to hand it to her. Nicely done. But, it had been only eleven days, and she'd spent a good part of that dining and playing cards. Had there really been enough time to write a play?

Although, so far, there had been nothing about a play being written during this time period, the books were very intriguing, which I had been happy to discover. Bless our good buddy Lance and his knowledge of the topic. Fairly recently, an admiring author had uncovered a treasure trove of notebooks while researching in Greenway, Agatha Christie's home in Devon. Lance had handed me the admiring author's book, which described what was in those notebooks and how the contents related to Agatha Christie's life.

Agatha Christie's Secret Notebooks sounded like a piece of fiction itself, although it was very real. I was fascinated to see how her famous novels had developed and something of the process she used. Better yet, while exploring the treasure trove of notebooks, the author had come across two unpublished short stories. Vera had alluded to those. I was glad to know how they had come to light. No one had even guessed they existed. But as one famous guy once said, the play's the thing. Of course, that hadn't ended well. So far there was nothing to confirm or even suggest a new play, although it now seemed more possible. So why had it taken over eighty years for this particular, and still hypothetical, play to show up? Where had it been? Why had it surfaced now? What were the chances that this wasn't someone trying to con Vera Van Alst out of what was left of her inherited stash? That seemed more likely to me. God knows I'd seen enough of that kind of thing. On the other hand, I'd been hired to find the stupid thing, not disprove its existence.

If I were a con artist, I'd sure be targeting obsessive collectors like her. Planting a rumor is an honored part of the con tradition. I knew all about collectors' lust from my visits to Uncle Mick's "antiques" shop. Vera Van Alst was a committed collector with deep pockets. Was she also a mark?

From what I'd seen, she was shrewd and tough. Time would tell. As I went back to the books, I was growing more and more curious about my predecessor. The postal carrier had said an accident. What kind of accident? Maybe he'd been eaten alive. I'd have to check that out.

In the meantime, I decided to celebrate my new digs with a bath in that amazing tub. The pipes clanged and rattled as I filled it. As least hot water was not in short supply in the Van Alst household. That was excellent. I was really glad that I'd brought my vanilla and amber bath salts. I let myself soak in the tub until I relaxed and the tight muscles in my neck recovered.

Later, I spotted a note on the small demilune table by my entrance door as I padded, yawning, through my tiny living room heading for bed. I hadn't heard anyone knock. But someone had clearly entered the apartment while I was luxuriating in the tub. For one thing, a Siamese was watching me from the club chair. I opened the door and peered out. The narrow staircase leading to my charming staircase was in utter darkness. Even when I flicked on the overhead light, there was barely enough illumination to see. I was pleased when the cat skittered past me, through the entrance and down the stairs. Had Signora Panetone teetered up the two flights of stairs again? Did she have any comprehension of privacy?

Thursday, May 17

Dear Miss Bingham,

I breakfast at eight in the conservatory and you will be expected to join me. We shall use the opportunity to go over your plans and strategies for the day.

Should you be unable to attend breakfast, please let Signora Panetone know the evening before.

Sincerely,
Vera Van Alst

I WAS JERKED awake by the phone near the bed. That was too bad because I'd been just about to marry Jake Gyllenhaal.

"Breakfast is at eight. Did I not mention that?" Vera Van Alst said in a tone that no one would argue with.

I glanced at the clock. Seven forty-five. "I'll be there."

In my experience, no one gets a master's degree without being able to shoot from bed to class in less than twenty minutes.

She said, "Good. I'm looking forward to hearing your strategies."

My strategies? What *were* my strategies? And why was there a cat in my bed? I had shown the cat the door. Had the signora stuck her head in this morning while I was sleeping? The Siamese seemed less than pleased to see me up and about and skittered toward the door, growling loudly. I dodged it, barely managing to avoid a slash of claws.

One of my early strategies would be getting a slide lock for my entry.

CHAPTER THREE

❖

SIGNORA PANETONE DEPOSITED three perfectly poached eggs in front of me. Bacon, lightly fried home-made bread, thick slices of tomato that must have been fresh from some unseen hydroponic garden, all appeared like magic. Steam rose from the *cafetiera* as the signora topped up my cup with fragrant espresso. I inhaled the rich aroma.

Maybe my predecessor had died of clogged arteries and caffeine intoxication.

I glanced over at my new boss. She was wearing another ratty ensemble from her yak-herder beige collection. The soft sunlight in the conservatory wasn't doing her any favors, and she obviously didn't feel like talking. In case I had been tempted to start up some idle pleasantries, the fact that her pointed nose was stuck in the *New York Times* would have been a clue not to. It's hard to compete with the crossword.

Well, never mind that. The conservatory with its view of the gorgeous east side garden of the Van Alst house more than made up for Vera's lack of social skills. I liked the ceramic floors, the three walls of windows that started at knee length and the French doors with their own security pads. I admired the large potted lemon trees, thriving. And was that a fig tree? I figured the signora cared for the trees, as well as the rows of some kind of seedlings on the wide, low window ledges. I felt like I was in heaven, even if Vera didn't share my opinion.

From my seat, I got a glimpse at a peculiar group of low structures in a sheltered spot near what I took to be the kitchen door. It was the only less-than-perfect aspect of the Van Alst garden. Of course, we Kellys do not garden, so what do I know.

Every now and then, I glanced at Vera. While I had wolfed my breakfast, not a crumb seemed to have moved on Vera's plate. The *NYT* seemed to hold her attention. It took me by surprise when she finally spoke.

"What are your findings thus far?" Vera's gravelly voice seemed set on permanent growl. It suited her.

Signora Panetone said, "Yes, yes, yes, no, no. You must eat. American breakfast. Why do you leave it there? Eat. Yes, yes. *Mangia. Mangia!*"

Vera swatted her away. "Findings, Miss Bingham?"

Playing fast and loose with the term "findings," I said, "Well, my initial findings are that this will require caution. We need to confirm the existence of the manuscript, and then we will want to rule out forgery, fraud and other gimmicks."

I saw a small flash from the dark eyes. "I'm glad to see you are not as naïve as you look."

"Well, thank you." I admire a well-aimed left-handed compliment as much as the next person and Vera Van Alst was obviously very skilled at lobbing them. I decided to take advantage of the moment. "I meant to ask yesterday, if you have any other Christie manuscripts or—"

"I do not."

So much for that. I could tell by her tone that she wasn't in the mood for small talk, and I didn't want to reveal how little I really knew about the topic of Agatha Christie and her work.

Luckily, Signora Panetone had plopped down yet another small mountain of still-sizzling fried bread. I reached for it.

Signora Panetone said, "Yes. Eat. Good."

There was something else I needed to know, though.

"I'm curious about my predecessor. Was he naïve?"

"No, no, no, no talk," Signora Panetone said. "More coffee?"

Vera scowled. "I don't remember mentioning a predecessor."

"More egg? Yes, yes."

"No," I said, to both. "You didn't. But your mailman did."

"Oh, that Eddie McRae. Never knows when to keep his mouth shut. None of anyone's business."

I couldn't have agreed less. "So what did happen to my predecessor?"

Vera said, "As it turned out, he went out with a bang."

I stared at her. That didn't mesh with Eddie McRae's comment.

"Coffee, yes, yes," said Signora Panetone, filling my coffee cup.

Vera said, "In that he managed to get himself hit by a train."

Signora Panetone stopped serving and made the sign of the cross. "Poor boy."

Vera ignored all that.

"The country mouse wandered into the city, stumbled into the subway, was attacked by a homeless person, lost his footing and plummeted onto the track in front of an oncoming train. I trust you have no balance issues and a rudimentary understanding of the laws of physics and how trains work."

Wow, cold-blooded. "I'm quick on my feet and have no problem using the subway safely. I'm good with planes too." Something was not right there, for sure. If he'd been smart enough to get the job, you'd think the poor doofus could take a subway without getting killed. And what kind of employer would talk like that after a tragedy?

Signora Panetone crossed herself once more to be on the safe side. Was that because of the death or merely Vera's untouched plate? Hard to know.

Vera Van Alst showed no empathy about his passing, and I didn't really appreciate the black humor. It would have been a nasty way to go. But then, Vera had all the warmth of a trout caught yesterday. Never mind, I didn't have to like her; I just had to cash her checks.

"And today's strategy?"

A cat brushed against my leg. I jerked away before I got scratched, but all I heard was a contented purr. A trick, no doubt. I wasn't likely to fall for that.

"I'll start with some online snooping and then begin to visit contacts. Shake things up a little bit."

She nodded.

"Do you have wireless Internet here?" I asked.

"No."

"Do you have any Internet service? I should have checked yesterday."

She shrugged. "Why would I? I don't need a computer. I despise all this electronic folderol."

I bit my tongue so I didn't blurt out, "Because you are not the only person in the world." Instead I said, "That 'folderol' will speed things up if I can do much of my computer research here. That would give me flexibility."

"You'll have to find another way. That will be all, Fiammetta. Stop hovering." She wheeled back from the table. "Good day to you, Miss Bingham."

Right.

AFTER GATHERING UP my materials for a day on the prowl, I headed out. I decided to detour and take a walk around the side grounds. I was curious about the structures I could see from the conservatory.

Up close the whole setup seemed to be made of leftover bits and bobs from other projects. I spotted pieces of battered fencing, some old wire hangers and a pair of plastic milk cartons, one red, one blue.

A middle-aged man in a straw hat was leaning against a shovel. I recognized him from the ride-on mower, and I figured he was the same guy who'd been working in the tulip beds.

"What is this?" I said.

This time he grinned at me. "It's Fiammetta's vegetable patch."

Of course, it could only have been Signora Panetone's garden; nobody else would have had the nerve to carve out this untidy little patch amidst the immaculate Van Alst gardens, let alone eat produce grown on the property of the most hated woman in Harrison Falls. Even I knew that gardens were full of plants in neat rows. I'd seen pictures. I said, "It's not like other gardens."

He nodded. "It's a Fiammetta special. It's like nothing else in the world. That's why it's tucked out of sight, so that Vera can't see it messing up the grounds."

What was I missing? "It's different. Why aren't there any plants in it?"

"I guess you're not a vegetable gardener."

"That's an understatement. In my family we believe that vegetables come from cans. Fruit too, although some of it seems to grow in Jell-O and Pop Tarts."

He chuckled. "Well, until this week, the weather's been bad. It's been too cold and wet to plant much for most of the spring. Once we're past Memorial Day, you just watch. She'll grow tomatoes like you've never tasted in your life."

"I can't wait." I wasn't sure I really believed it, but I was looking forward to being proved wrong. "And I'm Jordan Bingham, by the way. I work here now on Miss Van Alst's collection."

"And I am Brian Underwood. I take care of the grounds and the gardens, and I do repairs and maintenance. Nice to meet you, Jordan. And good luck to you. You'll need it."

For all I knew Brian would go running back to Vera with whatever negative things I said. I kept it neutral. "I'm enjoying it so far."

"Well, look out. You never know when Vera's got a black mood coming. Been like that for the twenty-five years I've been working here. You just have to grow a thick skin. And watch your back. She has a dangerous streak. Fiammetta, now, she's thrilled to have you. Says you're a real good eater."

I STROLLED BACK along the elegant driveway that wound around the Van Alst house from the spectacular wrought-iron front gates to the rear entrance. I stopped at my vintage blue Saab, as pretty today as when it first rolled off the line in 1960. It had been passed from my grandfather to my mother and had been waiting for me the day I got my license. My Uncle Paddy dabbles in classic cars and kept it purring like a kitten. That car was the closest I'd ever come to having a pet.

Harrison Falls being what it is, I was back at Uncle Mick's in fifteen minutes. I kept my eyes on the road during the steep drive up the hill. It was a gorgeous spring morning: the sun was bright, the sky blue, the air full of promise and the scent of fresh green leaves and grass. Everywhere I looked, peonies were delivering their spectacular blooms. Spring in upstate New York seems to take too long to arrive, but it never disappoints when it finally does. By nine thirty that morning I was settled in Uncle Mick's cluttered back office, ready to start creeping around the Internet. I turned down his offer to enjoy a double feature of Froot Loops and Count Chocula for breakfast. Ditto the instant coffee. Despite their fondness for "antiques," my uncles are early adopters of every form of electronic communication, including some that are less than legal, but never mind that. I figured I'd get one of them to hook me up in the garret without Vera being any the wiser, but in the meantime, I needed access and privacy.

I was eager to get to work. I did hope to ferret out some scraps of information about this play. I needed some hint about its existence. There had been no inkling of a previously unknown play, even in Agatha Christie's own notebooks, as far as I could tell. Of course, I hadn't had time to make a real dent during my first evening of burrowing through the pile of information I'd gathered. Still, the right search engines can pull up information that is unofficial, unverified, as well as inaccurate and downright dangerous. I looked forward to it.

But first, I wanted to check out my predecessor, the country mouse. And now I had enough information to do that.

It didn't take long for Google to spit out a number of articles related to deaths in the subway. My predecessor had been Alexander Fine, a twenty-eight-year-old recent graduate of Ithaca College. He was from Darby, just ten miles away from Harrison Falls, and his parents still lived there, so naturally our local paper had covered his death thoroughly. I had missed the drama, being in the middle of end-of-term madness and marking, studying and writing like a maniac.

In the article, my new employer was interviewed and showed her usual level of compassion. She did manage not to make a joke, so I supposed that was to be commended in a limited way: *When reached for comment, his employer, prominent Harrison Falls resident Vera Van Alst, said, "It was a stupid thing to happen. A waste."*

And then I assumed she released the hounds on the reporter.

Witnesses said during a hostile encounter with a deranged homeless man, Mr. Fine was pushed into the path of an oncoming train. His fiancée, Miss Ashley Snell, tried unsuccessfully to save him and had to be held back. The homeless man had already fled the scene with Mr. Fine's laptop bag.

Another article featured a photo that showed the devastated fiancée, long dark hair disheveled, her face distorted by grief, weeping, while emergency workers milled around. What a powerful illustration of the tragedy. Of course, it wasn't the best circumstance for a flattering photo. It appeared that Ashley Snell was a donkey-faced girl with unfortunately close-set eyes and more teeth than mouth, but I put that down to a nasty photographer on some kind of a power trip. Some people are like that. The paper went on to say that Miss Snell was still suffering from shock and was requesting that people respect her privacy.

No kidding.

I couldn't even imagine dealing with those vultures after you'd been coping with the horrendous death of your fiancé. And what kind of unfeeling monster would use that photo?

I didn't know the victim, his parents or his fiancée, and I still felt bad for all of them.

The picture of Alexander Fine showed a man in his late twenties with dark hair, a receding hairline, large expressive eyes fringed with dark eyelashes and a slightly feminine pointed chin. The dark circles under the expressive eyes added a few years to his age. In his photo, he looked like he was about to apologize to the photographer.

I wondered what he'd been doing in Manhattan. Had he had a line on the Christie play? If so, why hadn't Vera mentioned that? She must have known if he'd been in the city on business for her.

I reminded myself that it took only a few hours to drive to New York City. It could have been a romantic outing for a young man and his fiancée that ended in tragedy. But somehow I wasn't buying that.

As I was the new Alexander Fine, it seemed a good idea to make sure I knew what had really happened to him. Apparently the police didn't. Later articles showed there were no leads on the homeless man and the police had no suspects, although Alex's empty laptop bag had been discovered in a Dumpster the day after his death. Had it been a random theft of a laptop for a quick buck, or was there something more going on?

I wondered if it was too soon to run into Miss Ashley Snell, accidentally, of course, while still respecting her privacy.

I bookmarked a couple of articles and got on to strategy number two.

Sal.

Flipping open my phone, I zipped off a quick text to Tiff. *Number 10 Bridge Street.*

SALVATORE TASCONE'S NAME was nicely scripted in gilt on the door of Number 10 Bridge Street. I opened the door and walked in. Like everything about Sal, it was discreet. No indication, for instance, of what line of work he was in, if you know what I mean. The reception desk was decorated with the Marilyn Monroe look-alike filing her red nails. Sal appreciated that era. Once past the platinum-blond guardian at the desk, I found myself in a room that was as far from an office as any I've ever seen. A pair of tufted green leather club chairs faced each other. I tried not to drool at the sight of them. A polished French occasional table held a crystal candy dish and Sal's highball glass, also crystal. Probably Waterford. Uncle Mick had mentioned that Sal was partial to it.

Sal looked good in his green chair. He stood up as I entered and kissed me on both cheeks. He was six feet tall, slender, elegant in his custom-tailored suits, a gentleman transplanted from 1959. Seventy, looking fifty, you'd swear he just stepped out of *Ocean's Eleven*, the original. He has always looked exactly the same: silver waves, thin face, sharp cheekbones and jaw, perfect but subtle manicure, black pencil-thin mustache, French cuffs, this time sporting Art Deco green tourmaline cuff links, a thousand bucks if they were a penny. Sal was a handsome man and one you knew you should be wary of. Forget the handmade leather shoes. Concentrate on the tight lips and the expressionless eyes. I managed not to shiver, but only barely. Sal is the go-to guy for coins, stamps, Georgian silver and anything missing from museums pretty much anywhere on the planet, despite his cozy setup in plain-vanilla Harrison Falls. In fact, Sal's face was the first thing that came to my mind when I heard *The Scream* had been stolen.

He never says much. Long pauses are a specialty. Most people start to sweat as soon as they get over their shivers.

"I hear you're looking for something, Jordan."

"Oh, you spoke to Uncle Mick."

"Not recently." He indicated the guest chair with a courtly wave, sat elegantly back in his own chair and smoothed the immaculate creases in his trouser legs.

I got the message. He already knew what I was looking for without hearing it from me or my uncle. I sat down too. "I am looking for something, but I don't know if it exists."

Sal liked that approach. He raised his eyebrows in interest, and I continued. "A matter of an unknown play by Agatha Christie."

His eyes narrowed. Sal's intense stares and long pauses tended to give me verbal diarrhea, never a good thing.

"Never produced," I said, fighting the urge to blurt.

Sal permitted himself an almost imperceptible nod.

"Maybe the only copy in the world."

He fingered his tourmaline cuff links.

"Could even be in Agatha Christie's own handwriting." Now where the hell had that come from? I wasn't even sure that Christie had written her novels and short stories longhand. Perhaps she'd typed them. Or dictated them. I reminded myself that I still had a long way to go researching what I was supposed to know.

Sal flicked an imaginary speck of dust from his snowy white French cuff.

I said, "What do you hear about it?"

Sal unbent elegantly from the chair and said, "I'll let you know."

I recognize when I've been dismissed.

I FROZE WHEN I spotted the cop idling across the street from Sal's office. Was he following me? Plenty of reasons for the cops to keep an eye on Sal, although wearing a Harrison Falls Police uniform and sitting in a marked car was a bit too obvious. But why was he smiling? Why was he getting out of his squad car? Instinctively, I flattened myself against the wall in case I'd blundered into the middle of a takedown. Caught between a cop and a bad place. But if I was trapped, then so were the three blue-haired ladies with walkers who had just emerged from the bingo hall. They clustered around Officer Smiley, looking like they were about to pinch his flushed cheeks or ruffle his wavy blond hair. He was over six feet, so they'd have to stretch to manage that. I think they were won over by his twinkly bright blue eyes. Beware, ladies, I thought.

He disengaged himself from his new fans and crossed the street. His admirers hurried to catch up. He reached out his hand toward me, and I froze in slow-motion horror as he took my hand and shook it.

Now the old ladies clustered around and turned to me. I swear they giggled. "Is this your girlfriend? Oh, she's beautiful! Childbearing hips."

"No!" I gasped, but my protest was drowned by the rattle of the walkers as they headed down the street.

Why the hell was he still holding my hand?

"Tyler Dekker," he said. The tips of his ears were glowing red. He had the kind of fair skin that was born to blush. The small chip in his left incisor just added to the charm of his smile.

I stared at our entwined hands. This couldn't be happening. And why was I feeling the heat? I hadn't done anything illegal, but there was that lifetime of conditioning.

"And you're Miss Jordan Bingham."

There was no point in denying it, but I couldn't think of a thing to say. He could, though. "Just visiting?"

"Just passing by, Officer," I said curtly, hoping that Sal wasn't watching this encounter.

I managed to be on my way fast enough that the most suspicious watcher couldn't imagine that anything like an actual conversation had taken place.

CHAPTER FOUR

J ORDAN BINGHAM, WHY am I being graced with your gorgeous presence so soon after the last visit?"

I smiled.

That Lance DeWitt was so dreamy that if the Harrison Falls Public Library decided to charge fifty bucks a reference question, they would probably have plenty of takers. I kept my voice even and overlooked the small flutter in my chest. Other women in the library glared at me. Maybe it was the double-cheek kiss. Even though there was absolutely nothing between us, I still got a rush when my handsome friend worked his flirtatious magic.

"Rare manuscripts and books, where would I find the people who know about them?"

"Still on Agatha, are we?"

"You know me, like a dog with a bone."

"Well, you could go online, but for the real inside story, let me help. There are some people you should stay away from. You think drug dealers and gangbangers can be violent, try crossing a rabid collector for his first-edition Dylan Thomas."

I knew my uncles had had a few close calls with obsessive collectors, but would that hold true for book collectors? "Just books, Lance."

"People get addicted to anything, dear Jordan, like I could get hooked staring into your gorgeous eyes."

I flushed foolishly. "Oh, come on, they're—"

"Some collectors won't part with their prizes unless you pry them from their cold, dead hand. But they'd be happy to pry a desired object from yours. No matter what the cost to them. Or you."

"I find it hard to believe there's much danger in this business."

"Where there's desire, there's always a dark side. Just be careful, Jordan."

Ten minutes later, I left the library with a fistful of brochures and a pair of trembling knees.

Ridiculous really.

I TEXTED TIFF. *Back at Mick's.*

Uncle Mick was just about to serve up Kraft Dinner for lunch when I dropped in. KD was the foundation of the food groups for the Kellys. I am a Bingham, but I've had my share. Still, only day two in the Van Alst employ with Signora Panetone's cooking and I was already being ruined for my uncles' cuisine.

I accepted some anyway. I didn't want to bite the hand that had fed me for so many years. My purpose was to make the best use of the top-of-the-line printers owned by Michael Kelly's Fine Antiques to run off some attractive business cards. It is great to be connected. And we all need the right credentials. But first, I had to spend a little time with family. Uncle Mick was in a chatty mood, not unusual. Lucky was playing his cards close to his chest. Nothing new there.

Mick couldn't wait to talk about Agatha Christie. I guessed he'd been doing his own bit of research.

"Right, my girl. You know Agatha Christie wrote *The Mousetrap*."

I was aware of that. "That's the longest-running play in history."

I knew that my uncles would have images of cash dancing in their heads. I added, "In her heyday, she had a string of hits in London's West End."

Of course, Uncle Mick had to ask the question that had been bothering me. "I know that too. So what are the chances that nobody knew about this so-called play, then?" Mick did the asking, but Lucky raised his eyebrows.

"That's bothering me too. The woman was under a microscope. I've been reading all about her. I don't know how she survived all that attention."

"So why wouldn't this play have been produced? Problems finding a backer?"

"I doubt it. I don't really know how her productions were funded, but investors would have been falling over themselves."

"Maybe she wrote it up and it was no damn good. And she threw it away and some joker found it."

"That's possible. But I get the impression from my research that she didn't throw things away. She kept all her notes and notebooks. She just reworked ideas and plots until they suited her. Sometimes it took years. And she knew what people liked."

Uncle Mick topped up my Kraft Dinner. I didn't protest. I have a fast metabolism.

"But she didn't keep rewriting this one?"

"I have no idea. I haven't come across anything that references it. And I haven't been told the story behind it by my employer." Best to keep the Van Alst name unspoken in Uncle Mick's kitchen.

Uncle Mick and Uncle Lucky exchanged meaningful glances.

I said, "It will take a while for her to really trust me and confide in me, but it will happen." I could tell that they liked the sound of wearing the mark down. "So if there is a seller and if there is a manuscript, it will have some background. There has to be a tale behind the play or no one in their right mind would buy it. Once we've heard that, we can make some kind of decision."

Mick said, "What if it just turned up in her old papers? That happens all the time. You should see the stuff that people bring in here. Some things that look like crap turn out to be worth a lot. Letters, documents. If a play turned up, I might not know it was worth something. How would I? Maybe some dealer got hold of it with a pile of whatever and just happened to decide to check it out."

"Mmm. Not too likely in this case. She had only one daughter, and the daughter had one son. So there weren't dozens of family members rooting through things, and the close family knew all about her writing business. Plus Agatha Christie's papers were kept together. Researchers have gone through everything, recently even her notebooks with little jottings. Dozens and dozens."

"No sign of a play?"

"Well, like I said, she was always reworking things, playing around until they suited her. So there are plays that turned into stories and stories that turned into plays, but I haven't come across anything that indicates that there was a play like we're looking for: complete and unproduced. I find it hard to believe it was among her papers or in her home."

Mick wasn't one to give up. "Maybe it was somewhere else."

Well, that went without saying. If it existed, logically it had to be either among her papers in her home, or somewhere else. But where and why would it be somewhere else when there seemed to be a tight lid on the Christie output? Never mind, I respected my lovable and larcenous relative too much to make a sarcastic remark at his expense.

I said, "You may be right."

Actually, I hoped he was.

After lunch, I made myself some nifty business cards on a classy heavy cream stock, with a lovely italic font. My name, Jordan K. Bingham, and my cell phone number. No more than anyone needs to know. Uncle Mick always says leave them wanting more. That made sense. Before I left, Uncle Mick accompanied me to the boxes of used books kept at the back of his shop. Someone was always turning in the contents of their late parents' bookshelves. It was a good day.

"Jackpot," he said. "Look at these, not a whiff of mildew in any of them. They're yours." I left carrying a Neiman Marcus bag with two dozen Agatha Christie titles to take home.

I also picked up my basic tool kit that had been stored with my uncles. Pink-handled tools in a matching tote. That kit was worth its weight in gold for a girl on her own. Next I stopped on Main Street at the A1 LockMaster to get a sliding lock for my bedroom door.

I headed home to my garret to check out the background materials on book collectors' gatherings that had now been added to my mountain of Christie reading. There was a note on the demilune table. The note was on deckle-edge paper, the kind Emily Post would have recommended to a young woman forty years earlier. I figured that Vera Van Alst probably had a lifetime supply of it as it would cost the earth these days. The sight of the note reminded me not to delay in getting that lock installed.

Dear Miss Bingham,

I customarily dine at eight in the formal dining room.
*   As a rule, you will be expected to join me and bring me up to date on your progress. Should you be unable to attend at any time, please inform Signora Panetone the day before.*

                                   Sincerely,
                                   Vera Van Alst

* * *

DINNER AT THE Chateau Van Alst was no porkandbean-palooza. I assumed that I was expected to dress for dinner. And dress I did. It gave me a chance to wear my mother's black silk sheath dress and her favorite black Alaska diamond cocktail ring. Simple, chic and the price was right. My mother would have been proud of me. The look was ruined somewhat by the goose bumps rising on my bare arms. It may have been a gorgeous and warm spring day, but the heat hadn't reached this part of the massive Van Alst stone dwelling. The dining room was freezing, and I should have worn a wrap. I'd definitely know better the next time.

Even though treasures were obviously vanishing from the house, the dining room was still intact. With its acres of Sheraton furniture, it could have been on display in an exclusive museum. I couldn't begin to put a price on that black oak sideboard with the dragon's head knobs, or the sterling silver serving pieces that sat on it. I tried not to stare at the pair of Chinese dogs, museum quality again, I was sure. Boy, what Uncle Mick could do with those. Molded? Reproduced as fast as you could say "Ming Dynasty" or whatever they were, authenticity guaranteed.

Vera Van Alst and I sat at opposite ends of a table that was longer than the first floor of the average family home. Although maybe it just gave that impression. Vera's wheelchair was parked by the side, and she actually sat in the chair at the head of the table. She kept her back to the swinging door that led to the mysterious and magical kitchen regions inhabited by Signora Panetone. I stared down the damask-covered table at Vera. I was glad I didn't have to iron that cloth, even happier that I didn't have to polish the Francis I sterling flatware and thrilled I still had good vision, otherwise I would have missed Vera's latest exercise in beige. I wondered how many beige sweaters with holes in

•

the elbows she owned. Nobody appreciates vintage more than I do, but Vera's wardrobe had never been enviable. Where would she have even found those sweaters? And why?

This was a table for sixteen in a room where captain-of-industry grandpa Van Alst would have hosted governors and senators and other creaky robber barons. Of course, now it was dim with only wall sconces to light the room. The elaborate silver candelabras remained unlit. I guessed we were conserving candles. But I had a full place setting of sterling silver, three crystal glasses and Royal Crown Derby china. I didn't need to turn it over to know what it was. Thank Uncle Mick for that.

"Lovely," I said, "reminds me of home."

I didn't mention the absence of Kraft Dinner, cigar smoke or whiskey.

I also didn't refer to the presence of the dangerous-looking Siamese cat that suddenly landed in the middle of the table. Vera hadn't appeared to notice, but then as she so rarely ate anything, she wasn't too concerned with germs. I fought down thoughts of toxoplasmosis and worked out a plan to keep my plate safe. The cat leapt gracefully from the table and disappeared seconds before the swinging door swung and Signora Panetone descended with a tureen of aromatic soup.

Fine sense of self-preservation, cat, I thought.

"Eat. Eat. Eat. You eat."

"Okay." I could hardly wait. The soup turned out to be a broth with some kind of small dumplings.

Signora Panetone turned to Vera Van Alst. "Yes. Yes. Vera. You eat too."

Vera said to me, "I am eager to hear what you have discovered to date, Miss Bingham."

Discovered? Wasn't this day one of the job? I had barely unpacked my bag. "Not much so far. It is a bit like chasing a ghost."

"Really? I understood you were up to the task."

"I am up to the task. First I need to find out if I am looking for something that really exists first."

Was that a flash from Vera's eyes? Scary. Things got so
quiet at both ends of the table that I thought I could hear the
gilt peeling off the antique mirrors. Of course, I may have
imagined that.

"I like results, and that's what I pay for."

Signora Panetone said, "No, no business. Eat soup. Soup
is good. Vera, you must eat. Yes."

I was grateful for the distraction. And the soup was good.
As Signora Panetone swung through the doors yet again to
scoop up my empty soup bowl and Vera's full one, I decided
that I wouldn't be joining Vera Van Alst again without something more concrete. Even if I had to pour that concrete
myself.

Minutes later the door swung open again. Signora Panetone swooped in with a platter of pasta. Spinach and cheese
and, unless I was mistaken, just the right amount of basil.

"This you eat," she said to Vera. "Yes. Yes. Tonight you
must eat."

She didn't have to ask me twice.

I realized as the last of the pasta disappeared that Vera
Van Alst was still waiting for something of interest from
me. Her own plate showed no signs of having lost as much
as a forkful of pasta. A tragedy if you ask me.

By the time Signora Panetone whisked the plates (one
full, one empty) off the table and vanished behind the swinging door yet again, I was in an excellent mood as I'd been
well fed and perhaps had even overdone it just a bit. I decided
to drop a few tidbits from my day to foster some type of
conversation. "I have been making inquiries."

Even down the length of that ridiculous table I could see
the Van Alst nostrils flare.

"I trust you were discreet."

You could be nothing but discreet with Sal. And Lance could be trusted with your life. Librarians are like that.

The cat reappeared out of nowhere and landed on the priceless sideboard. I felt a flicker of fear for the Chinese dogs. The cat shot me a contemptuous glare and licked at its fur. I knew I imagined the whispered threat in its glance. Vera paid no attention to it.

"One thing you can count on, I am always discreet."

"Yet to be proven."

The cat leapt from the sideboard and vanished into the corridor just as the swinging doors swung open again. That vanishing trick was a good one. I decided I could learn a bit from the feline.

Meanwhile, Signora Panetone was bearing down on us with her tray, containing a gorgeous antique platter— Limoges, unless I was mistaken—laden, and I mean laden, with some kind of cutlets, a serving dish with steaming rice and another with green beans.

She was somewhat dwarfed by the vast quantity of food. Delivery number three might I add. I jumped to my feet as she teetered closer. "Shouldn't I help you with this? I mean it's—"

Vera Van Alst waved her boney hand dismissively. "Save your breath."

I almost said, "What?" But I knew that wasn't the sort of thing one said to Miss Van Alst.

I did say, "But I think she must need help with that heavy—"

"No, no, sit, sit, sit. You eat, now. Sit, Jordan." Signora Panetone managed the whole platter as if by magic. I sat. I was surprised that she'd learned my name.

"You eat," she said menacingly to Vera.

Vera shrugged.

I felt I was sitting in the midst of some surreal movie. Postwar Italian perhaps, only with more food and less sex.

Aside from fending off Signora Panetone's attempts to put food on my plate, I spent the rest of the surreal movie scene trying to get some more information from Vera Van Alst about the possible play (as I still thought of it). She was nothing if not elusive.

By the time the three dessert choices arrived, I had begun to wonder if my predecessor might not have flung himself in front of the oncoming train out of absolute frustration with his employer. But I am not only a Bingham, I am also half Kelly, and if there's one thing we love, it's a challenge.

AT LEAST MY garret was warm and cat free. I sifted through the stack of promotional material for antiquarian book fairs and settled on the Antiquarian Book and Paper Fair, twenty minutes away in Grandville, at Saint Sebastian's Hall. It seemed to be a large enough fair, and I was betting that there would be lots of good stuff there. I leafed through a few of the Christie paperbacks that I'd picked up from Uncle Mick's shelves. I knew better than to try to actually read any of Vera Van Alst's treasures. I began with *The Mysterious Affair at Styles*, the book that started a mystery empire. I already knew that Agatha Christie had tried to have it published for a couple of years without success. Who would have guessed that this little book would kick off her career? I expected to be bored by it, but in fact, found myself drawn into the world of the upper-crust English for whom entertaining an endless parade of pretentious visitors seemed to be a way of life. There was something appealing about M. Hercule Poirot. I was caught up in the mystery and, to my surprise, enjoying the sly wit of the author. I put that book down and went back to the nonfiction. Sure, it was good to get to know Agatha Christie, her tricks and her trade, but I needed facts to help me find out about this play.

As I read through the reference materials, I decided one thing: Agatha Christie's life was at least as exotic and mysterious as anything she wrote. I made notes as I read late into the night. Perhaps I should have stopped long enough to install my new slide lock.

"CLEAR AS A bell!" Tiffany's grinning face shone through my screen.

She tilted her laptop to and fro trying to show me her new quarters. "These are the bunks, just me and two other girls."

"Stop moving, Tiff! It's worse than *The Blair Witch Project* on my end." I eyed the now still room. "It looks like a cold storage unit, only not as cozy."

Tiffany's face popped into view. "Oh, she thinks she's funny, does she? Well, we can't all be living in the Van La-Tee-Da Mansion, missy."

"Van Alst." I slowly pointed my iPhone around the room to let Tiff get a peek at my digs.

"Sweet mercy, Jordan! It looks like Laura Ashley and *Antiques Roadshow* were massacred over there!" All the way from northern Alberta, Tiffany's laugh filled my apartment. I missed her gentle southern teasing.

"Well, you won't hear me complain."

Tiffany panned down to her concrete floor with a single teal chair. "You'll see that we too have some items of note in our décor, my friend. For example, this chair is early nineties dental waiting room and still retains its original mock Naugahyde upholstery. It's sure to fetch tens of thousands of cents on the open market."

"Well, tens of cents anyway. Hey, I've got to get back to reading about Agatha Christie now, but I wanted you to see my new place. I love it."

"Ah, research on the dead mystery writer. Sure beats what I have planned."

I happened to know that she was headed to a bar for pipeliners that would have a ratio of one woman to every thirteen men. Tiffany practically cackled in glee.

"Cackling is not attractive in a woman, Tiff. Same with gloating. But have fun, be safe. Text me the name of the bar *and* let me know when you get back."

"Will do, sister."

I AWOKE FROM a nightmare in which Hercule Poirot was expressing his outrage as I had apparently sat on his hat. "Of course, you didn't see it, mademoiselle. You are as oblivious to my chapeau as you are to what you seek. You need to look where it will be."

As my eyes refocused, I noted the sunshine streaming through the windows. I blinked at the black-clad figure staring down at me and screamed. Leaping to my feet, I was nearly tripped by a cat circling my ankles, but I'd already used my scream on Signora Panetone.

"Why you scream, Jordan? Bad for you! Eat. Eat. You eat enough, you don't need to scream."

No arguing with that logic. Anyway, my heart was still thumping. I am not used to having people invade my space. That goes double for cats. My uncles always had a healthy fear of a teenage girl's room when I was growing up. They never came closer than the bottom of the stairs.

Never mind. There was no way I would complain about the aromatic caffe latte and the china plate of sugary pastries, fresh-cut Granny Smith apples and chunk of cheddar on the silver tray. It had all been delivered by Signora Panetone, as unexpected and boundary free as she was.

"I thought we took breakfast in the conservatory at eight," I said. "Isn't Miss Van Alst waiting for me?"

"No Vera today. Vera not well. Read notes."

Notes?

Signora Panetone pointed to the next room. Presumably, sometime during the night a note had materialized and I had been expected to read it in my sleep. This place was going to take some getting used to. Installing the lock had moved way up the list of priorities.

The tray of food was enough for a family of four, but it wasn't the only unusual element. I never thought I'd be greeting the second day of my new job with breakfast in my feather bed surrounded by cabbage roses on the wall and Agatha Christie novels and reference books piled around me, but life has a way of bringing little surprises. Signora Panetone was just one of them. The cat was another. This morning it was playful and purring, wanting a scratch behind its ears.

As I worked my way through my breakfast, I tried to get Hercule Poirot out of my mind until I realized, he was right. I did need to look where it would be, "it" being the play that might or might not exist.

But where would that be?

I didn't know, but thanks to Lance and my research, I had an idea where to find out.

CHAPTER FIVE

———❖———

A T ANY GIVEN time, I keep five outfits that can be used to bend all occasions to my favor. They have a vintage vibe, and they fall under the headings "classy," "brainy," "don't mess with me," "sexy" and "clueless." I was going for classy on this day, channeling my inner Jackie Kennedy. Everything but the pillbox hat.

The classy bit took a hit in the endless hallway as I collided with a tall woman who came around the corner as I tried to dodge the cat that had shot out at me from nowhere. Alarmed by the collision, the cat scurried back toward the front foyer.

The woman squeaked in surprise. I squeaked back.

She must have been six feet, with broad shoulders, big hands and a close-cropped salt-and-pepper haircut in an old-fashioned pageboy. She didn't seem at all pleased to see me.

"Watch out," I said, "the feline has a fondness for ankles."

Someone has to take the high road.

The cat made a liar out of me by returning and attempting

to rub up against her while purring like an outboard motor.
She stood stock still. Cat phobia, perhaps. I saw no sign of
friendliness, and I was in a hurry. But once I was out of her
sight, I wondered not just about that totally bipolar cat, but
about the woman. I assumed she'd come from the elevator
that led to Vera's private quarters on the second floor. Or
had she been in the library? Whatever, it was very peculiar.
By the time I got to the front door, there was no sign of her.

I attempted to hunt down Signora Panetone and find out,
but that proved fruitless too.

THE ANTIQUARIAN BOOK and Paper Fair was a new
experience for me. I wasn't sure what to expect. So, M. Poirot,
I thought, let's see what we can turn up. I anted up for my
ten-dollar ticket and made my way through the double doors
into a room where everyone spoke in hushed tones. Maybe
some of the sound was absorbed by the thick floral-patterned
carpeting, but I thought there was more to it than that. Even
the scent of the room was soothing: old paper, old ink and
Old Spice.

At first glance there were about thirty booths, mostly
U-shaped arrangements of tables. The tables all seemed to
be discreetly covered in royal blue cloths and skirts that
probably hid empty boxes, extra material, handbags, back-
packs and other miscellaneous and unsightly gear. From the
door all the booths looked pretty much alike, but as I began
my rounds, I could see that each one had some kind of
specialty. I would have liked to remain and finger every
historic map and faded print, but I needed to stay on task.
Three booths down, I was distracted by a display of children's books. I already was lusting after a first edition of
Where the Wild Things Are, a book I had loved as a child.
Even with the slightly faded cover and a tiny tear, it was still
nearly five hundred dollars. I couldn't afford it, but I wanted

it. I was beginning to understand how intoxicating this game could be. If it was behind glass, that just made it worse.

I made the rounds once, doing reconnaissance, something I'd learned from my uncles as a child, and discovered that two of the dealers dealt solely in mysteries. Without looking too keen on anything, I drifted back the second time. Looking too enthusiastic is the worst thing you can ever do to yourself, short of emptying your wallet down a sewer grate. I stopped at a booth called Nevermore Mysteries. Poe would have approved.

The silver-haired middle-aged dealer, with his reading glasses perched at the end of his nose, looked up at me with mild interest and then turned his attention to an alarmingly tall man in a floor-length trench coat. Or was that possibly two smaller men in that trench coat? Where would you even find one of those coats if you needed such a thing? The dealer watched with narrowed eyes as Tall Trench Coat reached down for one of the pricier items on the top shelf.

I picked up a mass-market Dell issue of *Red Harvest*, by Dashiell Hammett. Of course, I liked the sixties retro cover of the reprint. It was in moderately good shape with protective plastic on its faded cover and reasonably priced, probably because of the fading. My guess was there were still plenty of these to be had, but I knew it was a classic and decided I wanted to own it for the cover as well. I thought that I'd seen a red morocco-bound copy of an omnibus of Hammett's work in Vera Van Alst's library. I couldn't imagine how much that would have set her back. I reminded myself that my interest was in Agatha Christie's possible play, and not in one of the billion or so inexpensive Christie paperbacks that were still easily found, many of them stacked on my coffee table and beside my bed. I reached for a hardcover first edition of *The Body in the Library*. It seemed appropriate. The dust jacket looked to be in nearly perfect condition. A hand appeared over my shoulder and whisked *The Body in the Library* from my grasp. The dealer appeared to be able to teleport himself. With a tight smile and an upper-class British accent he said, "Maybe I can help you find something in your price range?"

The smile didn't reach all the way to the eyes behind the reading glasses.

"Why? How much is this?" I resisted the urge to remove his condescending head from his shoulders, knowing that he was just sniffing out weakness and enjoying the superior feeling. I made sure that feeling was brief.

"Fifteen hundred. It's a first edition in mint condition. And, of course, it's a bargain at that," he said in a voice like melting British butter.

I managed to look unimpressed, but really I was doing the math. Was this the price range that Vera paid for the thousands of books on her treasured shelves?

I said, "Nice. Of course, I have one at home without a trace of foxing and a brighter dust jacket. I couldn't resist a comparison." As if I would ever go on a scouting mission without picking up some lingo. That would have been a rookie mistake. My uncles would have been disappointed if I'd made such a slip.

He managed to keep his face from falling too far, but I'd scored my point.

He held out his hand and said, "I should have introduced myself. George Beckwith."

I had his attention now.

I added, "It has sentimental value. I bought it on a trip to London, from Ash Rare Books. Always quality, of course." My research was starting to come in handy, but I reminded myself that I had also been taught to keep the lies simple. Too much detail will always trip you up.

"In that case, you may be interested in some better quality Hammetts."

"No, I'll stick with this one. I put my money on the British authors."

He cleared his throat. "I have a lovely copy of *The Nine Tailors*, first edition, second impression only. Very little wear on the jacket. It's a bargain at five hundred dollars." He reached for and held out a book, reverently. The words "immensely successful" appeared on the yellow jacket in red. I loved it. There's nothing like confidence.

Even so, I waved it away and managed to look bored. That was on the outside. Inside I was screaming, "That's a lot of loot!" It wouldn't take many books like that to fund the next stage of my education. But I had to keep my mind on task. "I don't know. I'm in the mood for something different."

"Like what?"

"Not sure. My daddy has a lot of these, so they might as well be mine. I'm looking for something more unusual, something different. I can't describe it, but I'm in the mood for something . . . theatrical. A statement piece, perhaps."

"And your price range?"

"I want something that appeals to me. It's not about money, really, is it?" And it definitely wasn't about *my* money, not that I had any. I needed to make an impact. I knew for sure that these people talk. They whisper. They gossip. They deal in innuendo and rumor. In fact, I was beginning to suspect that Vera and poor dead Alex had fallen for this very trap.

I wanted to get some tongues wagging. And my uncles had taught me to always walk away leaving them wanting more.

"Money's not an issue. I might be back," I said, drifting toward the aisle, trying not to smile at the forlorn-puppy look that had settled on his old-dog face.

He followed. "Is there a way to reach you if I find something of interest?"

"I suppose," I said, with just the hint of a yawn.

He said, "You never know when I might find something worthy of your collection."

I sighed and pulled out my newly minted business cards. Works of art if I do say so myself. It's amazing what you can do if your relatives have the right equipment. I left him staring at it, pondering the gilt-embossed seal on the top center of the card. An Uncle Mick special. Gorgeous and devoid of any useful information except for my name and cell phone number.

I resumed my drifting about, knowing that I had his interest. So many delicious objects, so close, so tantalizing. This research was fun, and I was getting paid.

At each booth I tried a variation on my patter, dropping hints about something different and perhaps dramatic. I wanted to get some talk going in this community, and nothing gets people talking more than money and misinformation. I made sure that no one knew that Vera Van Alst was puppet master.

A half hour later, I had checked out a number of published plays. One of the dealers had a nice line of Samuel French publications.

I let myself be enchanted by some Beatrix Potter, including *The Tale of Jemima Puddle-Duck*, at eight hundred dollars, and some vintage *Rolling Stone* magazines. There was a treasure trove of *Life* magazines. I loved the stuff from the fifties and sixties, like the moon landing and Beatlemania and above all, the fashions.

Toward the end of the second row of booths, I came across the Cozy Corpse, the second mystery specialty dealer. There was no sign of the seller. Given the level of book lust in the room, it seemed unwise to leave all those delicious collectibles just screaming "steal me." I picked up a pristine copy of Minette Walters's *The Ice House*. I wondered if Vera owned a copy. I didn't remember seeing any Walters in the collection, but with twenty thousand books, it was too huge to check out with a quick visit, and I hadn't really spent much time on the mezzanine. She certainly had a lot of Sayers and the Cozy Corpse had some lovely versions, although nothing as grand as *The Nine Tailors* first back at Nevermore. There was, however, a fairly new copy of *The Mousetrap and Other Plays*. I decided I did need that. It would be a great way to get a sense of how the plays read. In short, a big help. If I could buy it. I glanced around again, but still no dealer. I decided to come back for a chat in a few minutes.

The best maps in the place were in the booth directly behind Nevermore, and I made a point of concealing my interest in the mystery bookseller, who was in a lively phone conversation. George Beckwith seemed to be groveling for all he was worth. I examined a wonderful print of "downtown" Harrison Falls in 1848 while keeping my ears open and straining to hear. He was following up. I like to stir the pot. Beckwith's buttery voice rose. "I assure you. This is the real thing. Nothing like the last time." A long silence followed and then he said, "Shall I. . . no really, I'm sure there's money to be had here. I can smell it."

I put down the print and picked up another one, smiling at the proprietor of the booth. Things were starting to get interesting.

It's thirsty work checking out gorgeous books. I headed over to Yummers, the concession stand directly across from The Cozy Corpse booth, to get a cup of coffee and a spectacularly overpriced Danish. When I bit into the Danish, I was immediately offended by the product. Maybe it had been freeze-dried? The girl at the cash register had a long, sad face. Her black-and-white uniform wasn't doing her any favors and emphasized her small, red-rimmed eyes. Her shoulder-length hair was in need of a trim. I guessed she'd noticed the look on my face because she said, "I know. Those are, like, really disgusting."

"And yet you sell them."

"Yeah. We do. And people buy them. I'd like to find better suppliers, but it's not easy around here. So what can you do?"

I tried not to be irritated and take it out on her. She was working at the concession stand, not making the decisions. I've had jobs like that too. And I didn't want to interfere with any potential source of information. There was something familiar about her. I was pretty sure I'd seen her before. Oh well. I didn't have time to keep track of everyone who might get on my nerves. Life's too short and busy. I figured she had her own troubles if those red-rimmed eyes were anything to go by.

I said, "I suppose we're a captive audience."

"Well, that's it. Where else are you going to go? I'm here all the time and believe me, there's nothing. *Boring.*"

I tossed the Danish into the nearest trash and sat down at one of the round tables with my coffee. I checked out the brochure of the event and tried not to listen to the girl on her cell phone. "I told you, people are complaining about the food. I think we should . . . What?" She lowered her voice, but I could tell her attempt at increasing customer satisfaction hadn't gone well. She had my sympathy. Times are tough in this part of upstate New York. Jobs are scarce. I could have ended up behind a counter getting an earful from customers about stuff that I had no control over instead of playing happily at a book fair. I drank my coffee and reminded myself of how lucky I was. Vera Van Alst might be difficult, but the rest of the gig was a dream.

I decided to forget the coffee and give my ears a rest. I could hear the counter girl sobbing on the phone by now. Time to move on. I hoped she wasn't sobbing because of anything I'd started, but I didn't think there was much I could do for her. I indulged myself for the next twenty minutes checking out the postcards and Edward Gorey prints. They reminded me of nights watching *Mystery!* on PBS as Uncle Lucky read *I'm OK, You're OK*, which really should have been titled *I'm OK and You Should Have Insured Your Jewelry.*

This time I found a worried-looking woman inhabiting

the Cozy Corpse. She was squinting through gold-rimmed glasses as though she were expecting a cobra to pop out of an open box of books. But as I arrived at her booth, her face lit up and she tidied the flyaway strands of wildly curling red hair that had escaped from her loose clip. She had the widest smile in the place. You can never tell by first impressions. I, of all people, should know that. In addition to the Janet Evanovich and Sparkle Hayter books, there were rows of Christies with covers I'd never seen before. British? Most of them were quite inexpensive. I had plenty of Christies still piled on my bed to be read, so I decided to look around before buying the plays.

She bubbled, "The Evanoviches and Hayters are all signed firsts, if that's your thing."

"Not really. I am looking for something a bit unusual."

"Unusual?"

"Mmm. Surprising."

"Well, I was really surprised when I realized that my fine first of *A Is for Alibi* was apparently signed by Dick Cheney."

I said, "So now *A Is for Absurd*?"

"Absurd and absolutely no chance of resale. I often wonder how it happened. I'd like to catch the prankster who did it. Sometimes people are light-fingered, but this isn't the kind of crowd that's inclined toward vandalism." She stopped, frowned and stared at the ridiculously tall man in the floor-length trench who had sidled up a bit closer to her booth. He must have felt her stare, because he sidled off in the opposite direction. For sure, there were some unusual types around there. When I had her attention again, I said, "I bet there's a market for something like that. In fact, I'm looking for an unusual piece myself."

She leaned forward, her smile growing wider. "Like what?"

"I'm not even sure. I love my rare books, but lately I'm thinking maybe a manuscript. A colleague is bragging about getting his hands on the original script of a play, handwritten.

I was jealous when I heard that. I have a nice little collection of movie scripts, but who doesn't? I like the idea that other people wouldn't own a copy of the same item."

"One of a kind. I get that."

"Something that the author would have touched personally."

"Hmm."

"I don't suppose you've got any inside scoop on that type of artifact."

"Not so far, but I'll sure have fun checking it out."

I liked her big smile and wild red hair so much, that I let my guard down. She passed me her slightly crumpled card.

Karen Smith. A nice name for a nice lady. I purchased the copy of *The Mousetrap and Other Plays* for ten dollars and watched Karen pop the money into a red metal cash box. I handed over my snazzy business card and said, "In case you come across anything that might make me happy, please call me."

In retrospect, that might have been my first big mistake.

CHAPTER SIX

❖

ONCE AGAIN, I stared down the length of the Sheraton table at Vera Van Alst as Signora Panetone hovered behind her with yet another heaping platter of mouthwatering food. Vera waved her away. But I was really hoping she wouldn't leave the room. She rumbled toward me, muttering, "Eat, eat, yes, yes." I knew that Vera was the target for that. I fully intended to eat. I'd been smart enough to wear a cashmere sweater and my boots this time. I enjoy my food more when my teeth are not chattering and there are no new scratches on my ankles.

The platter had lovely homemade fettuccine and what looked like mushroom sauce. "Porcini," she said mysteriously, "from friend."

I nodded, but made a point of not looking too interested in case that would set Vera off. I said, as the signora was heaping, and I do mean heaping, the fettuccine on my plate, "I did meet some potentially productive contacts at the Antiquarian Book and Paper Fair over in Grandville." I tried to make my efforts sound more successful than they actually had been.

Vera raised an eyebrow.

I said, "I met George Beckwith at Nevermore—"

Vera said, "A sniveling sycophant in a suit."

I blinked. Her characterization didn't sound much like the handsome silver-haired man with the buttery British voice. Snooty, maybe. "I think he wants to connect me with something. I heard him asking around."

Vera inhaled dramatically. "You didn't tell him about the play, did you?"

"Of course not. I let him think that I have money to spend, I know my stuff and I am looking for something different. I think he'll act on it."

"Humph."

I took a measured breath. "I also met Karen Smith from the Cozy Corpse."

Vera snorted. "Small-time operation. She can't be that good a contact."

"Nevertheless, she seemed interested." There was no point in telling Vera that Karen seemed very nice and helpful and had a great sense of humor, plus all that dramatic red hair and the wonderful smile. Vera would probably hold those things against her.

"Interested?"

"Yes. I bought a nice book of Christie plays from her and said I was looking for something special. Unusual."

"Did you say you were working for me?"

"Not a word. I didn't say anything I didn't have to. I think I'll get further being aloof. I did let it slip that I am a collector, like my daddy."

Vera frowned. "Is your daddy a collector?"

"No," I said, "he's dead."

That nipped the topic in the bud, as it was intended to.

"Be careful not to overplay your hand," Vera said. "Every single person you meet will just want to separate you from your money."

I was pretty sure in her case that would be true, with the exception of Signora Panetone, who was unaccountably devoted. For sure, I was there because it was a job, not because of an emotional bond. And in fact, I couldn't imagine any kind of bond developing.

I took that moment to work on my fettuccine.

Just as I was finishing, the door to the kitchen swung open and Signora Panetone teetered in with the next platter. Sole in parsley and lemon sauce, served with fluffy Italian rice. Nice.

The door was behind Vera, and I thought I spotted movement in the kitchen. Was it the cat? A tail waving? No, not the cat, something man sized. I squinted as the door closed again. Was it my imagination? The dining room was long and dim. Easy to make a mistake.

As the serving and "eat, eat, yes, yes" routine continued, I waited.

Vera grudgingly accepted about a tablespoon of food. I didn't hold back in any way. I did keep my eye on the door as Signora Panetone swung through it again. A pale, thin man, but a man. Sure enough. Leaning against the table, stood the unassuming postal carrier, looking quite at home. What was his name? Eddie? Yes. Eddie McRae, a pastel and reedy man. What was he doing in the kitchen on a Saturday night? Did Vera know he was there? She certainly didn't seem to. Should she be made aware of it? It wasn't any of my business. She was a lot of things and stupid wasn't one of them. When the door opened yet again for the arrival of dessert, something Signora Panetone called *zuppa inglese*, there was no sign of the pale postman. I knew that *zuppa inglese* meant English soup, an alarming name for a dessert, but it turned out to be a wonderful combination of ladyfingers, custard, chocolate and liqueur. It was very distracting. I didn't give the mysterious Eddie another thought.

*   *   *

SATURDAY NIGHTS USED to be for parties. Now they were for finding out what made Agatha Christie tick. They were also for fishing out my girly pink tool kit and installing that slide lock. I figured I was far enough away from Vera that she'd never hear the whine of the adorable pink drill. Of course, a cat had managed to materialize before that job was finished. How did that happen? I reminded myself that I should be more vigilant as I didn't want to end up like my predecessor. For all I knew, a Siamese cat had pushed him in front of that train and blamed the homeless dude. I stared at the cat nervously, wondering if it was planning to slash my legs as soon as I relaxed. But, despite my efforts to escort it from the room, it only wanted to purr and stick close to me. If the stakes weren't my legs, I could have relaxed and enjoyed it. But this cat's mood swings were doing my head in.

After finishing the lock installation, I set up my pile of reading, planning once again to alternate reading stories and biographical material. I was most interested in the period in 1926 when Agatha went missing. That had to be the center of this whole mystery. Eleven days. What had happened? And why?

I settled in and decided to focus on the story behind her disappearance. I knew what it meant to have a man decide you didn't matter to him. In my case, the creep maxed out my credit cards at the same time he was shredding my heart. In Agatha's, her husband made sure she knew he didn't love her. Here was a woman who had captured the attention of the world with her clever and entertaining mysteries. Yet, she was all alone when it came to her love life. It seemed that Archie Christie had treated her with contempt and considered her writing as nothing more than frivolity. I sneered at the pages as I read about his flagrant affair and his coldness to Agatha. There were theories about her disappearance. Had she tried to make him look like a murderer? He had certainly fallen under suspicion by the police. I liked that idea. Some specialists suggested that Agatha had been in a fugue state, whatever that was. I'd never heard of it. A bit more research told me that a fugue state is a rare psychiatric disorder characterized by reversible amnesia. It usually only lasts a few days.

Eleven, maybe?

According to my sources, it also involves unplanned travel or wandering, and can be accompanied by the establishment of a new identity. Of course, if you were a noted mystery writer with a husband who'd announced he was leaving you for another woman, you might be plunged into a mental state like that. Or you might be prepared to fake it. What had it been for Agatha Christie?

If she'd been in a so-called fugue state, could she have written a play and left it somewhere? Tucked under a loose floorboard in her hotel? Hidden behind a bookcase? She might have had some form of amnesia, but she wouldn't necessarily have been without her formidable skill at putting together a mysterious drama. Perhaps she'd written a play in which Archie Christie got what was coming to him. I chuckled at that idea. Slow-acting poison? A favorite. Perhaps that was wishful thinking on my part. I felt lucky that I'd been able to hang out with my best friends, drinking red wine, eating chocolate and throwing darts at pictures of my ex. Tiff had been thoughtful enough to give me a voodoo doll with some pins strategically placed for maximum effect. That's a true friend. Agatha could have done with a Tiff in her life.

By midnight, I had decided that Agatha could have written the play. In fact, I was counting on it. I got myself a glass of water and decided to hit the pillow.

The evening air was still warm, and it was an ideal night for an open window. I figured the garret would be like an oven in the summer, but now, it was perfect.

As I stared out at the garden, I saw movement. Someone

was slinking along the path toward the wrought-iron gate. I leaned forward. A thin, stooped figure. Eddie? I was pretty sure it was. Whatever he was doing here at this time of the night, he sure wasn't delivering the mail.

I WOKE UP on Sunday morning prepared to face my biggest fear. No, not the cat that was hissing at me from the end of the bed. What happened to all that purring and cuddling up? This was Psycho Kitty. I bolted for the door, unlocked it and let the ferocious feline escape, but not before it made another one of its slashes at my bare legs. For a minute, it took my mind off what I had to face. Today, I needed to find out what had happened to Alex Fine's research material. I had checked every inch of my small garret, but it sure wasn't in my quarters. I already had tons of notes, but I was sure Alex would have had his own. Wherever they were, they would be incredibly useful to me. Vera hadn't been forthcoming about them.

BREAKFAST WAS AT eight in the conservatory. I smiled at Vera as I arrived with one minute to spare.

She lifted her gaze from the *New York Times* and raised an eyebrow as if my smile had about the same appeal as a slap in the face.

"It was a beautiful night last night," I said to no one in particular as the signora hovered with pastries and coffee.

Vera grunted.

I guessed a beautiful night is really in the eye of the beholder.

"I was wondering if Alex Fine left any information here that I might build on. I am surprised I haven't found anything."

Signora Panetone leaned in close and whispered, "Eat."

Vera said, "He did not. You'll have to find out for yourself. Unless you are really less competent than you suggested in your interview. Other people wanted this job, you know."

I smiled again. "Did they?" I doubted that too many people who were capable of doing the job would be happy to put up with Vera and her surly ways. "You know, I am asking myself if Agatha Christie didn't write that play while she was in a so-called fugue state, and put it somewhere that she didn't remember afterward. That would account for the fact that no one has found it until now."

Vera glowered, but I knew she was interested.

"It might have been hidden or given to someone who didn't realize its connection to her. Perhaps someone found it in their grandmother's attic and it went out with a box of old books or papers."

She shrugged.

I said, "And Christie herself might not have been aware. If she'd been in this fugue state."

Vera nodded, trying to look totally unenthusiastic, but not quite pulling it off.

I said, "Did the person offering it for sale give you a title?"

"Perhaps I didn't make myself clear earlier. There is no 'person offering it for sale.' There is only a rumor that the play exists. No name. Just that it was never performed. No other original copies exist. And no real details. That is, if you remember, why I am paying you and providing you with comfortable accommodation."

So much for my attempt to squeeze a bit more information out of her pursed lips.

"Very comfortable accommodation," I said as I spotted a tail and tucked my legs in out of harm's way. "Excellent food too."

I grinned at Signora Panetone.

"You eat. More? More. Yes, yes. Coffee. Yes."

Vera managed to escape with barely a mouthful.

Breakfast came and went without any new information.

But it was delicious. And the coffee just kept on coming. Bliss.

What were these little games with Vera all about? Was she testing me? Why? Was there really a play? I couldn't see what she was getting out of any of it. Aside from the obsessive desire to own something that no one else could have, what was driving her?

I had more reading to do and wanted to see my uncles' mischievous faces, but I also had to make a plan to find out what my predecessor, the very dead Alexander Fine, had learned before his death.

I had two friends on Facebook: Uncle Lucky and Tiffany. Tiff was outgoing and loved to socialize, making friends with everyone who crossed her path. People clamored to be her friend, write on her wall and get her to join their groups. I occasionally received FarmVille and FishVille requests from Lucky. But I loved to watch Tiff bubble online. Still, I had felt it necessary to join this social network under a forbidden "assumed name" of Kelly Jordan.

I commented on some photos from her night out. At this moment I doubted my decision not to join her in Canada. I could be swimming in cash and pursued by hard-bodied lads too. Except for the ever-flirtatious Lance, the only attention I seemed to attract lately was that of local law enforcement and I had mistakenly mentioned both sightings of Officer Smiley to Tiff on the phone. Now, a late-night inbox message from Tiffany referred to him as "Officer Hottie" and included this helpful suggestion: *Get your fine overeducated butt down to the police station and ask for a date.*

Call me when you sober up ;) was my reply.

SUNDAY AFTERNOON JUST after two, I walked up the path to the neat, white Cape Cod–style house. The short drive to the village of Darby had been pleasant and uneventful. I figured I might be on a winning streak. I knocked on the faded red door. As I glanced around, I realized that the grass was growing over the hose. There were hangers for flower baskets, but no baskets hanging from them, and the planter boxes were sitting empty. I hoped the lump in my throat went away before I had to ask my questions.

Alexander Fine's parents looked older than they probably were. That was no surprise after the death of their son. It was a house soaked in sadness and loss, and I remembered the feeling well.

To my surprise, they were pleased to talk about their son and his work. They didn't even ask what I wanted. I'd barely said my name when I found myself welcomed into their home. No elaborate cover story needed, it seemed.

"I am so sorry for your loss," I said again, when Mr. Fine ushered me into their home.

Mrs. Fine said as I took a seat in the flowery living room, "We were proud of Alexander."

Mr. Fine said, "Very proud."

I could have figured that by the number of photos of the young Alexander that were clustered around the room. An only child, Alexander had clearly been the center of his parents' world. This boy with olive skin, huge dark eyes and amazing eyelashes. He hadn't been much of a smiler. He looked like a worried little boy. There were graduation photos, spelling bee photos, and some from what looked like a chess club. Alex had a faint air of anxiety in every one. It made me wonder if he'd had some kind of lifelong premonition that something very bad was going to happen to him.

In the foyer, I'd passed the annual progression of school photos. Intricate model airplanes and finished puzzles decorated every surface in sight.

"Something to eat?" Mrs. Fine said.

"Oh, no thank you, I'm—"

"We have cookies." She nodded at her husband, who shot out of his chair and disappeared in the direction of the kitchen.

I said, "I love that you still have Alexander's pictures up. He sure was a cute kid." That got me off the conversational hook of saying he sure was an attractive man, as he really hadn't been. He'd had, however, a quiet niceness about him, like his parents. They seemed like the type of people who would stop and help you change a tire on a dark night while they were wearing their best clothes, at the same time the rest of the world might ignore you and rush home to watch *Dancing with the Stars*.

Mr. Fine arrived back with a plate of cookies. Pepperidge Farm Pirouette Rolled Wafers. I am very partial to them.

Mrs. Fine smiled. "Did you go to school with our Alexander?"

I felt so comfortable with these people, that I didn't even feel the need to lie. Mistake, as it turned out.

"No, actually, but I am . . ." I hesitated. I didn't want to say his replacement. Nothing was going to replace Alexander with these gentle people. "I am now working as a researcher for Vera Van Alst."

The temperature in the room dropped by ten degrees. The soft, sweet pallid people seemed to develop sharp edges. They stared at me with narrowed eyes. Mr. Fine crossed his arms. Mrs. Fine moved the Pirouette Wafers out of my reach.

"So you're saying you didn't go to school with Alex and you work for that horrible woman?" Mrs. Fine said.

In my family, honesty is never the best policy, but I had nothing to lose and I felt bad about bothering these grieving people. "No, I didn't go to school with Alex, and I do work for the woman you clearly despise, but this is my job now and it's a job I love and respect." I decided against mentioning that I was sure Vera was keeping information from me for whatever bizarre reason. It might have been true, but I didn't think it would help my case. "I am missing some information, and I was hoping that you might have some of his notes or—"

They exchanged glances, and I figured the answer would be no.

Mr. Fine said, "Well, I guess it takes integrity to be truthful."

Mrs. Fine said, "Not everyone is." She pushed the cookies back toward me.

I pulled something out of thin air. "I am sure that Alex wouldn't want to leave his work unfinished. Did he love the job too?"

That hit the spot. The mother gasped. I felt a frisson of guilt, but I fought it.

I pressed my advantage. "Did he keep research materials? Books? Anything relevant? I didn't find anything in the apartment, and I believe he was there before me. I was hoping that he might have left some things here with you."

Mr. Fine glanced at Mrs. and nodded. She said, "Most of it is gone, but what he had left is still in boxes in his room. We haven't been able . . ." She stopped, choked up.

Grief flooded both their faces.

I felt like I'd dropped a bag of misery on the doorstep of these already stricken people. I said, "Don't worry about it. I don't want to cause you any more distress."

They exchanged another glance. Mrs. Fine nudged the cookies further toward me, and Mr. Fine said with a tremor in his voice, "Would we be putting you out too much to ask you to go through the boxes by yourself? It would be just too painful for us."

Mrs. Fine's eyes filled. Mr. Fine reached over and squeezed her hand.

I wondered if I was actually lower than dirt. Would there be a special place in hell for people who took advantage of bereaved families?

I managed to stammer, "No, no, please don't put yourselves out. I should never have bothered you." I considered sprinting for the door but realized that would just make things worse.

Mr. Fine got to his feet and said, "You'd be doing us a favor, and you are right, Alex would want his work finished."

Mrs. Fine handed me the plate of cookies. "You may want to take these too."

There was no backing out now.

ALEXANDER FINE'S ROOM, spotless and minimalist, was sparsely decorated in IKEA furniture. The walls still held every merit badge and honor roll certificate, as well as a chess trophy and a fine selection of summer camp photos featuring the solemn olive-skinned boy. To make things worse, he was smaller than the other boys around him. I sure hoped these early years hadn't been hellish.

I spent an hour sifting through what was left of Alexander Fine's life. Much of it was research for his dissertation. There was no mention of Vera, nothing about the play or even Christie. No books by or about Agatha Christie. No files. That seemed strange to me. It was such a compelling project that I found it hard to believe he hadn't written a single word about it anywhere. Where was his notebook? Had it been stolen with his laptop bag? Or did he even use a paper notebook? I have always kept a dedicated paper notebook, quite aside from any computer files. Life is safer that way. Electronics get fried, lost and upgraded, or like Alex's laptop, stolen. But maybe Alex didn't think that way. Maybe he had everything on a desktop computer. If so, where was that? I checked the box. Sure enough, a printer, and a small webcam, but no other computer, iPad or mini.

I turned back to the room. The saddest thing was a strip of photo-booth pictures of Alex and his fiancée, Ashley. They were the happy kind where everyone clowns around. Ashley was as tall as he was. She had her face turned toward him. Alex was smiling. Alive. Almost carefree, but not quite.

The Fines were waiting for me at the bottom of the stairs. I said, "I didn't find any notebooks here. Is there anyplace else they might be?"

Neither one said anything, but I could tell that the question had upset them. I waited for a few more seconds and said, "Would they be with his fiancée?"

Both parents looked like they might have just smelled something very bad. It crossed my mind that with all the photos of Alex in the living room, there wasn't a single one of him with Ashley. Maybe they had had trouble letting their only son leave the nest. Perhaps his fiancée deserved even more sympathy if Alex had been still tied to his parents.

Silence.

"So no chance there's anything with Ashley?"

Mr. Fine said, "She wasn't interested in Alex's work."

His wife said gently, "But she loved our boy."

Mr. Fine nodded. "For anything else, you should ask your employer. After Alex died, we brought his things back here from the apartment at the Van Alst house. We wanted everything that was connected to him. We were . . ."

"Of course, you were."

Mrs. Fine blurted out, "And then Miss Van Alst called and was very unpleasant. She asked us to send everything about the project to her. Books, notes, everything. She said that she'd paid for them and therefore they were her property and if we didn't cooperate, she would take legal action."

He added, "We were so shocked that we didn't seek legal advice ourselves. We just packed them up for her. I'm surprised she sent you here, after that."

Well, this was embarrassing. "She didn't send me. Actually, she doesn't even know that I am here. I took the initiative. Alex was doing the same job as I am, and I'm sure he really cared about the project. I thought I might learn from his work. I didn't ask Miss Van Alst about his materials. And I didn't mean to upset you. I am so sorry."

Mrs. Fine patted my arm. "It's not you, dear."

I was going to burn forever for bothering these people. But Vera was definitely going to a deeper, hotter level.

ON THE SCENIC drive back to Harrison Falls, I asked myself what Vera could possibly have gained from not telling me about Alex Fine's research materials. Was there information she didn't want me to have? Either Alex hadn't found anything useful, in which case I could save time by not following the same leads, or he had found something and Vera had chosen not to share it with me. What would be the point of that? What game was Vera playing? Why would she have been so cruel to the Fines? Obviously, things weren't as they seemed. I had to find out what was really going on.

Alex Fine's fiancée seemed like a logical place to start.

I SPOTTED OFFICER Smileypants in the distance in his squad car and managed to veer off the main road and take a diversionary back-road route to Harrison Falls. No point in asking for trouble, even if trouble was kind of cute.

After arriving at Uncle Mick's, I skillfully evaded my uncles' questions about Vera's finances and general lifestyle and scampered off to do some online research. I looked over the articles on the train accident, and it dawned on me that all the information about the project might have been in the stolen laptop. I gave a little shiver. If Ashley Snell didn't have any information, I was going to have to discard this line of inquiry and start again. It was easy enough to get an address for Ashley Snell. You can find anything online. She might have wanted privacy, but she'd left a trail of bread crumbs right to her front door.

I promised the uncles that I'd dish the dirt on Vera on my next visit, and I asked Uncle Lucky to figure out a way that

I could have Internet at the Van Alst house. I was in the Saab and on my way before they could mount a counteroffensive. If I knew Lucky, I'd have service by nightfall and no one would have even seen him come or go.

OF COURSE, IT would have been wonderful if Ashley Snell had actually been at home, but she wasn't. Ashley rented apartment A, the first floor of a small two-story house on the outskirts of Harrison Falls, not far from Grandville. I banged on the door extra long just in case. It wasn't like I was the sleazy media. I convinced myself that Alex Fine would have wanted this. Officer Smiley, on the other hand, was right behind me, with his roof lights flashing as I walked away from Ashley's house.

The fact that I hadn't done anything remotely wrong had no impact on my aversion to the law. It was automatic. I was well trained. Anyway, it wasn't as though I liked Officer Smiley or anything, I reassured myself. Cute, yes, but too pink cheeked. Too blond. Too pretending to be nice.

But since he was also too in my face, even if it was to smile in my face, I decided to use Uncle Mick's "take the upper hand" method and question the cops before they could question me.

"What can I do for you, Officer?"

He laughed. "That's what I was going to say. Hey, do you have a lot of experience with the police?"

Now what did he mean by that? I didn't want to look flustered, but a weird sound came out of my mouth. Real smooth, Bingham.

"Is there a problem?" That came out all right, more or less like a normal person without criminal connections.

"I just stopped to say hello. It's a lovely afternoon."

"You just stopped to say hello? To me?"

"Well, yes." He leaned forward to sniff a cluster of low-hanging lilacs. My palms had started to sweat. Should I be flattered? Or worried? Did lilac sniffing symbolize anything? Why did I find that chipped incisor so adorable?

He said, "So, visiting a friend?"

"No. Yes. Well, not exactly. I'm following up on some research."

"Anything I can help with?"

My car was so close. My instincts told me to push past him, jump into the Saab, gun it and be out of sight in two seconds. My rational side told me those actions wouldn't look good or end well. Some other part of me noticed the little freckles on the bridge of his nose and wondered what it might be like to be tackled by him. I gave my head a shake. "I don't think so. Thanks." I made a beeline for my car. I had just settled in and snapped on my retrofitted seat belt when he tapped on my car window.

I rolled it down.

Apparently he had never stopped smiling. "By the way, who's your friend?"

"What friend?"

"The friend you were visiting here. The one who's not at home."

I reminded myself once again that I had done nothing wrong. And I needed to avoid telling fibs out of habit and inclination. "Not really a friend, just someone I need to speak to."

"Oh sure, but anyway. It's a small town, I might know them."

Fine. He might have some useful information. "Her name is Ashley Snell."

A small shadow clouded his sunny smile. "Right. Wasn't her . . . ? Oh boy. That was an awful thing. That poor girl witnessed it."

Of course, he would know all about Alex and his terrible death. The fiancée too. Harrison Falls was indeed a small town, and everybody knew everything about everyone's every action. It wouldn't have surprised me if my uncles were already aware that I was having this conversation.

I said, "I have to go now."

He nodded. "I am glad that Ms. Snell has good friends like you."

He sounded like he really meant it. For a second I wondered if I was dreaming.

I SPENT THE rest of the afternoon plowing through my stack of research material on Agatha Christie, her disappearance and her plays. I worked undisturbed for hours, if you don't count Signora Panetone arriving with an afternoon snack of prosciutto, melon and fresh Parmigiano-Reggiano. The cat, of course, came and went like magic. I quite liked it when it was in a good mood, purring and wanting to snuggle up, but when that leg-slashing business started again, I was prepared to try to chase it out, while keeping a safe distance.

I now knew that *The Mousetrap*, Agatha's most famous play, began life as a radio play, which was itself based on a short story. It seemed to me that indicated there was hope. She'd done that with *The Mousetrap*, so she might have done it with something else. She'd asked that the short story not be published in the UK as long as the play was running. I assumed that was not to spoil the ending. But it was an interesting approach. She could have experimented earlier and for some reason not wanted to release this other play. Perhaps she'd based a book on it. Or a short story. Or it might have been too close to her real life. She'd been going through an intense crisis. Maybe, if it existed, this play would shed light on her unexplained eleven-day disappearance. Dramatize it. What if it showed her in an unappealing light? That would make news even after nearly a century. People love a good mystery, and this one would be a spectacular story.

Lots of sources mentioned the two unpublished Christie short stories that had shown up in her notebooks, but if the play existed and if it had been written during her disappearance, it would be in a whole different league.

I now had three possible theories: theory one, that she'd written a play in a fugue state; theory two, that she'd reworked it into some other pieces, short stories, radio plays, even an early version of a novel; and theory three, that someone was prepared to make a fool out of a collector who would pay the big bucks for the privilege.

Someone would pay the big bucks, no question. Would someone even be willing to kill for it?

CHAPTER SEVEN

I WAS GETTING smarter about dinners with the crabby and deceitful boss. I always brought a wrap. I wore my boots in case the cat was under my chair and in a mood. As I headed down the steep dark staircases from my garret and walked along the corridor to the dining room, I was steeling myself for battle. Not even the gorgeous room and the food could take my mind off the fact that my employer was somehow playing games.

Vera Van Alst, a vision in frayed beige once again, raised a beige eyebrow as I arrived. It may have been the hand-tooled cowboy boots. I smiled at her, all confidence. Two can play games. Even so, I reminded myself that I had to tread carefully. I needed this job. And I loved my funky garret and cabbage rose walls. Plus there was something to be said for living in the Van Alst mansion and having platters of delicious food placed in front of you three to five times a day.

The downside was not knowing what Vera was up to. I

didn't mind grumpy, but I wasn't crazy about deceitful and manipulative, when I was the target.

If she really wanted this play, why wouldn't she want me to benefit from Alex Fine's work? Why would she have asked his parents for his research notes and then not mentioned it? I realized that I hadn't been bright enough to ask them if they'd read the materials that they'd turned over to Vera Van Alst. It had been an uncomfortable conversation. Knowing how distraught they must have been, I was pretty sure they hadn't.

As Signora Panetone burst through the swinging door from the kitchen, carrying a tray of something that smelled delicious, I tried a preemptive strike.

"I have had a quite productive day. Finding leads, but I don't really want to waste time going over old ground. I'm puzzled by the lack of research notes from my predecessor. How long did you say he worked on the project?"

Signora Panetone set down a steaming soup plate (Spode, I thought) in front of Vera. How many sets of antique dishes did Vera own? Vera scowled and attempted to bat her away without success.

"No, no, no. You eat. Must eat."

I didn't plan to push the signora away. She settled a plate of delicious-smelling broth with tiny pasta stars in front of me and plunked down a small bowl of what looked like freshly grated Parmesan cheese. "Parmigiano-Reggiano," she muttered. "Yes, yes, eat."

I couldn't wait to eat. But instead I gazed at Vera expectantly. "I wondered if they might be tucked away somewhere."

She shot me a look that might have turned me to a block of ice, but, of course, I had that wonderful soup to keep me warm. I took the first spoonful while I waited for her.

Nothing.

I said, "Perhaps they were packed up when Alexander's things were cleared out of his rooms here."

Signora Panetone, who had been attempting to pile some

cheese onto Vera's soup plate, stopped and glanced from Vera to me and back again.

Vera said nothing.

Signora Panetone threatened, "Eat cheese," before she vanished through the swinging kitchen door.

Perhaps the look had nothing to do with Alex or papers.

I said, "Or if not, they could be with his family. I may drop over and express my condolences. I can ask them while I'm there. I'll find a nice way to do it."

I left that hanging in the air and got busy with the soup. It was fabulous.

Vera glowered. "That won't be necessary. I'll have a look and see what there is left here. Probably a box somewhere."

"Excellent."

As I waited for Signora Panetone to come bursting through the door again with yet another taste sensation, I had to wonder what Vera was hiding. And why.

In the meantime, I said, "I look forward to that."

As the main course arrived (turkey cutlets with lemon and wine sauce, orzo and fresh beans), I felt my iPhone vibrate. I'd made sure it was on vibrate as I knew instinctively that there would be a Van Alst aversion to the technology and an unspoken rule against having one on your person in the dining room. But who would be calling me? My uncles were much too savvy. They knew where I was and with whom. Tiffany might text, but we kept our talks for later in the evening. Who then?

Signora Panetone staggered around with the giant platter, managing to get the bare minimum onto Vera's plate and a man-sized portion onto mine. I got to my feet and said, "Please, let me help you with that. It looks very heavy and . . ." I fully expected Vera to order me to sit down again, but I moved fast.

"You eat!" Signora protested, but I had wrestled the plate from her in a preemptive strike and hustled through the door of the kitchen, leaving them both with astonished expressions. As the door swung closed behind me, I put the platter on the counter and whipped out the phone.

The Cozy Corpse showed up in my call history. That was good news, but most likely not an emergency at eight thirty on a Sunday night. I figured Karen Smith must have finished packing up after the Antiquarian Book and Paper Fair closed and decided to call me with a bit of news. It could wait until after I finished dinner and tried to pump Vera. I slipped the phone back into my pocket just as Signora Panetone had puffed through the door after me. "Go eat. No one in the kitchen!"

That wasn't entirely true, I knew, as I clearly remembered Eddie being there the night before.

I raised my hands in surrender and returned to my cutlets.

Vera said as I settled in, "Signora Panetone doesn't care for anyone in her kitchen. I thought I made that clear before."

"My apologies. I thought she looked like she was struggling. Some of those old ironstone platters weigh a ton. She's not a young woman."

"She's strong as an ox and twice as stubborn. You'd do well not to get on her bad side."

I knew that my healthy appetite meant that wouldn't happen. But I said, "I'll be careful.

Vera grunted.

I tried something different. "And I'll be really glad if you find any of Alex's papers around. That would certainly save you time and money. If I don't have to follow any false leads, that would be great. And maybe he'd actually uncovered a line on the play. I do have to ask myself why he would scamper off to the city with his fiancée when he was in the middle of this project, unless he was on to something."

I ate the rest of my dinner in the shadow of her long glower. Didn't bother me. I paused every now and then to make a comment about the food, the weather and the china. There were many more challenges at dinner when I was growing up with my uncles, including the police at the door every so often.

As soon as dessert was finished (an excellent cheese plate), I dashed to my garret to see what message Karen Smith had left. I reminded myself to keep an eye on what was happening at foot level on the steep stairs.

I locked the door behind me, then turned around to see that the Siamese had managed to get in first. I kept my distance as the last scratch was still throbbing. But now, apparently, all was forgiven and the sneaky creature just wanted to be friends. As I plunked myself on the bed to check the message, the cat jumped up to join me and rubbed its head against my arm.

Karen Smith's message was intriguing. "Hello, Jordan. I have some information that will interest you. I'm quite worried and I think you will be too. It will be of concern to your employer. Can you meet me at Saint Sebastian's? I had to leave early to check something out. I'm here now finishing packing up my booth. The front door of the hall is locked, but if you come to the loading area on the far side of the building and ring the bell, I'll let you in. I should be here until about nine thirty. Otherwise, call me and we'll make it another time."

Wait for another time when I'd been without any leads whatsoever so far? Not a chance.

Bring it, I thought. It was nearly nine and about a twenty-minute drive. Would she be gone already? I called her back to let her know I was on my way, but it went straight to message. Just to be on the safe side, I left a message saying that I hoped to be there soon. I had a mountain of reading to do, but I knew that Agatha and her mysterious story would still be waiting in my garret when I got back.

I WRAPPED MYSELF in a lightweight camel-colored cashmere cardigan, yet another flea market treasure, then topped it off with a punchy Pucci scarf from the sixties.

Twenty minutes later, I pulled into the parking lot at Saint

Sebastian's and drove around to the back. The chain-link fence had been camouflaged by rows of lilacs, all in bloom. I loved this time of year.

I hurried toward the door. A van with "The Cozy Corpse" painted on it and a cute waving skeleton was parked close by. I could see that it was half full of boxes of books. Karen had left the back door to the hall propped open with a strategically placed carton. I popped in rather than ring the bell. She was probably busy packing. I could give her a hand. She was a nice person, and I appreciated her getting back to me so quickly. I didn't think it was just business on her part, but as the uncles like to point out, sometimes I can be a patsy.

The hall was empty. The booths had all been dismantled except for the three tables forming the last unit at the end: the Cozy Corpse location. I noticed I didn't make a sound moving forward on the soft, thick carpet. I didn't want to give Karen a shock, so I called out to let her know I was coming.

"Hi! It's me. Jordan."

No answer.

I figured she probably had her head in a box of books. I ambled in, amazed at how the room had lost its old-fashioned charm now that the dealers were gone.

"Karen?"

Again, no answer. But a little flutter in my gut set me on edge. The smell of lilacs clashed with the dank odor of the empty hall.

She couldn't be far. Her van was still here. Two boxes of books had been stacked on the small blue metal dolly, ready for the truck. Maybe I could do something to help while I waited. Next to the red cash box, the credit card receipts were neatly stacked in two piles, as though she'd been working on them. She couldn't have gone far. She was probably in the ladies' room. As I stepped around the far table, thinking it would be fun to check out some of the still-unpacked books, I tripped over an upturned chair and careened out of control. I was stopped by the farthest table and swore as I slammed into it. The cash box and credit card receipts went flying. What the hell? I'd never thought to look for overturned chairs. But nothing prepared me for what I saw next: a leg and foot sticking out from under the blue-skirted table.

I screamed. At the top of my lungs.

Of course, I was alone with the leg and foot.

Get a grip, I told myself. It must be Karen. I snapped out of screaming gear and into Good Samaritan mode. What could have happened to her? Perhaps she'd hit her head and crawled under the table? That didn't make sense, but this wasn't the best situation for thinking clearly, or at all. I forced myself to bend down and flip the table skirt back so I could see.

Please don't be dead, please don't be dead. It took a second for my brain to sort it out. It was indeed Karen Smith lying motionless. Her wild red curls had come loose and spilled behind her. The gold-rimmed glasses lay twisted near her hand. Her cheeks were gray, and her fair skin now seemed nearly transparent. I leaned forward and knelt. There was a red wound on her forehead. There was a slowly spreading pool of blood, soaking into the plush carpet under the table. I gasped. I was kneeling in it! I heard myself screaming again. I forced myself to stop and pull out my phone from my handbag. With shaking hands, I dialed 911.

The dispatcher was calm, reassuring. This was to his credit as it must have sounded strange to have someone yell, "A leg! I saw the leg under the table!" I did get myself under control enough to say that I thought the woman I was meeting had been hurt. "I'm sorry, I'm pretty rattled. You have to send help. There is a lot of blood. She's badly injured."

"Keep calm, ma'am. We need your location, first of all."

"Saint Sebastian's Hall in Grandville," I yelled. "The rear door's open!"

"Help will be there soon."

I lifted the table skirt again. I was only vaguely conscious of the dispatcher's disembodied voice. My heart was thundering. Was Karen dead? I managed to keep my eyes open and peer under the table. Instead of the 911 dispatcher's calm and measured tones, I imagined my uncles' voices, advising me to keep cool and get out of there before the cops came. I knew that wasn't the best advice, except for the "keep cool" part.

"Ma'am? What is happening?" I suppose dispatchers are trained to keep level heads. That was good. I needed that.

I touched Karen's arm. She was still warm and breathing.

"Karen Smith has been injured, possibly attacked. She has a gash on her forehead, and she's bleeding."

I bent closer to Karen and whispered, "Karen. I'm here. You'll be okay. Help is coming." I swept some curls off her face and did my best to be soothing.

What had happened? She couldn't have banged her head and then crawled under the table. What then? I patted her hand and stroked her arm. Was I just fooling myself? She was clammy but not cold. There was blood on her sleeve. I stared at my hands. They were streaked with red. The blood had come from me. I had marked her arm with it. For some reason, this seemed like the worst thing in the world. In the back of my mind, a rational voice said, if she's alive and badly injured, she'll be in shock. Stay calm. Try to staunch the bleeding. Keep her warm. It finally occurred to me that was the dispatcher. How did Tiff deal with this stuff on a daily basis? I was getting freaked out from the knowledge that Karen's blood was getting all over me.

For the only time in my life, I wanted to hear a siren. I slipped out of my vintage cashmere cardigan and placed it gently over her. I took my scarf and pressed it gently to her head wound with one hand. I held her limp white hand with the other. Was it too little too late?

"Karen," I whispered. "Please stay with me. Help is coming."

I sure hoped I was telling the truth.

I found myself blinking back tears at the first sound of a siren. It seemed they'd gotten here very quick. Maybe Karen's luck would hold, although she sure hadn't been lucky that day. Let it be paramedics, I thought.

I heard a voice calling.

"Over here at the end," I shouted. "Hurry."

But of course when I looked up, it wasn't the paramedics. Officer Smiley's round innocent face had shock written across it. He stared at me and knelt down beside me to check out Karen. He reached out for me and recoiled at the blood on my hands.

I managed to say, "Her name is Karen Smith. She's still breathing. I've already called 911."

He snapped into cop mode. "You're going to be all right, Karen. The paramedics should be here any minute." His usually bright face was deadly serious. His voice dropped and took on a tone that I might have melted for, under different circumstances. He spoke soothingly, reassuring us that everything was under control now. I don't know if it was helping Karen, but it was really working on me.

The welcome scream of the ambulance cut through our conversation. Officer Smiley jumped to his feet and raced to meet the paramedics at the door. I peered up over the table and watched the emergency team rumble toward us. Were they moving in slow motion? This was a life or death situation. "Hurry up!" I yelled. "She's here."

At least Officer Smiley was hustling. He ran toward the table, bent down again and pried my hand from Karen's. I protested as he pulled me to my feet. He put an arm around my shoulder and gently led me out of the way. "They have to be able to reach her," he said.

I knew he was right, but I hated letting go and hated waiting while they worked on her. The paramedics radioed the hospital, assessing Karen's condition.

"Lost a lot of blood."

"Checking vitals."

"Let's get that bleeding stemmed."

They seemed to work as a hive mind, completing each other's tasks and sentences, buzzing over Karen as they prepped her to go to hospital. I knew they would do everything possible to save her.

By the time she was loaded on the gurney and being wheeled toward the door, I found that I was shaking. Officer Smiley's arm was still around me. He led me to the foyer where there was a comfortable sofa and a table. "You'd better sit down," he said.

I sat, stared at my knees and shuddered.

Officer Smiley waited for me to gather myself a bit. I was even beginning to feel a bit grateful for his presence. "What happened?" he said in a low voice.

I turned to stare at him. "I don't know."

He nodded sympathetically. "But you were here."

"What? No, I wasn't here."

He patted my hand. "Jordan, you might be in shock. We'll get you seen to before they take your statement." That took care of any misplaced warm fuzzies I was feeling.

"Take my statement? Why?"

"Because a woman has been seriously injured and you were here."

"I told you. I wasn't here."

He nodded sadly. "We'll get you seen to."

"Karen."

"What do you mean?"

"Her name is Karen. She's not just 'a woman.' She's Karen Smith. She runs the Cozy Corpse. I told you that. She was really nice to me. I like her."

"I'm sorry. You're right. I didn't intend to diminish her. My point was that you were here with Karen when she was critically injured, so we will need to know what happened."

He made it sound so reasonable. It was really hard to be mad at him and his cute little chipped incisor, but really, I could not give a statement. No way. I was pretty sure every cop in upstate New York had a file on my felonious family members. For all I knew they had one on me too. Maybe this smiling policeman was familiar with it. That would explain why he was always showing up. But why would they have a file on me? I hadn't done anything. I was the law-abiding one. I'd gone to college. I had paying jobs. I filed my taxes.

Oh right. I had just taken over the job of a man who'd died mysteriously. And now, I'd stumbled over a woman who looked to be critically injured. But I had no idea what had happened. Making that point wouldn't do me much good. It was the Kelly family curse: even when we are doing the right thing, we exude guilt. I could see how it looked. I was in an empty hall after nine o'clock on a Sunday night for no reason that made much sense, and I'd been found holding Karen's hand with both of us covered in blood. I glanced at his innocent pink-cheeked face. I decided I was better talking to him than some stranger who might have a history with my family.

He said, "Look, I know you're upset. But let's get you some medical care and—

"I'm all right. No need for medical care. I'll tell you what happened."

"Are you sure?"

"Of course I'm sure. You're with the Harrison Falls Police and I—"

"Yes." He nodded at me and waited.

I said, "Does the jurisdiction of Harrison Falls Police Force extend to Grandville?"

"Are you kidding? I'm pretty sure I'll get my butt seriously kicked for being here in uniform."

"Well, um, why are you here in uniform?"

"I got a call."

"A call about?"

"That someone, who didn't identify himself, wanted to meet me to give me information about a series of crimes in Harrison Falls."

"And he wanted you to meet in Grandville?"

"Yes."

"At Saint Sebastian's?"

"Exactly."

"And that seemed like a good idea to you?"

"At the time."

"Huh."

His flush got deeper. "When you think of it, it turned out to be a good idea. I was here to help you."

I bristled. "I had already called 911 by the time you got here."

How deep could a flush get? He didn't say anything.

I said, "I'm sorry. I'm being a jerk. I am really glad you showed up. You calmed me down."

Damn good thing my uncles weren't around to hear that little speech. I'd be cut off Kraft Dinner for years. To my own surprise, I'd meant it.

"So what happened before I got here?" he said. I guessed he didn't hold a grudge, not like my family. His flush was subsiding, and he seemed to have forgotten my outburst.

I'm sure police officers have people blowing up at them all the time, and probably far worse than myself. All this caught me off guard, though, and I found I was willing and able to spill every detail, especially as I had a choice. "If I tell you what happened, then may I check up on Karen and go home after?"

"Right. Of course." If he'd nodded any faster, his smiling blond bobble-head might have fallen off. "So do you mind filling me in?"

Why not? I really didn't have anything to hide. "I got a call from Karen to meet her here."

"What time was that?"

"During dinner. We dine at eight." I was surprised at how naturally that very Vera Van Alst phrase slipped out of my mouth.

"Oh, we do, do we?" Was he smirking now?

"We can check my phone for the time." My hand was now rifling through my satchel where I'd dropped the phone.

"Did she, Karen, say why?"

"Just that she had interesting information."

"What kind of information?"

"She didn't give any details, but I assumed it had to do with a collectible that I might buy."

"You didn't ask her?"

"I didn't take the call. I was at dinner and my employer refuses to have any modern electronic devices in the dining room. I checked the message just before nine and drove over."

He blinked. Perhaps it was because of the "dining with my employer" thing.

"She asked you to meet her at that time?"

I stopped to think about what exactly she *had* said. "She said she'd be here packing until around nine thirty. I'd left her a reply saying I was on my way."

"Were you worried?"

"What? No. I was excited. I was really hoping to find out what she'd learned. And it's a beautiful Sunday night. This is the fun part of my job." I shivered. "I can't believe I said that."

"You didn't mean it that way."

"No, I meant finding leads and tracking down books is the fun part of my job. I had no idea that I'd find . . ." I trailed off, picturing poor Karen barely alive.

"What did you find, Miss Bingham?"

I thought back. "The parking lot had only the Cozy Corpse van. I didn't see any other cars anywhere around the building. So whoever it was must have attacked Karen and then driven off quickly, or if they were on foot, disappeared into the neighborhood as quickly as possible.

He blinked again. What was he thinking? I wanted him to nod in agreement or say yes or something else reassuring. I reminded myself that the police are—if not the enemy—at the very least, a force to be wary of. "We need to consider both possibilities," I added. "There's no way to know for sure."

He blinked again. I decided that he blinked whenever he was keeping something from me. Good to know. I said, "Is there any way to find out? Surveillance cameras? Witnesses?"

"No working cameras here, believe it or not. And *we* shouldn't be considering anything. You leave me to worry about that."

Like I wasn't going to worry. Normally it would be all I could do not to laugh at that comment. Just like a cop to pretend it's run-of-the-mill to stumble upon a victim of a violent attack. As if. But I didn't laugh, because there was nothing funny about tonight.

"I think I will worry, if you don't mind."

He said, "The police will look into all this." Before I could protest, he said, "Weren't you nervous meeting her here? Alone?"

"Nervous? Why would I have been nervous? It's a bright night. You could still see well enough. It was a church hall in a lovely residential area. I was meeting a friend after a book fair. This is Grandville, for Pete's sake. It's hardly the mean streets."

"People have been killed."

"Killed? What people?"

"Well, Alex Fine. You were going to see his fiancée earlier."

"That's one person. And he was killed by falling in front of a subway train in New York City. Why would that make me nervous here?" I realized that my voice was pretty high-pitched for someone who wasn't nervous. "Anyway, I wasn't worried. I wasn't nervous. It hadn't occurred to me that I should be. I went in and—"

"Did you see anyone?"

"No. Just the—"

He said, "How did you get in?"

"Didn't I say that? The door was open. It had been propped open by a box of books. I assumed she'd done that because she was loading the van. I just went in. I didn't want her to come out and get me. I saw"—I closed my eyes to recall the scene exactly—"the room was empty except for her table and some boxes of books, stacked."

"And you saw her, um, Karen Smith?"

"No. I thought she'd left the room to go to the ladies' room or something. The cash box was also on the table. And stacks of credit card slips."

"Was there cash in the box?"

"I don't know. It was closed. I imagine she would have had a float at least. The box got knocked over when I tripped. That's when I found her."

"You tripped?"

"I fell over that overturned chair and I went flying." I stood up to demonstrate, showing him where the table had been in relation to the chair. "And I crashed into the back table. As I was getting up, I saw Karen's leg sticking out from under."

"What did you think?"

That was just annoying. "I didn't know what to think. Have you ever had anything like that happen to you? It was bizarre and frightening. Then I saw the blood from her head wound and started to make sense of it. Not that it makes sense. I got down to check if she was . . . all right. I called 911. The rest you know. Oh, wait a minute. When did you get the call?"

"It didn't take me long to get here. I was at the edge of town, so maybe ten minutes. I must have taken the call ten minutes before I arrived."

My eyes widened. "But I would have already been here."

"Yes."

"So someone called you over in Harrison Falls to come here and find me kneeling in Karen's blood. Does that not strike you as strange?"

It struck him as something. I could tell by the look on his cute pink face.

I saw his eyes flick behind me to a man looming in the doorway. This guy could only be a detective. There was a granite edge to his features, and my guess was that would be reflected in a hard, edgy personality. The sick feeling in the pit of my stomach was because I knew I'd be giving him my statement next. Even from a distance, I could tell he lacked Officer Smiley's apparently sincere and pleasant nature.

One thing I was glad of, I could give the Van Alst mansion as my address, rather than the digs I recently shared with my uncles, who would be, as they say, known to the police. It would be a good time to be a Bingham rather than a Kelly.

CHAPTER EIGHT

※──❖──※

I F YOU FIND yourself in an interrogation room, you will probably do better if you have not spent a bit of time kneeling on a blood-soaked carpet. And it would be especially good if you didn't have any of that blood smeared on your clothing and your hands. I'm just saying. A word to the wise.

Detective Fenton Zinger had brought me a bottle of water. This seemed like an act of kindness, but I knew better. I'd been coached by my uncles, that should I ever find myself being interrogated, I should not accept an offer of water, as the police were just trying to get my prints and DNA. They advised if I was too thirsty to refuse, to make sure I took the bottle or paper cup with me. Leaving it behind made it fair game for the fuzz—Uncle Mick's words, not mine.

I felt my insistence that I'd had nothing to do with Karen Smith's attack, or maybe that would be her murder by this point, was not having the right impact on Detective Fenton Zinger.

"Tell me again," he said. "Start from the beginning. You got the call . . ."

"Yes. I got the call."

"You didn't know what it was about."

"I *did* know what it was about. She had found something she thought I would be interested in. I just didn't know what that item was."

"Maybe it was her cash box?"

"What?"

"The thing she keeps her money in?"

As Uncle Mick likes to say, everyone's a comedian. I said, "I know what a cash box is. I'm pretty sure the call wasn't about that."

"But she had one."

"Yes. I saw it on the table when I came in."

"Any idea where her cash went?"

I didn't like the sound of that. "Wasn't it there?"

He couldn't hold back that sneer.

I said, "The cash box got knocked over when I hit the table. If there was a roll of bills, maybe it rolled under the table. Her cash was probably in a pouch or something like that. Did it fall into one of the boxes?"

"Nope."

I shrugged. "I imagine she kept it separate from the credit card receipts, along with her float. I hope it went to a safe place. Her home? Her shop? Her car?"

"And why would you think that?"

"Because she was a smart lady and there was no reason for her to keep her cash at the hall. The security wasn't that great. The credit card receipts were different. And anyway who is going to walk in off the street to a church hall thinking there was even anything to steal?" Of course, some of my relatives could make hay with credit card receipts, but I didn't plan to mention that.

He said, "But this was more than a casual thief off the street."

"Have you searched her van? What about her—?"

"Let's review a bit. Who asks the questions here?"

"I take it that's a no." I paused to consider. Had Karen Smith been attacked by an opportunistic thief? A kid who couldn't resist? A loser needing drug money? It would be a relief to know it was not connected with me or Agatha Christie or Vera Van Alst's quest in any way. But I just didn't buy it. Karen Smith was pleasant and gentle, but I'd gotten the feeling she was an astute businessperson. She wouldn't have taken a foolish risk like carting her cash around practically begging someone to steal it. She'd been in and out of the hall loading her van. No. It was out of the question. She would have put her cash in a safe place.

"Was she worried about anything?"

"Why are you asking me? I just met her yesterday at the book fair. I didn't know her personally."

"And yet you went back to the hall at nine o'clock to see her. And you keep referring to her as your friend."

"Haven't I explained this already? She was warm and friendly and had found something for me. And no, I don't know exactly what it was, but I'm pretty sure it had to do with Agatha Christie."

"Are you being funny?"

"No. When I'm funny, I'm a lot funnier than this. I was looking for an artifact, and she had a line on one. She sounded upbeat. She didn't sound worried about anything. Then I left her a message and—"

"And?"

"Oh my God."

He rolled his eyes. "And?"

"*And* where's her phone?"

"You tell me."

I heard my voice go up. My uncles have always urged me to remain calm should I find myself being interrogated. But it's one thing to hear it and another thing to manage it. I was new to interrogations. "How would I know? I never saw it.

I don't even know what type of phone she had. I only know that she didn't answer it at around quarter to nine."

He opened his mouth, no doubt to make some remark that would put me in my place.

I got in first. "Did you find one in her clothing? Pockets? Handbag?"

"One more time, we ask the questions. Just so you're clear about that."

"Well, I sure hope you asked yourself who might have taken her phone. I called her after dinner. It kept ringing until it went to message. She might already have been injured. So someone must have taken her phone. But why would anyone do that?"

"People will steal anything. Cash boxes. Phones."

"I guess. But hitting her in the head was a serious crime. Most casual thieves wouldn't do that. She was badly injured. Don't the police have ways of tracking down cell phones? You could get the phone records and use that to—"

He leaned forward. "Next time you're looking for a new position, you could come on board with the department and give us workshops on how to do our jobs."

"Oh. I suppose you already know that."

"That's right. And you and every other citizen who is smart enough to power up the television think that watching an episode of *CSI* makes them an expert."

"I don't actually watch *CSI*. I prefer . . ." I quit while I was ahead. Detective Fenton Zinger might have had a point.

We went around and around the questions, and the interview never really got any better. It must have been eleven o'clock when I was finally released.

Officer Smiley offered to drive me home. Or drive me to my car and then follow me home, whichever I preferred. I didn't want to admit that once again I was glad to see him. It had been a rough night, but there was no way a half-Kelly could give up her mother's car to the cops.

"If you drive me back to my car at Saint Sebastian's Hall, I'll get myself home."

Detective Zinger stuck his head out the door and called to me as we headed out the door. "Oh, and don't leave the area. That means Harrison Falls, Grandville and the region. We'll need to ask you questions."

Was he kidding? I didn't plan to leave my bed for at least two days.

"SO, OFFICER. WHAT'S the news on Karen?" I asked Officer Smiley when we finally escaped the Grandville Police Station.

"My name is Tyler," he said. "I wish you'd call me that."

"Sure," I said, not really meaning it. "What have you heard about Karen Smith?"

"I checked with some colleagues. They've taken her to the regional hospital here in Grandville. Her condition is critical. She'll be operated on tonight." He bit his lip. It might have been adorable if he hadn't been a cop. But he was a cop, so it was just plain weird.

"What?" I said.

He shook his head.

"Don't just shake your head. Say what it is that you're shaking your head about."

"No need to yell," he said, looking like a wounded teddy bear. "It's just that . . ."

"They don't think she'll make it."

"It doesn't look good."

I felt a wave of nausea. "I have to go home. Now."

OFFICER SMILEY ("CALL me Tyler") did his best to walk me right to my door. I insisted that I was fine and made my way down the long, dimly lit driveway to the back door.

Vera definitely wasn't squandering money on exterior lighting. The Van Alst house looked like a fine setting for a ghost story at that time of the night. Lucky I'm not superstitious, I reminded myself as the ancient back door opened with a creak.

The click of my heels echoed in the back hallway of the empty first floor. "Ridiculous," I said out loud. What? Was I channeling Vera Van Alst now? Vera was far away in her own private second-floor wing, and Signora Panetone was, well, wherever she went after running the kitchen and the house for eighteen hours or so.

I didn't spot a cat and planned to keep my cool in case a tail brushed against the back of my leg. After what seemed like a year, I reached the top of the two dark, narrow flights of stairs, unlocked my door and practically tumbled into the safe cocoon of my garret. It was a cat-free zone. I bolted the door and ran for the tub.

AFTER THE BATH, I settled in for a chat with Tiffany, planning to leave out key details. She'd be instantly more alarmed than necessary, and I was too tired to recount my evening from hell and reassure Tiff that all was well. I had violated our pact, by not texting *Grandville Police Station* as my location earlier. Before I finished my "Hey, Tiff," she interrupted. "What's wrong?" Dang. I really hate Tiff's intuition.

"Just what is going on, Miss Jordan *Louise* Kelly Bingham?"

"You really don't have to middle-name me, Tiff. I am trying to tell you what happened." My voice cracked a bit, thinking about poor Karen lying in her hospital bed.

Tiffany softened. "Are you okay?"

I started at the beginning.

When I finished, she said in her most reassuring health practitioner's tone, "And Officer Smiley just happened to be the cop who got this alleged anonymous phone tip?"

"Well, yes, he did, but I'm sure it's a weird coincidence."

"Hold on, aren't you the one who doesn't believe in coincidences?"

I sputtered, "But he was nice enough to escort me back here. I didn't see anyone else at the station offering to get a bloodstained woman home after she'd been grilled for hours by a detective." Hmm, maybe I should have left out that part.

"What?" Uh-oh. Tiffany's voice was flat. "Did you say 'detective'?"

"Um, yes I did."

"It's going to take me a moment or two to absorb all this information, Jordan." A long pause ended with a very deep and disappointed sigh on the other end of the line.

"You have had this 'job'"—I could just see the sarcastic finger quotes—"for less than a week. You're being interviewed by detectives and narrowly escaping a bludgeoning, to seek a possibly nonexistent pile of papers for a mean old bird in a wheelchair. That right?"

"About sums it up."

Tiff pressed on. "You know I don't like that your boyfriend the cop was the first one on the scene. He's been 'on the scene' a little too often as far as I'm concerned."

Now that my head was clearing a bit, and I was no longer consumed by the need to bathe, I saw what Tiff meant. Officer Smiley had been bumping into me daily since I'd started to work for Vera. My stomach knotted. Was that a gut warning? Or had it simply been too long since Signora Panetone popped in with my bi-hourly snack?

"If you ask me, he's gone from cute to creepy. It may be time to tell your uncle Mick that this guy has been sniffing around."

I laughed. "Oh yes, I'll run right out and do *that*. Just let me check on my flying pigs first." The uncles would not be inclined to feel pity for someone who has withheld information regarding the police. Family or not.

"Okay, I get that you're between a rock and a hard place

with those guys. Better yet, just tell Lucky. Let him track down some online stuff. It helped last time."

Ah yes, last time. Uncle Lucky had been the one who found the proof needed to keep me out of jail after my horrid slug of a boyfriend committed credit card fraud. Lucky was brilliant with code if not words.

"And how many times have you seen Officer Stalker this week?"

"Maybe four, give or take."

Suddenly Tiff's volume rose. "*Four?* Jordan, how could you have let him take you home?" I thought I could hear her pacing on the concrete floor of her bunker.

"I had no choice, Tiff. I really didn't want to have to call Mick, and can you imagine if I'd tried a cab? I may have traumatized someone." I left out the part about not being able to afford a cab at that exact moment.

"I know you must be exhausted. I'm sorry. I don't mean to Mom you. I'm way the hell up here. I can't exactly get to Harrison Falls to get you out of any trouble. I am worried about this, so take me seriously. I'm asking myself what kind of research job this is. You should be asking yourself the same question. Remember that I'm your friend and I love you."

"Love you too."

I sighed deeply after we hung up. Tiff's question was a good one. What kind of research job was this? At that moment, I spotted some dried blood under my nail, missed when I scrubbed down earlier. Karen's blood. What kind of job was it? A dangerous one, apparently.

AFTER TALKING WITH Tiff and a long read of Agatha's biography, I finally dozed off. My eyes popped open at two. If the person who hurt Karen Smith had her phone, then that person had gotten the message I'd left for Karen. I might be in danger from him. I felt confident thinking it was a man.

Her attacker was far more likely to be male given the statistics on violence. Anyway, the person who had called Officer Smiley had been male. He'd said "he." Tiff's voice echoed in my head. If there'd really been a call. Despite Tiff's meltdown and my family's predisposition against the law, I couldn't really believe that this sweet, blushing man had attacked Karen Smith. It didn't make sense.

I wasn't crazy about the idea that someone else had my telephone number and maybe had accessed my message, and I was really glad I hadn't thought of it when I was clattering up those isolated stairs from the empty first floor of the Van Alst house. I'd been jumpy enough. I tossed and turned, wondering if Karen had been attacked by an opportunistic thief. Or did that attack have to do with the call to me? If it did, had the attacker found my response to her and planned to have me take the rap for it? Take the rap? For sure my uncles were still living in my head.

I lay on the pillow trying to distract myself and get to sleep. No joy there. What would Agatha Christie do? I'd gotten sucked into her biography and had not expected to find such a kindred spirit in a dead mystery writer, but her life was so much more. She'd become like a new companion to me. Maybe I could count on her for some inspiration about what to do next, as my shattered nerves would never let me sleep.

Agatha would certainly take action. I thought about her mysterious departure. Life had served her lemons as her husband Archie consorted quite publicly with his mistress, Teresa Neele. Had Agatha made lemonade with her disappearance, assuming Teresa Neele's name in her hotel while the world searched for her and looked suspiciously at Archie? I knew from her notebooks that she kept poking at an idea, working and reworking until it succeeded. It didn't always come easily or quickly, but she didn't give up. That's what I needed to keep in mind.

Agatha may have lost Archie (lucky her, in my opinion),

but she continued to be a huge international success, married again and had adventures the rest of us could only dream of. Except for the huge international-success thing, I felt like I was on the same path. I was still in the process of healing from my humiliating breakup. I decided to start with my own notebook in the morning. It's always cathartic to put pen to paper.

But first I needed to find out what had happened to Karen.

CHAPTER NINE

❖

I OPENED MY eyes to find the May sun streaming
through the window and a cat on my pillow. How had I
missed that the night before? I guessed it just showed how
upset I was. And it may have partly accounted for my miserable night's sleep, although flashbacks to Karen's injuries
were responsible for the rest.

I was sure the cat wasn't really smirking. It just seemed
that way. I kept out of its reach as I hurried to get ready for
breakfast on time.

Despite the bright day, the tall windows, the exuberant
plants and the cheerfully faded floral coverings on the furniture, that morning breakfast in the conservatory was a
gloomy affair. I decided this was because Vera could suck
the sunny morning out of any space. The mood was warmed
only slightly by Signora Panetone's frantic cries. "Eat! Eat!
Now!" Followed by, "You! Coffee!"

I was very glad to get that first cup of espresso. Like a
peevish child, Vera kept her eyes on the *New York Times*
and pushed away her plate of breakfast pastries without even

glancing at it. I hardly felt like eating a thing. Karen Smith's white face kept popping into my head.

I found myself staring at Vera, a shapeless mass of beige as usual. How much had she failed to tell me about what was going on? If I'd known the real story, whatever that was, would it have prevented what happened to Karen? Only one way to find that out.

"So," I said as Signora Panetone plopped a warm sweet roll and some fresh cheese on my plate, "I suppose you've heard."

Vera shot me her best glower. "Heard what?"

"Karen Smith was badly injured last night."

Signora Panetone stopped serving and made the sign of the cross.

"Should I know who Karen Smith is?"

"I think you should." That earned me a raised eyebrow and an expression that said "I am the employer and you are the indentured serf. Don't forget that."

But I had already made up my mind. As much as I loved my garret and needed this job, I needed a fair, respectful employer more. I needed to know that I wasn't doing things that would get me or other innocent people killed. I needed Vera to be honest with me.

"She's the woman who owns the Cozy Corpse mystery bookstore over in Grandville. I've told you about her, although I'm sure you already knew."

Vera said nothing.

I did, though. "She arranged to meet me to give me some information, possibly about the Christie play. When I got there, I found her with a serious head wound. They're not sure if she'll make it."

Vera pursed her lips and glowered a bit harder. She seemed to think it was the most effective of her five facial expressions (scowl, glower, sneer, utter boredom, and reverence, although reverence was reserved for books in her collection). The glower had stopped working on me, though. I doubt it had ever made a dent in the signora. But the news about Karen Smith had. Vera might be pursuing an "I know nothing" attitude, but she was the only one.

"That means she might die. In case there was any lack of clarity on my part."

"None whatsoever. Did she tell you anything about the manuscript?"

"No, she was too busy being clubbed."

Vera said without a blink, "I mean when she arranged to meet you."

"She did not. She left a message. But really, I think it's time that you told me what you know about the manuscript. I do not want to be flying blind anymore." I stopped and sipped my espresso while I observed the impact.

Vera's nostrils flared. I had hit a nerve. "Miss Bingham—"

I held up my hand. "Miss Van Alst. People are being hurt. One person has already died. I do not intend to die, and I do not intend to put anyone else in danger. You must accept that, and if you want me to continue, you will have to be open with me. What do you know about who might have this manuscript, and who would be willing to prevent you or me or the late Alex Fine from finding it?"

Vera added a new expression to her list. Ambivalence? From the tormented look on her face, I concluded that she knew something and didn't want to share it with me.

Signora Panetone leaned over and filled my espresso cup. "Drink," she said with a hint of sympathy.

I resisted the urge to say something and gave my attention to the coffee, which I polished off.

Finally, with a massive sigh, Vera said, "I don't know."

I kept quiet.

"It is true, Miss Bingham. I do not know who is doing these things, and I would very much like to. You are correct. I have indeed met Karen Smith and purchased some excellent items from her. She did not deserve to have this happen. I have no idea what the connection is. That is the truth."

"But is it the whole truth?" She could scowl, sneer and glower all she wanted, I needed to know.

"Most of it."

"How about the rest then? This would be a good time." I held out my tiny espresso cup for a refill and probably earned Signora Panetone's affection for the rest of my life.

Vera sighed again. "Well, it's not much, but I know there is someone involved."

I barely kept myself from screaming, "Out with it!"

"In the collecting world, there is a shadowy figure known as Merlin. No one knows who he is, but he often is the broker in complex acquisitions."

"Ah," I said, knowingly. I took complex acquisitions to mean stolen items.

"That's it."

"If that's it, why did you choose to mention him?"

"I believe he was involved."

Control, I whispered to myself. "In what way?"

"Very well. He had been in touch with Alex Fine about the manuscript."

"In touch?"

She shrugged. "Well, through an intermediary."

"Were you aware of who the intermediary was?"

"In fact, I was not. Alex Fine played that close to his chest. But I believed him."

"And do you still believe this Merlin is somehow connected to the Christie play?"

"I do."

I waited. And waited. Finally, I said, "And you think that Merlin might have been responsible for the attack on Karen Smith?"

"That I don't know. But she is very well connected in the world of collections, liked and respected, but I suspect not overly, shall we say, scrupulous about her business dealings."

"You mean that she might have been willing to take part in a less-than-honest transaction."

"I don't know that for sure."

"So she may have been in touch with Merlin. Or with the intermediary."

"Exactly."

I suppose it had taken me a ridiculously long time to really question how Alex's death might be connected to his work with Vera. I was used to con games, but I was a stranger to violence. Murder was a new situation all together. "I think it's more than coincidence that Alex died working on this file and now Karen has been attacked."

She nodded. I'd expected a bit of an argument, but apparently I wasn't the only one who had been thinking that.

I said, "Stepping back a bit, do you think that Merlin might have been responsible for Alex Fine's so-called accidental death?"

Signora Panetone crossed herself three times in rapid succession. I thought I spotted tears in her eyes.

"It would seem possible, Miss Bingham."

"And you have no way of knowing who Merlin is?"

"Exactly. I don't even know if he's only one person. Or if he's a group that uses the name to conduct its business under the radar, for a variety of reasons."

"Theft from other collections? Pillaging of museums? Is Merlin some kind of high-end fence?"

"To repeat, I do *not* know and I don't think many people do. He's perhaps a construct, a foil, but Alex had made contact with him. Or so he said."

"He didn't give you details?"

"He claimed not to have any. But as I said, I believed him."

"Now Alex is dead, apparently after an encounter with a homeless man who stole his computer. And Karen was certainly left to die. Looks like someone wants to prevent you from getting that manuscript."

"Perhaps. I truly have no idea why. I am willing to pay

whatever Merlin wants to possess the play." I thought about the bare spots on the walls, the missing artifacts and the need for repairs in the house. But even so, Vera would spare no expense to have this play. That said less about the play than about Vera.

I said, "Why not just sell it to you? You'd keep quiet even if the provenance wasn't, um, clear."

"I'm afraid that is so."

"There's a real viciousness at work. I saw the damage to Karen Smith. It was very disturbing. Seemed personal somehow."

I heard the signora gasp.

Vera said nothing, but behind her latest scowl, I thought I caught the flicker of genuine emotion, the first I'd ever seen in her.

"So who wants to keep you from the manuscript?"

She shrugged. "That comes under your job description, Miss Bingham."

"How do I know that whoever is trying to prevent you from getting the manuscript won't come after me? Am I the sitting duck in this case?"

"I trust you will take good care to keep yourself safe."

Thanks a lot.

I shot back, "And I trust you will do the same."

Vera flinched. She was worried. Now I could see that.

"I am never really alone, and I don't leave this house, as you know."

"Let's hope that works out for you. Tell me, have you found anything of Alex's research? That would have to help."

She shook her head. "Nothing,"

"Would you tell me if you did?"

She paused, then nodded. "Yes. Now I would, but there is nothing."

Signora Panetone stuck her face in front of mine. She gestured toward a platter of fluffy scrambled eggs. "Eat now." She patted my shoulder in what I thought was supposed to be a kind of reassuring gesture. "You, eat, eat."

For some reason, I just couldn't.

I BREEZED INTO the hospital at eleven o'clock, as soon as visitors were allowed. I did my best to look distraught. That wasn't hard.

I inquired about Karen Smith at Information.

"Are you a relative?" the pleasant volunteer with the frizzy yellow hair asked.

I didn't hesitate. "She's my aunt. We're all so terribly worried." I considered saying that I'd driven all night to get there, but my uncles had always warned me to keep my stories simple. Less chance of tripping up that way. "Can she have flowers? I'd like to get some."

She squinted at the screen. "I think so. She's postoperative, but there's nothing to say she can't. Room 503."

I hustled to the gift shop where a small refrigerator held arrangements in vases. I picked out one that I thought Karen might like: small, bright iris and baby's breath. Five minutes later I stepped out of the elevator and headed for room 503.

There was no police guard outside her room. I guessed the police were still sticking to their crime-of-opportunity theory.

Karen lay there on the bed, wan, bandaged and swollen. I whispered her name. Was this a good idea? What if she was shocked to see me? What if . . . ? Get a grip. You need to know what happened, I told myself.

"Karen?"

Her eyelids flickered.

"It's Jordan."

I whirled at a sound behind me. A nurse's aide had entered the room. I nodded and turned back to Karen. "Aunt Karen? It's me, Jordan."

Her eyes opened. It took them a few minutes to focus.

"I am so sorry you were hurt. I brought you some flowers." I showed her the bouquet and watched it register.

"Glad you like them," I said with a grin. "You don't have to force yourself to talk. I just wanted to see that you were all right." I put the flowers on the window ledge and returned to her bedside. I squeezed her hand while the nurse's aide fiddled with the IV drip. Karen managed to squeeze back.

The aide flashed us a gap-toothed smile. "A good sign," she said.

Karen whispered, "Dog."

"Sorry, what?"

"Dog."

"Your dog?"

Another squeeze.

"You want me to walk the pooch?"

"Feed."

Feed? "Of course. I'll go right away. I didn't realize that no one had done that. The poor thing."

A look of relief crossed her damaged face.

"Aunt Karen," I said, "who did this to you?"

Her forehead puckered.

I tried again. "Who hurt you?"

The barest of whispers. "Don't know."

Oh great. I knew better than to badger her in her fragile state.

"Please. Feed Walter. Walk."

"Leave it to me," I said.

I glanced at the aide. "I'll need her keys. Do you know if they'll be in the drawer?"

"Patients are not supposed to keep any valuables here. There's all sorts of lowlife roaming around pretending to be something they're not. Someone gets your keys and they know your name, guess what happens next?"

"That's really terrible," I said, opening the drawer in the bedside table. No keys. Not for the van. Not for the house.

Wherever that was. Not for the store either. Where could they be? I remembered seeing Karen's handbag on the floor in the hall. Had the police taken it? Did they have the keys? Would they have been there? Would they have called animal control about the poor dog?

I said. "You rest. I'll be back after I've checked on the pooch."

The big problem was that I didn't know where Karen lived, and I could hardly ask when the aide was standing there, as I was supposed to be her niece. Luck was with me and with Karen and presumably Walter the dog. The aide straightened Karen's pillow and tapped at the various fluids and machines beside the bed, then, apparently satisfied, headed briskly out the door.

"Where is, um, Walter?" I whispered.

"Home."

"Where's home?"

But Karen seemed to have slipped back to sleep.

I stopped in the lobby to check the phone book by the pay phone. No luck. No Karen Smith listed. Of course, she could live anywhere in our patchwork of tiny communities. I tried my iPhone. No luck there either. The Cozy Corpse did show up with a street address in Grandville.

I climbed into the Saab and headed south. I sure hoped that some neighbor with a key had taken pity on that poor dog. If the dog really existed. I hear that morphine can make you spin quite a tale.

I felt a bit of guilt about the project. Vera Van Alst was paying me to work for her, not to walk dogs. But the connection with Karen was a lead to the coveted manuscript, so I could rationalize the dog walking. Maybe a visit to Karen's home would also help connect some of the dots.

CHAPTER TEN

❖

I CASUALLY DROPPED in to my uncles', even if it was out of the way, as I'd decided to use some of my surplus clothing. I changed into an old pair of cropped jeans, a pair of classic Keds in hot pink and a black T-shirt that could be tossed afterward if need be. I wasn't sure what I'd find at Karen's or what I'd have to do to find it. Be prepared, that's what my uncles always taught me, although they're no Boy Scouts. They'd also trained me in self-defense, evasive driving and the age-old art of getting past locked doors. I grabbed my lock picks, a gift for my sixteenth birthday. Until now, I'd never used any of the pieces except to practice.

Not willing to miss an information opportunity, I asked if there was any word on the street about the attack on a woman at Saint Sebastian's Hall the night before.

Lucky shook his head sadly.

Mick sputtered, "What's the world coming to, my girl?"

I took that as a no, which was, I supposed, a good thing.

*   *   *

I PULLED UP in front of the tiny shop on the first floor of a narrow Victorian-era redbrick house. The short street was just one block over from a trendy shopping area full of flower shops, gift shops, small bistros and decorators. It was too cute for words with all that brick and gingerbread. The sign said "The Cozy Corpse: Used and collectible crime fiction," and underneath it added, "By appointment and by chance." In the window, a skeleton in a jaunty red cap reclined in a comfy garden chair. A great afterlife.

No one else was in sight, but I wasn't going to take a chance. I drove around the corner and parked the Saab well away from prying eyes.

I returned to the shop and pressed my nose to the glass in the door. Not sure why, as I was well aware that the owner was in hospital a good drive away. The store was done up in Victorian style: velvet wingback chairs, polished round tables, swag lamps. Too cute for words and I wanted desperately to get in. Maybe I'd find some Christie material that I hadn't seen yet.

I glanced around, but this street was mainly residential and quiet. It was just about eleven. I decided to canvas the neighbors until I could find someone who knew Karen and better yet, knew where she lived. I was just about to set out when I thought I heard a strange faraway gurgle. I stopped. Listened. There it was again. I banged on the door and the gurgle echoed. A dog? I wasn't sure. Was it drowning?

Maybe Karen lived above the shop. That would make sense. There was no vehicle in the narrow driveway, but there wouldn't be, would there? The Cozy Corpse van was probably considered evidence by this point.

I stepped around the side and didn't find a doorway. If Karen did live upstairs, how would she get in? A fragrant row of French lilacs hid a chain-link fence around a small grassy yard in the rear of the building. I tried to look like I belonged there as I opened the gate, stepped in and spotted the back entrance to the house. It's all in the training.

A dog bowl filled with water sat near the steps. Was Walter in the house?

The row of lilac trees kept me from being too visible to neighbors, or so I hoped. I didn't see anything that resembled a security camera. Again I pressed my nose to the glass window in the door. Boxes, shelves, papers. What else? Was that a staircase? Hard to tell.

I tried the door. Locked. Of course, it would be. I banged and banged and listened to the forlorn gurgle yet again. Time to fish or cut bait, as the uncles said. They'd taught me how to pick a lock when I was sixteen years old because you never know. Another Kelly motto. I'd learned quickly when Mick and Lucky started locking the treat pantry during Uncle Danny's failed foray into Weight Watchers. Danny was always worth ten bucks a pop.

I pushed my pick carefully into the keyhole and raked at the pins in the lock. I found the pin with the most tension and wedged in my other pick, searching for the bottom pin, while still keeping the others from slipping. Sweat started beading on my upper lip. This part is the kicker. If you mess up and turn the lock in the wrong direction, you have to start from scratch, and I was at least five minutes into this operation, regretting it more with each stinging drop of water accumulating on my face. I increased the torque and held my breath long enough to hear the sweet click of the lock. I wiped my face on my T-shirt. Certainly I was leaving more than a little DNA on the scene. I scooted in, closing the door behind me. No security pad was flashing. Looked like I was good to go. The stairs ran up from the cluttered back office. I followed saying, "Don't worry, doggie. You'll be all right." What should I expect from this Walter? Would it be grateful to be let out, or would it try to protect its turf?

The door at the top of the stairs wasn't locked. "Hey, boy," I called as I opened it. Maybe that should have been "Hey, Walter."

The gurgle turned into a series of snorts and snuffles.

The racket stopped midsnuffle and two jet-black bulging eyes peered at me from a flat wrinkled face. Walter the Pug whimpered and wagged his strange curly nub of a tail at me. The pooch didn't know whether to hide or seek. "Poor thing," I said, glancing around for a leash. "Let's get you outside."

I was quite lucky that I didn't get knocked down the narrow stairs as the pooch squirmed past me. I galloped after, panicked that the poor creature would escape down the street. But Walter just wanted his patch of grass after having been shut up for nearly fourteen hours. Now that's control. I was impressed.

I said, "Now let's get you some food, buddy." He wriggled past me up the stairs, and I set about to find his dog food. Once he was eating, I thought, I'd search the place to see if there was anything that linked Karen to whomever she'd been in touch with, possibly even the sinister Merlin. I located some kibble in a large container and dished out what looked like a reasonable amount. From the enthusiastic snorts and snarffles I concluded that the dog was ravenous and thrilled to get extra. I put some fresh water into his empty water dish. He seemed to have the capacity to inhale food and water. Signora Panetone would have loved him. Maybe I could bring him home. No, the cat would chew him up and spit him out.

As I made my way around Karen Smith's apartment, the pooch followed me, wagging his tail. I stopped and bent down and gave his tiny velvety ears a scratch and his belly a rub.

"Gotta get to work," I said. "I hope you understand."

He seemed to accept that and sat watching me as I inspected Karen's dim and jumbled living room. It must have doubled as an extra office. Files and papers were piled

THE CHRISTIE CURSE 123

around, some tumbled over. Books were stacked and used
as tables here and there. Karen obviously lived for books,
although her approach was a lot less obsessive than Vera
Van Alst's climate-controlled library. Every flat surface in
the room had something on it. Mostly books, but also a
surprisingly diverse collection of ceramic and china jugs.
Every piece of the soft furnishings had quilts or throws or
cushions or afghans or all of the above. It was quite dizzying.
I didn't find any useful notes along the lines of "In case of
my death, so and so did it."

I would have settled for a phone message. Or a phone.

Karen's cell phone wasn't there.

I took my time and carefully checked every cluttered
surface. I kept my eyes open for anything to do with Agatha,
of course. There were some sweet little Fontana reprints of
early Christies in a teetering stack on the dining table. *The
Mirror Crack'd from Side to Side* was on the top. I hadn't
read that yet. I resisted it and kept going.

The compact kitchen was a bit neater. I was surprised to
see the avocado green fridge and stove still chugging along.
As Uncle Mick says, they don't make 'em like they used to.
You can't get too vintage for me. I found no sign of cooking
activities, but a row of vintage cookbooks took pride of
place. *The Joy of Cooking*, *The Moosewood Cookbook*, *The
I Hate to Cook Book* and some well-worn, dog-eared *Mar-
tha Stewart Living* magazines.

A box of Peek Freans sat open on the counter.

I saw no dishes in the sink.

Ah. That reminded me of something. I returned to the
living room and spotted a Spode china teacup resting on top
of a copy of Margery Allingham's *The Crime at Black Dud-
ley* beside the largest armchair. One single cup. It didn't look
like Karen had entertained anyone before leaving to go back
and meet me.

I glanced around again. The empty cradle of the portable
phone caught my eye. Where was the receiver? I checked

around the table, under the sofa and under the chairs. I lifted every large and small piece of paper.

Then I headed into the bedroom. The ornate four-poster bedstead was made up with an antique quilt with a dog-sized indentation in the middle and about a gazillion pillows. Karen Smith liked being surrounded by stuff, I could tell that. Dozens of bright scarves hung from the closet door. Purses were arranged like art on the walls. Shoes were parked in tumbled pairs around the perimeter of the room.

Receiver, receiver. Where was the receiver? It wasn't in the living room or the kitchen, so the bedroom was the best bet.

The pooch came along and leapt up onto the bed and into the dent. I bent down and peered under the bed. No receiver there. As I backed away, I tripped over a pair of shoes discarded in the middle of the rug and barely kept from landing in a heap. How had I missed those? And what were they doing there? Had Karen decided to change in a hurry? Why? Someone must have contacted her. But who?

As I twirled around, surrounded by so many distractions, I thought I heard a noise outside. What was it? Oh no. Not a siren. Yes. A *whoop* and the slam of a door. I peered through the ruffled curtains on the window. Cops all right. I was toast. I watched as two officers marched up to the front door of the shop. It was then that I spotted the receiver on the window ledge and picked it up.

I suppose it was instinct. After all, I had been raised to be no friend of the law. "Come on, Walter," I said. "Time for a walk."

I hoped I had enough time to make it before the cops came around the back of the building. I tucked the receiver into my shoulder bag and pounded down the stairs with the dog on my heels. We both scampered out the door and into the yard. My heart was thundering, and I imagined the neighbors could hear my heavy breathing. The fence kept the dog in, and as climbing it to flee would be a clear admission of guilt, it was keeping me in too. I had just enough time to pull my lock picks out of my shoulder bag and slide them under a large ornamental rock in the middle of a bed of peonies. Just in case. It is always wise not to be found with breaking-and-entering tools in one's possession. I tucked the receiver there too, as it was nothing if not incriminating. I picked up a Frisbee I'd spotted in the grass and tossed it to the waddling Walter. He caught it in midair and raced around dropping it at the other end. I had just retrieved it and tossed it again when the cops called out to me.

"Oh hello," I said innocently.

"Ma'am," one of them said.

"Officer," I answered.

He cleared his throat. He looked even younger than I was.

"We got a report of a break-in at this address, ma'am."

"A break-in?" I said, wide-eyed. "Really? When?"

"Now, ma'am."

The cop stepped toward me, and Walter panted at him, with attitude, his hackles raised.

I bent down and said to the dog, "It's okay. Friends."

Walter seemed to accept that. If I said they were friends, that was good enough for him. I guessed he didn't see through my lie.

I straightened up and said, "Now? But I was in Karen's apartment and I didn't see any sign of a break-in."

As there was no threat from the cops, Walter barked to have the Frisbee tossed to him again and I complied.

"The person matched your description, ma'am."

"What?"

"Woman. Twenties. About five six. Dark hair. Wearing jeans and pink shoes."

"That's a weird coincidence," I said.

The first officer stroked his chin speculatively. The other one gave me a dirty look.

"Well, don't you think?" I said.

Walter returned with the Frisbee and dropped it at my feet. snorting bossily.

The first officer said, "No, ma'am. I don't think it is a coincidence."

The other one said, "Is this your residence, ma'am?"

"No. It's my friend's."

"And your friend's name?"

"Karen. Karen Smith."

"And where is Karen Smith, ma'am?"

"I don't know."

More chin stroking.

"But . . ."

"I came by to see her and I could hear Walter here in distress and I thought I'd take him out. Sometimes Karen gets tied up in business things and doesn't get back. It's really hard on Walter. And it must drive the neighbors crazy. I could hear him when I got out of my car."

I could tell they wanted to believe this, but I know their training tells them to be skeptical.

"Do you have a key, ma'am?"

"I don't."

"Then how did you get in?"

"Sorry?"

"How did you get in without a key?" A bit of edge in his voice this time.

I smiled as if it was the most logical thing in the world. "Didn't need one. The door was open."

"Open?"

"Yes. Karen must have forgotten to lock it. She's a bit . . . absentminded sometimes."

The first cop said, "Your car, ma'am."

"Yes?"

"Where did you park it?"

"Ah. Yes, it's around the corner and down a bit."

They exchanged glances. I should have had a sensible reason for parking the car there, but I'd not been prepared for that issue. Be Prepared 101 and I'd flubbed it.

I said, "The last time I parked here a bunch of kids were skateboarding on the street. I drive a vintage Saab. It's in mint condition, and I don't want anything to happen to it. It was my mom's."

Their eyes flicked to each other. That could have been true. But the whole thing probably seemed off to them, which of course it was. By now I was kicking myself for having picked the lock and weaving this web of lies. How many times had I had it drilled into me? Don't lie too much, you'll always get caught up in it. Stick as close to the truth as you can.

"You have ID, ma'am?"

I felt my mouth go dry. I hoped that my words were clear. Clear and unconcerned. "Of course." I reached for my shoulder bag and fished out my driver's license. "Here you go. But I think if you get in touch with Karen, she'll tell you that she often asks me to walk the dog. She'll be in soon I'm sure. She had a big show on this weekend."

"Is this your current address?"

"No. I've just moved back to Harrison Falls. I work for Miss Van Alst."

One of the officers said, "I'm sorry to tell you this, but your friend Karen Smith is in the hospital. She's been attacked."

I gasped.

The other officer moved to check the door. He turned back to me. "This door wasn't left unlocked. The lock's been picked."

I said, "Picked? But who could . . . ?"

They both turned and looked at me.

I let out a little whimper. I felt quite proud. "What if he's still up there?" I swayed a little bit for dramatic effect. "I could have been killed!"

They exchanged glances, and I figured the jig was up.

"Oh, here you are," an unexpected voice said.

The three of us whirled. I don't know which of the three of us was the most surprised to see Officer Smiley. Walter was delighted. Instead of barking, he jumped for joy and ran in circles wagging his ridiculous tail. Officer Smiley scratched his ears.

"Oh, it's you," I said. Had he been sent to pick me up? Drag me to the slammer? I'd been right all along. The policeman is *not* our friend, children.

"I'm sorry it took so long," he said with a dazzling smile at me. He might be pudgy and cute, but some orthodontist had done an excellent job on his pearly whites, except for the chipped incisor.

I said, "Don't worry about it."

He said to me, "I got caught up with a shoplifting incident. Guy's going down for a couple of rib eye steaks."

"Shocking," I said.

"I didn't even have time to change. I didn't want you waiting, so I hope you don't mind a detour before we go out." He shrugged cutely.

"No problem for me."

He nodded at his two colleagues. These guys didn't even live in the same jurisdiction. Did all cops know each other? If so, that was very creepy. "So, what's going on, guys?"

The first one said, "Reported break-in. Lock was picked."

The second one said, "She'd been inside. Seems to have apprehended the family dog."

I said, "Apprehended? We call that 'walked the dog' where I come from. Walter was upset and—"

Officer Smiley said, "But I'm sure Karen would have asked Jordan to take, um, Walter out."

"Exactly," I said. "I knew this would get straightened out. Glad you finally got here."

"You know her?" the first officer said to Smiley.

"Of course. We see each other all the time," Smiley said,

smilingly. "Since I moved to Harrison Falls and she moved back."

"Okay then. Guess the neighbor overreacted."

I said, "Probably driven to the brink of madness by Walter's sounds of distress. Really, Karen shouldn't keep him cooped up in that small apartment."

Officer Smiley turned to me. "So, you ready to go?"

"More than. But I'd like to take Walter for a proper walk. I hate to put him back upstairs. And Karen's lock has been picked. What if whoever did that is still up there?" I turned to the two cops. "Are you going to check out the apartment? And you really should take a look at the shop too."

Reluctantly, they headed into the building, leaving me standing there with Smiley and Walter. Walter shook the Frisbee. Smiley said, "You in a little hot water here?"

"Not anymore. I'm glad you showed up. They got it into their pointy little heads that I burgled Karen's apartment."

"Do you think anything was taken?"

"Hard to tell, really. She's a bit of a pack rat, and there's stuff everywhere. Stacks of books and sweet little collectibles. Nice stuff, but it's hard to tell if there was even more stuff earlier, if you know what I mean."

"Hmm."

"I suppose we should wait to see what they find. I'd really like to go, but I don't want to leave Walter here alone. Karen's—" Lucky I caught myself in time. Smiles or no smiles, he didn't need to know that I'd been in to see her. "What is happening with Karen? Do you know?"

"She's out of intensive care, but not out of the woods yet."

"I can't leave this dog in there. It's cruel. I think Karen worked out of her house and shop and he's not used to being alone."

"I suppose not."

"But I don't think I can bring him to my place. I live in a house that's ruled by a bipolar cat that can walk through walls. I don't think he'd be safe."

He scrunched up his face, something he does when he's thinking. I don't imagine he'd ever win a poker game. "Bipolar cat? That sounds bad."

The two cops took that moment to emerge. One shook his head in disbelief. "If anyone got in there, looks like he brought stuff in instead of taking things out."

The other one said, "Looks like the only thing missing is the receiver to the phone."

I managed to keep my expression neutral. "The receiver?" With my luck someone would pick that exact moment to call Karen and the stupid thing would ring from under the rock. I'd lose my lock picks.

He said, "Yeah. Although it's probably in there somewhere."

They ambled off, exhibiting those cop walks I am so not fond of, leaving me with my new best friend, Officer Tyler "Smiley" Dekker. And also leaving me to wonder exactly why he'd showed up at Karen's house while I was there. I imagined Tiff asking, *Have you seen Officer Stalker today?*

Was it a coincidence? How could it be? Karen's place was in Grandville, ten to twenty minutes from Harrison Falls. Neither his jurisdiction, nor his business really. He'd been prepared to lie to his Grandville colleagues, and he'd done a surprisingly good job of it. They'd gone away thinking that somehow Officer Smiley and I had met on schedule. Huh. My brain formulated three explanations: (a) he'd known I was going to be there; (b) he'd followed me; and (c) he had some reason for wanting to get into Karen's business or apartment. I wasn't crazy about any of these. I wasn't even sure that I'd trust him with Walter.

I said, "I know someone who'd be happy to give Walter a place to stay until Karen's out of danger and home again. No cat. Home all day. No problemo."

I could tell he was relieved. We headed along the side walkway to the street to give Walter a bit of a waddle with me thinking fast. He hadn't been in the building, and he wasn't showing any interest in it. Unless, of course, he'd already been through the place. Walter had seemed quite comfortable when Smiley arrived. Had they met before, say when Smiley was going through the apartment? The door had been locked when I arrived, but what if he had Karen's keys? He could have picked them up when we were waiting for the emergency team. I'd been so distressed I wouldn't have noticed. All this was entirely possible and, really, no more unlikely than anything else that had happened in the past day or so.

Now I needed to know how to get rid of him so that I could get back to the yard and retrieve my lock-picking tools and Karen's receiver from under the rock without an audience of cops. But what if he followed me?

I stopped. "We can't leave the door like that." I was really surprised those two cops would just leave. Of course, Grandville was the kind of town where folks probably didn't even make a habit of locking their doors, possibly laboring under the delusion that the police might be looking out for them.

He shrugged. "It's the homeowner's responsibility."

"The homeowner, who is in the hospital probably not even conscious? That homeowner?"

"Well, yes, but . . ."

"We need to do it. And yes, I realize that the person who picked the lock could come back and pick the new one, but . . ."

"We don't have the right."

"Okay. I hear you. I'll do it. As her friend. I'll do it and I'll take responsibility for it and I'll pay for it and I'll make sure that the keys are taken to her in the hospital. It's the right thing to do."

"But I don't know if I can let you do it."

This was really starting to irk me. "Really? Well, let me point out, Officer Dekker, that this is not your jurisdiction and you have already told a double whopper to your colleagues about meeting me here, so you can bend a little more. Now, how about you go take Walter for a bit of exercise and I'll call a locksmith and you won't know anything about it."

It all came out huffier than I had planned, but my tone went unnoticed.

"Good thinking. But there's no phone."

"I'll use my cell. You don't have to be a witness to that. And I'll find a bag and clean up after our friend here."

As they strolled off, I used my iPhone to locate a locksmith and made a quick call. I glanced around. What kind of nosy neighbors were there? I guessed no one had spotted me hiding the lock-picking tools under the rock, but in case someone had resumed their watch, I used the guise of picking up after Walter and managed to snag the tools and the receiver and tuck them below the waistband of my jeans. I held my bag in front of me to hide the lumps.

Five minutes later Officer Smiley was back with Walter. I said, "We're good. I'll wait here for the locksmith. No need for you to hang around."

But of course, he did. I wondered what the neighbors had thought about the so-called burglar hanging around with the persnickety Pug, who had just been walked by the uniformed police officer. Now that would be a dinner-time story.

When the locksmith arrived, Smiley was keen to observe. I had to use Walter a second time. I suggested that Walter was really behind on his walks and should have another outing. I hoped to distract nosy Tyler Dekker long enough to get the locksmith to make an extra key. By the time Smiley and Walter sauntered back, I already had my copy in my pocket. And Officer Smiley promised to see that the official newly minted key got to Karen right away.

"I can do it," I said, sweetly.

"Better if I do. I am a sworn officer of the law."

"I'll go with you." I didn't say, "Because I don't trust you."

* * *

I TOOK THE blanket that I always kept in my trunk and spread it over the passenger seat of the Saab. I couldn't believe I was letting a dog into my precious vehicle. I felt a bit like Vera might have if Walter had been lurching through her library knocking first editions off shelves and chewing on the rosewood table legs. I hoped my elegant mother wasn't rolling in her grave, wherever that might have been.

It was cool enough in the covered parking area to leave Walter in the vehicle (as Officer Smiley called it).

When we reached the fifth floor, we discovered that Karen was now in an induced coma to allow the swelling in her brain to subside. And I'd thought I was having a bad day. I reminded myself of just how bad things were for Karen and how much worse they'd turned out for Alex Fine.

Officer Smiley turned on the wattage for the staff at the nurses' station and arrangements were made to take care of the keys. He made sure Karen would be given numbers to reach him and me when she was conscious again. Luckily, no one remembered me as her visiting niece.

After that, I decided it really was time to give him the slip. Whatever reason he had for sticking so close, it wasn't my problem. I had places to go and things to do. Starting with dropping Walter off with Uncle Mick. That would also give me a chance to return the lock-picking tools without arousing any suspicion in whomever was following me, and I was pretty sure that would be Officer You-Know-Who.

CHAPTER ELEVEN

❖

I SAID GOOD-BYE to Officer Smiley and drove off, try-ing not to think about the nose prints that Walter was making on my pristine passenger-side windows. I couldn't believe he'd made himself comfortable on the driver's side instead of the nicely protected seat I'd assigned to him. Even though I'd relocated him to his proper place, he kept trying to worm his way back to my side. I hoped he couldn't create too much chaos in the time it would take to get back to Har-rison Falls. At least he wasn't snuffling and missing his new best friend with the suspicious smile.

I was desperate to get the dog into someplace that wasn't my car. And I needed to get back to searching for the Chris-tie manuscript and seeing what I could dig up about Merlin. Of course, I knew that Karen's attack was connected even if I couldn't figure out how.

When I opened the door to Michael Kelly's Fine Antiques, the bell jingled, Walter lurched ahead of me as if this were the best place ever, and Uncle Mick didn't even blink.

As usual, it would take more than the unexpected arrival of a strange, and strange-looking, dog to throw Uncle Mick off his stride.

"Very practical, my girl. We'll put him to work keeping out the thieves," Mick said.

Walter had not the slightest talent in that direction, but I kept that thought to myself as well as the related thought that the thieves were all on the inside. You have to be careful with relatives.

Of course, the next time the door jingled and the long arm of the law appeared, Uncle Mick almost blinked. Really. I saw it with my own eyes.

"Tyler Dekker," my new nemesis said, giving Uncle Mick what looked like a very firm handshake. Did I detect a flinch from my uncle? "Jordan's told me so much about you. It's a real pleasure to make your acquaintance, Mr. Kelly." He turned toward Uncle Lucky, now looming silently in the doorway to the back room, eyes narrowed. Uncle Lucky shook his head in what I assumed was astonishment.

I turned and mouthed, "I didn't tell them a thing."

Officer Smiley moved briskly across the crowded shop to the back door. "And you must be Uncle Lucky. Great to meet you." He shook Lucky's hand vigorously.

Uncle Lucky stared at his hand as if someone had squeezed a caterpillar into it.

I barely managed not to yelp, "I've been framed." I was definitely going to have some explaining to do, although I had no idea how to explain it.

Smiley glanced around the shop. "Great little business you got going here."

I felt doomed.

Fortunately, Officer Smiley couldn't stay long, and Uncle Mick and Uncle Lucky seemed to recover.

"Not my fault," I said as soon as the door closed behind him. "And there's no need for a lecture if you are thinking of that. I am not encouraging him in any way, and I am certainly not talking about any of the Kellys to him. I never gave him your names. I don't know what he's up to, and whatever it is, I don't like it either."

With that settled, except for a number of wounded looks, I decided to get about my business. First, Karen's phone. Of course, it was useless. Too far away from the base.

At least I got a serving of canned chicken noodle soup from Uncle Mick for lunch. He served it with pop-up dinner rolls—a culinary triumph. Perhaps that meant all was not lost in the family department. Unlike Officer Smiley, Walter was a hit with the Kellys. This came as a serious surprise to me because my uncles had never had a pet. I had never had a pet, even though I'd wept and pleaded for one as a child. But Walter had his own lunch, which was exactly like mine, only served in a bowl on the floor. I wasn't sure what the vet would say, but then again, the vet wasn't there.

When I was finished, I said, "I have to go back to Sal. He's kind of let me down."

They exchanged glances.

"It's not good to push Sal," Mick said.

"Not pushing, just bringing him up to speed. Thanks for lunch. Now, can you help me ditch the cop? He can only go in one direction at a time."

Nothing would give either of them greater pleasure. Ten minutes later, with my blue Saab still sitting conspicuously in front of Michael Kelly's Fine Antiques, Uncle Mick drove off in the white van of the same name. He headed west toward the interstate with Walter sitting in the passenger seat looking out the window, snorting and expecting adventure.

Immediately after, Uncle Lucky got into his classic Town Car and headed east. At about the same time, I took a few moments to change back into my original outfit: wide-leg dark denim trousers with a sharp white tee and Uncle Mick's poor boy hat, and lip gloss, of course. I let myself out the back door. I sauntered two doors down to the garage where the uncles keep an extra vehicle for exactly this type of situation. It was an unremarkable Ford Focus wagon in faded black. I figured Officer Smiley would be either watching for me to emerge from the store and get into my own car, or he'd be following one of my uncles assuming that I was in that vehicle. That's what I would have done in his shoes.

I headed back downtown to Sal's and parked a block past the office. I arrived to find that Sal was his sartorially splendid self. I was glad I'd changed.

"Sorry to arrive on short notice," I said, accepting the double-cheek kisses. "Circumstances are evolving and I need to deal with them."

Sal would know about evolving circumstances. Dealing with them was how he stayed in business, whatever that business was.

We sat in the green leather club chairs, facing each other.

"Merlin," I said.

Sal raised a well-groomed eyebrow.

"Does that ring a bell?"

He shrugged his elegant shoulders.

"You see, my contact who was going to give me information about the manuscript I am seeking was badly injured just before she was supposed to meet with me."

A furrow appeared between Sal's eyebrows. I figured this was high emotion for him.

"Who is this contact?"

I explained about Karen and what had taken me to the hall Sunday evening. Had it been only last night? I felt like I'd lived a week in one day.

"So you don't think it was just a random robbery."

I continued. "I believe it's all connected. I think the person left her for dead. I may have been set up. The police think I had something to do with it, and I am being followed everywhere. Did I ever mention that the man who had my job previously was probably murdered?"

"And this Merlin is involved?" Sal said.

"Yes. I have heard that someone named Merlin might be the person behind the object of Vera Van Alst's desire."

He nodded. "And Merlin would be?"

"I don't know. I think a fraudster, a con artist or possibly a thief. Now maybe a killer. Or he's doing something to cause a killer to act. I thought with your connections in the world of, um, business, you might be able to help me out with information that will lead to him."

Sal reached forward and took my hand. That gave new meaning to the word "unnerving." "Jordan, my dear. I think you should back away from this one."

"Thanks for the advice, Sal, but I really can't. It's my job, and Miss Van Alst will fire me if I don't keep going."

"Maybe you have to walk away from the job too."

Oh boy. I didn't think that Sal would understand how I felt about my perfect cabbage rose garret and the fabulous collection of books, the amazing meals and my opportunity to drive around in my Saab tracking down books while looking like vintage money. So I said, "It's a matter of honor."

I would have added "principle," but I wasn't sure it would carry any weight. Honor, now, that was different.

Sal nodded. "You are going to have to be very careful."

I took a deep breath. "So you know something about this Merlin then?"

"I know nothing about him. Nothing at all. But there is one person dead and another one injured and you are connected to both of them. This is not something that happens every day in business. I have known you all your life, Jordan, and I would not like any harm to come to you. You must think of your family, your uncles. They lost your mother before her time. How would they feel if something happened to you? Do you not feel this responsibility?"

I hadn't been feeling it up until that minute. I worried about my family running into trouble of one kind or another, not me.

"I'll be careful," I said. "Really."

"It won't be easy watching out for someone when you have no idea who he may be. Or as these are modern times, perhaps Merlin is a she."

"I take your point. I won't do anything risky. But I would appreciate any information you can find for me." I felt a bit of déjà vu. Hadn't this visit been essentially the same as the first one, with the exception of the information about Karen Smith? I was surprised that Sal, who had a finger on everything going on in the state, had come up empty.

Sal got to his custom-shod feet and adjusted his impeccable jacket.

"I will see what I can find out. I can dig a little deeper."

I shivered. That phrase always makes me think of graveyards.

I was still feeling the chill as I left Sal's office and climbed into my decoy Focus. I looked in every direction but didn't see anyone or anything that looked unusual. Just in case, though, I made about two dozen unnecessary turns and drove down a few extra alleyways before I decided the coast was clear.

No sign of my new shadow.

MY CHALLENGE WAS to get into Karen's house for a good long search without getting myself either murdered or arrested. Avoiding these fates didn't seem as easy as it once had been. I lacked allies. My uncles could help protect me, of course, but with their track record it wouldn't be good news if anyone in authority came across them where they didn't belong. Tiff might as well have been on the moon. Vera Van Alst would have her own planet. I wasn't sure what Officer Smiley was up to, and I was really hoping that he'd stay in Harrison Falls where he belonged. My school friends had pretty much all left the area. I had the dog, of course, but he seemed happy with my uncles, and I was pretty sure he'd need more protection than he'd give. Of course, my uncles had always advised me, don't do what they expect. It was good advice if you could figure out what it meant.

In this case, I had an idea, and I decided to act before anyone watching caught on to the fact that while my Saab was parked outside the antiques store, I was not parked inside the shop.

I headed for the police headquarters (such as it was) in Grandville. I marched in and asked to speak to the officers who had attended the reported break-in at Karen Smith's home. To my astonishment, they showed up within ten minutes and parked their black-and-white in front of the station. Grandville is a quiet town. No question about that.

I went out to meet them, smiling as though my face might break. "I hope you remember me. I was at Karen Smith's place when you came along. I need to get back in, but I am very worried that whoever broke in might return. Might even be watching the place." This was true enough. I added, "I need to get a few things for her in the hospital, a nightie, and toiletries. The poor woman is going to be desperate. Can you help me?"

The first one scratched his head. "Why are you asking us?"

"I need protection. And I don't want anyone else to call the police on me. You see my problem."

"What about your friend? The guy from Harrison Falls?"

"He's been called in to work. And this is your town. Do you need to ask permission or something? I'm not in a hurry. I can wait if you do."

Of course they didn't need permission, and would never have admitted it to a civilian if they did. They swaggered off to their car, and I followed in my invisible Focus.

Shortly afterward, we arrived back at Karen Smith's. Luckily the officers were easily distracted. As they went ahead into the back office area of the shop, I produced the empty soda can full of change that I'd been carrying. I threw it at the farthest part of the first-floor shop. I was taught this trick by Tiff. It was supposed to be useful when encountering bears in the woods or dealing with drunken, groping frat boys. Shock and awe, with a zero percent chance of casualties. As they investigated the rolling clatter, it bought me enough time to head upstairs and slip the receiver back on the cradle in the living room and let it recharge. Meanwhile, I went into the bedroom and selected what I thought Karen might want when she woke up. I didn't want to think *if* she woke up. I found a small overnight case and filled it with the usual stuff: toothpaste, toothbrush, deodorant, face cream, two nighties, slippers and clean underwear. I also put together an outfit that she could wear when, not if, she came home. I figured the clothes she'd been found in would be sitting in the evidence room at the cop shop. As I gathered up everything, I checked each surface and under the bed, behind chairs, everywhere I could think of, searching for a clue to anybody she'd contacted recently. I knew that whatever she'd found out for me, it had to have been within the last day and a half as I hadn't even met her before Saturday. I found nothing. No messages. No notes. No scribbled telephone numbers. Nothing. Well, a note to herself. *Buy dog food* was scrawled on a napkin from Yummers, the concession at the book fair. I felt a little light go on over my head. That girl at the book fair, as mopey and dopey as she was, had a unique perspective because of her location. She could see everybody who came and went, and my guess was that most people bought something from her: coffee, water, rancid Danishes. Best of all, she had a clear view of Karen's booth. She was in touch, but not in the same business. But how could I reach her? Would the people at Saint Sebastian's have a contact? Would one of the vendors at the fair?

When I heard the cops arrive upstairs, I stepped into the living room.

"Nobody down there," they said, sounding quite disappointed. I said to them, "That's good, but I think I'd better go check the basement windows to see if they're secure. Just in case. Maybe a person could get access that way."

"We'll do that," the first cop said, putting me in my civilian place. As soon as they'd swaggered down the stairs, I picked up the receiver, which had recharged enough to use it. Karen had called only one number on Sunday, and she'd received only one call. As the cops didn't show any signs of coming back yet, I called that number. No answer. It rang and rang. Someone with no services, I supposed. Or someone who wouldn't answer the second line if they were on the phone. Then I tried again.

"Hello?" I said, when I heard the sound of a pickup at the other end. "I'd like to speak to you about Karen Smith. You called her yesterday."

Well, thanks for that dial tone, dude.

I tried the number again. A male voice answered. He didn't seem happy to get a call. I hesitated briefly and decided to go for it. I said, "May I speak with Merlin, please?"

"Who is this?"

I hesitated again. I didn't want to tell the truth, but I had to pick the right lie. "I am a friend of Karen Smith's. Who is this?"

"Why are you calling here?"

"I believe Karen spoke to you yesterday. I'd like to know what it was about."

"I didn't speak to her."

"Your number is on her telephone. Someone called."

A pause. "Are you calling from her house?"

Okay, this was tricky, but might flush him out. "I am."

"I told you I didn't speak to her. Don't call here again."

I listened to the dial tone. I was about to copy down the number when I heard the officers call out. On an impulse, I pocketed the receiver. It was time to head to the living room. The officers were already back upstairs and getting restless.

"That will do it," I said, smiling brightly. "I have everything I need. I appreciate you both helping me. I would have been very nervous here alone."

They both managed to look a bit bashful. That might have been cute if they weren't cops.

Outside, they asked about my vintage Saab. "Waiting outside the shop," I said, truthfully. "Sometimes I wish I was a mechanic," I added. That was true too. Sometimes. They nodded in understanding, and we all waved as we drove away. I took my invisible Focus around the block. High fences with sprawling vines, clumps of lilac, and tall cedar hedges made this street pretty, but also private and perfect for hanging around unseen. I returned and backed the car into the driveway of the house next door. I angled the car so I could see through the yew hedge without being too noticeable myself. No one was home, judging by the flyers sticking out of the mailbox. This couldn't have been the neighbor who'd called the cops. I hoped they would continue to stay away wherever they were. I wanted to be able to get out of the neighborhood quickly in case I needed to. I adjusted the poor boy hat, locked the car doors, slouched down in the seat and waited.

The minutes seemed like hours, but according to the clock on the dash of the Focus, it was less than a quarter of an hour later when I spotted a vehicle turning onto the street. A battered red pickup crept along past Karen's house. I thought it was a Ford, but that was just a guess. Trucks are not one of my interests, even vintage ones. The truck rolled along and parked two doors down. That was exactly the type of trick I was employing, so I wasn't really taken in by it. The person lumbered along, hugging the over-hanging lilacs and vines. I couldn't really see a face because he also had a baseball cap pulled low, but it was definitely a man and he seemed to have a limp. And I couldn't make out the license plate on the truck, mainly because of the shadows and the distance. I squinted, straining to see while at the same time trying to remain as invisible as my temporary car.

I was distracted by another car turning into the driveway across the street.

In the time it took to turn and glance, the lumbering, limping truck guy had turned into the path toward Karen's backyard and, I figured, the door leading to her apartment. I'd missed seeing his face.

Now what?

I was pretty sure that my phone calls from Karen Smith's place had led to this guy's arrival.

At that moment a *whoop!* cut through the air and a police black-and-white careened onto the street and parked, angled, blocking the path to Karen's backyard. As I sat there with my mouth open, a familiar cop bounced out, leaving his driver's-side door open. I heard him yell something. I rolled down the window—the Focus didn't have automatic anything—to hear better. As my own personal officer Smiley hurtled down the pathway, I spotted the truck guy pull himself to the top of the chain-link fence behind the lilacs and drop to the other side. He might have been sinister and he might have had a limp, but he was definitely in good shape. Officer Smiley did not return. I sat there scowling, trying to figure out what kind of hornet's nest I had stirred up. About two minutes later, I spotted a figure limp along the sidewalk, leap into the pickup and screech down the street.

Fifteen minutes later, Officer Smiley still hadn't returned.

Was he all right? Had the truck driver injured him? From what I'd seen, that didn't seem possible. The guy had practically catapulted over the fence. But where was Smiley? There was nothing to do in the backyard, so the obvious answer was, in Karen's apartment. Why was less obvious. And winning the prize for least obvious was, why was he here in Grandville again?

I started up the Focus. Lucky me, I still had Karen's receiver and it was close enough to her apartment to work. I made a 911 call and said nothing when it was picked up. I hung up, wiped off the receiver, tossed it into the neighbor's koi pond and drove off, leaving Officer Smiley to explain himself. It was only much later that I realized that I should have copied down the telephone number I had dialed earlier, in Karen's apartment.

I EASED THE car into my dusky parking area at the rear of the Van Alst house. I spied a note taped to the door and was focusing on it intently, stepping through the threshold of the back entrance, when Eddie, the mailman, appeared behind me. For that scary surprise he very nearly got a sharp kick in the shins.

"Jorduff, caan I spweechwff chew?" Eddie mumbled incoherently.

At first, I thought he might be drunk. Then I noticed the huge biscotti in his hand.

"Sorry." He swiped at the crumbs spraying past his lips. "I was waiting for you when Fiammetta ambushed me with snacks."

He held the homemade treat as evidence and smiled meekly.

I put down my bag and stepped back outside with Eddie. The early evening was casting heavy fuchsia shadows. He seemed shifty and nervous about being in the open. Perhaps he feared the ninja-like Signora Panetone would cram more biscotti into his empty mouth.

He looked me square in the eye and drew a long breath.

I would not have described this as a threatening situation, but I was very uncomfortable. "What is it about, Eddie?" I figured not a postal issue.

Eddie seemed to get even jumpier and edged away from

me now, pressing himself into a forsythia bush as if to stay out of sight. Who was he hiding from? Vera? The signora? Eddie began to sputter quickly. "You had better be more careful, Jordan. Not, not, not just for your sake, but Vera's too. She's all alone out here."

All alone out here? She was surrounded by paid helpers in a house with excellent security. Anyone who got past the gardener, the coded security system, Fiammetta and the damn cat, not to mention Eddie and me, would have to contend with Vera herself, who was about as helpless as a bear. On the other hand, she did live in a house that still held valuables, including her collection. How long would it take the police to get all the way out here if there were a break-in?

As if to answer my unspoken question, Eddie said, "The police would take ten minutes, minimum, to get here."

Of course, Officer Smiley seemed to be able to teleport himself, but if he wasn't available, the ten minute estimate was probably true, even optimistic. I was keenly aware that I was also "all alone out here" at the edge of town. Eddie's nervous behavior was unsettling me. Was he on something? He certainly was twitching, and also he'd been hiding in a forsythia bush, which seemed unusual. But what did I know of the strange people connected with the Van Alst house?

"Just watch yourself!" Was he threatening me? I wasn't particularly scared, but I was so frazzled, my instincts were suffering, but not so much that I couldn't snap a picture of him with my iPhone.

That seemed to make him even jumpier. Whatever it was he'd been trying to accomplish, he gave up, darted ahead of me and slunk off into the house, shaking his head.

What the heck was that?

I stepped into the back entrance and shut the door on anyone else who might be lurking in the bushes. I started up the stairs, uncrumpling the note I hadn't had a chance to read yet.

Dear Miss Bingham,

I would like to speak with you at my earliest convenience.
That would be at dinner. Please bring your notes and
research.

Sincerely,
Vera Van Alst

Oh yeah, that. I'd been so busy trying to figure out what
was going on with all the people around me, I'd forgotten
why I'd been speaking to them in the first place. Not for the
first time, I asked myself what kind of mailman comes to
your house at seven p.m.

This place was starting to give me the willies, and I
guess, the Eddies too.

CHAPTER TWELVE

THE THING WITH Vera Van Alst is that you always need to play from your strengths. I wasn't even sure what mine were as I headed for dinner, with my notebook tucked under my arm. I certainly didn't have any definitive answers for her. Questions, yes. I was going to be faking my head off, while trying to extract useful information from her.

I kept my head high but also kept an eye out for Eddie in case he jumped out of some alcove as I strode by. Didn't he have a home?

In the dining room, the table was set for one. The place setting was in my usual spot, so I could only assume it was for me.

The signora arrived, swooping as usual, as soon as I sat down.

"Eat," she said firmly. Tonight's temptation was a spinach fettuccine, homemade, with a dusting of fresh shaved Parmigiano-Reggiano.

"Sure thing," I said. "Where's Miss Van Alst?" I added as she heaped the fettuccine on my plate. I tried to limit the amount, knowing that this course was just the warm-up for the main event, but the signora ignored my pathetic attempts. Oh well. I didn't ask, where's the cat? But I did wonder.

"Vera sick."

"Sick?" How sick could she be? She'd just left me a typical bullying note.

"Bad back. Very sore. Pain. You eat. Eat!"

"But I just—"

"Doctor here. You want more?"

"No thank you. This is lovely. The doctor's here? Now? How sick is she?"

"Vera, Vera. Always sick. Always. Bad pain. Eat more. Get better."

Eat more. Get better. Words to live by. I got busy with the fettuccine and the extra bowl of lovely cheese for my health.

What was the history of the signora and the Van Alst family? Why did Vera treat her like an old shoe? Signora Panetone, although she took a little getting used to, obviously cared about Vera. Vera, just as obviously, needed people to care about her. She hardly ate. She never seemed to leave the house. She didn't appear to ever get any kind of exercise, nor have the slightest joy in life. I wasn't even sure the books brought her pleasure. Maybe they just took the edge off her misery. Vera was very lucky to have these people and this house, and equally oblivious to her good fortune. But I hear pain can change the way you view the world. Is that what had happened to ruin Vera?

Dinner was veal and lemon saltimbocca and fresh local asparagus. Hard to beat. I felt extra sorry for Vera, even though she was her own worst enemy.

Every time the door opened, I thought I caught a glimpse of Eddie, pacing. Come to think of it, what was his story? What role did he play in the household? What was he trying to do? Scare me? Warn me? Creep me out?

I figured I had a hope of getting some answers to the

Eddie questions, at least. I got out of my seat and headed for the kitchen, pushing open the swinging door expecting to confront him. Instead of Eddie, I found the signora, who chased me back to my seat with the dessert.

Sit! Eat!

Toasted angel food cake slices with lemon sauce.

Vera missed the toasted angel food cake too.

I WAS SO happy to flop onto my own bed, I didn't even care if there was someone (or some cat) lurking behind the door. If I hadn't been in such a zombie-like state, I would have had the presence of mind to let my buzzing iPhone go to voice mail.

"Oh good, you're home!" Tiff chirped before I'd even said hello.

"Barely. I feel like I'm still dragging some parts of me up the stairs." I propped myself against the feather pillows as Tiffany began to vent. My job was to listen. That's what friends are for. I did that. Despite my wonderful dinner, I was far too exhausted by the day's extraordinary and confusing events to rehash them and reassure Tiff that I was in no grave danger. This was something I had yet to convince myself. Better she didn't know.

Instead, I zoned out on my room, letting my eyes trace the cabbage roses and curlicues on the wallpaper while Tiff went off about the boom operator and how she loathed him. "He's reckless! We're out here in the middle of *nowhere* and he's injuring people." I wasn't even sure what a boom operator did, or even what a boom was, so I allowed my weary mind to saunter around the room once more. I paused to contemplate the alcove where the patterns didn't match up. Like a big knife had sliced all the beautiful roses in half. I didn't remember it being like that earlier.

"People could be killed!"

"What?"

"Listen, if this guy doesn't smarten up and stop partying his paychecks away, someone is going to lose their life. These pipes weigh about a ton each segment, and this hung-over guy is swinging them around on his boom like they are Lincoln Logs."

"Oh, well, yes, that sounds dangerous. Someone should tell his foreman."

"He *is* the foreman." As Tiff launched into another tirade, I was beginning to think I wasn't the only one finding my new employment stressful. Tiff was always consumed with the well-being of others and considered herself a "safety inspector to the world." Yet another reason to hold my tongue about all the creepiness on my end. It would only worry an already overloaded woman. Worse still, it would create more work for me.

Something fluttered in the alcove, and I pulled myself out of bed to shut the window. It was getting chilly now that the sun had set. Looking down beside my Saab, I could see a figure, dark clad. My arm hair stood at attention.

Behind me something rustled, and this time I did shriek.

"You okay?" Tiff stopped counting the flaws of her least favorite coworker.

"Yes," I said shakily. I'd spotted the source of the noise: a cat curling itself into a ball on my library books. "That stupid cat keeps getting into my apartment." I have been known to have an overactive imagination. Was this just another one of those times?

My mouth went dry. "Tiff, I need to catch this cat. Can I call you in the afternoon tomorrow?"

"Sure, sweetie, sorry for all the dumping."

"No worries. Talk soon." If I'd dropped one hint of what I'd seen, Tiff would have been on me to get out of there. It wasn't like she could have done much except worry herself sick up there in northern Alberta. I didn't want that. So I was on my own. When I turned back to the window, the lurker was now crouched almost out of sight behind some boxwoods. But he was definitely getting closer to the house. It wasn't Eddie. Too big. I strained to see. Did he have a limp? I couldn't be sure. Was he even real?

I opened the window and yelled, "Hey, get out of here. The police have been alerted and they'll be watching." I couldn't believe I'd said anything so ridiculous. The police were hardly likely to hang around watching Vera's place on the strength of one phone call. But it did the trick.

I figured an innocent man would have looked up in confusion. This one bolted. Of course, he could always wait and come back.

I double-checked the lock on the foyer door. Back upstairs again, I pushed the rolltop desk against my apartment entrance. I wasn't even going to bother to show the cat out. Felines were the least of my worries now.

I DIDN'T HAVE the best night's sleep. It was full of limping strangers, cats with keys, postmen wearing fright wigs and Miss Jane Marple hanging upside down like a bat. The signora pursued me with plates full of food, and all my vintage clothes were now too small. Nightmare alley.

When morning came, there was no sign of Vera in the conservatory. No sign of Eddie and for once, no sound of the lawn tractor or the busy-bee gardener. On the other hand, the signora was fresh as a daisy and in a mood to dish out food. Why not?

I DECIDED TO give Lance a call to see if he had any helpful information. I needed to keep digging about Christie and the unpublished play, but also I was troubled that I really did not understand my client. The uncles have a saying: know your mark. I suppose it's not such a bad thing when it comes to employers too.

"Harrison Falls Public Library."

"Hi, Lance. It's Jordan."

His tone switched from helpful public servant to flirtatious. "Miss Bingham, to what do I owe this delicious surprise?"

I found myself blushing like a schoolgirl, despite the fact that Lance and I were merely friends. He certainly had a way with the ladies, but I wasn't ready for a romance, let alone one that could mess up a friendship. "Suppose I was looking to find out the history about the Van Alst Shoe Company."

"Then you would have come to the right place." He laughed in his warm and charming way. I felt a little butterfly in my stomach.

"If I left that with you, do you think we could meet up for coffee, and I could get all the nitty-gritty details?" I was nervous. I'd been badly burned in my relationship, hadn't dated in a year, and even a fact-finding mission with a platonic friend was still too close for comfort.

"It would be my pleasure." Damn that smoldering voice. "Café Hudson for lunch? How long do you have?"

"For you I can take an hour. I'd like to catch up, hear about your time away."

My lip was getting annoyingly sweaty. I hurried to get off the phone. "Sounds good, buddy!" Everyone knows that calling someone your buddy is an immediate mood killer.

Lance just chuckled. We exchanged cell phone numbers in case plans changed.

I shot a text off to Tiff. *Meeting Lance for lunch at Café Hudson. Eat your heart out.*

Tiff and I had loitered at that café an entire summer, when we weren't "working" at Kelly's Fine Antiques. It was a miracle we'd had anything left for our college expenses. Lance had been a waiter there, putting himself through library school at SUNY in Albany part-time. He was like a bronze god with espresso. We were instantly smitten. But life had other plans for us all, and a strong friendship blossomed instead. This didn't affect how much Lance flirted, though.

I could just imagine Tiff's reaction. She would turn green. But she took the high road: *Wish I was there! Take a pic plz!*

The Café Hudson was still just run-down enough to be chic. Young, angry-for-no-reason, heavily tattooed and pierced people enjoyed six-dollar coffees and checked their Facebook accounts on their phones. The players had changed, but the place smelled the same. It felt like coming home. Lance was waiting in "my" booth by the smeared picture window. It was well outside the scope of his job as a reference librarian, but Lance wasn't one to be constrained.

For instance, I was unable to squirm out of a long hug. My relatives are not huggers, unless someone has something in their pocket that needs to be liberated.

"Sit down, tell me everything." Lance beamed at me.

"Actually, as much as I'd love to sit here and talk about myself for an hour, I really need that info about the Van Alsts and maybe some guidance in finding out where to sell very rare ephemera." Lance squinted his amazing green eyes, sizing me up. He could sense that I was all business. That sensitivity was one of his best traits. He let the personal update slide.

"Let me give you all I've got, and there is a lot." This was a man who loved to ferret out information, loved to learn and loved to help. He was a born librarian, the Harrison Falls Senior Women's Book Club must have thought they'd died and went to heaven when he walked in.

"The Van Alst Shoe Factory was founded by Herman Van Alst in the mid-1800s. Business was solid, right from the beginning."

"So, all the Van Alst money came from shoes?" Nothing too insidious there.

"From what I could gather, it was a very modest enterprise up until the end of the nineteenth century when business began to boom."

"That's when the Van Alst house was built."

"Then Van Alst was awarded a major military contract and his consumer business took off as well. The Van Alst shoes had style. After that there are records of expansions and upgrading to the factory." Lance slid a printout toward me. It was a newspaper ad from an Irish paper.

"They started advertising for staff in Europe near the turn of the century, mostly Ireland and Italy. I guess they were expanding so fast, they just needed workers."

"Wow, I wonder if the Kellys were among those who answered the call. I don't know much about my family's early days here." Maybe that's what had brought Sal's people here too. The signora, though, she was a much more recent arrival.

"It's possible, because Harrison Falls basically grew around Van Alst's factory. This town sprung out of all those new employees."

"I guess I've always known Van Alst basically founded the town."

"Herman's grandson, Leo, took over in the early seventies. He sold the company but it wasn't worth much by then. Times had changed. The Atlanta Shoe Company acquired the operation and turned the whole factory into a shipping warehouse." Lance handed me another stack of microfiche printouts, articles about the buyout. The headlines were about the factory closing and jobs being lost. "Of course, nowadays, we know that a lot of factory jobs are going offshore, but it was a shock back then."

"Okay, so the factory fell on hard times and a lot of people lost their jobs, but why is it that everyone hates Vera?"

Lance looked at me carefully. "Don't tell me you have a soft spot for your evil employer."

"Soft spot? Are you kidding? She's about as cuddly as a cactus. That would be one sore soft spot."

Lance laughed, and women around the café swiveled in their chairs. Nothing had changed with our Lance. He was still the Pied Piper of Harrison Falls.

He said, "I don't know why they hate her. I know she's the only one of the Van Alsts left. Maybe because everyone in this town suffered and there she is still in that huge house with her servants and her precious books. You're right, you know. She's not all bad."

I hadn't actually said that. "How?"

"Well, I know she's a major donor to Grandville General Hospital. She set up a small foundation and supposedly sheltered some of the Van Alst money there. I've heard she's grateful for her treatment after the accident that put her in that wheelchair. Before my time, of course."

"Mine too, but interesting."

"Give me a little more time. I'd like to check out some more sources and I'm still vetting the stuff I found online. Oh, and I haven't forgotten about the Agatha Christie info you were chasing either. I'm really enjoying the challenge of hunting for something unknown and possibly nonexistent." His eyes twinkled. Lance reveled in research.

"I appreciate it."

"The pleasure is mine. You know I always have fun getting embroiled in Jordan Bingham adventures." He squeezed my hand. "Anytime."

I could feel every woman in the café shooting molten-eye daggers at me from the corners of the room. I patted at Lance's hand. "Thanks, buddy."

He laughed. I grinned weakly.

DESPITE SPENDING A ridiculous amount of time sitting in my parked car outside the café trying to reach the organizers of the Antiquarian Book and Paper Fair, I struck out. I didn't give up, although once or twice I threatened to toss my iPhone out the car window in frustration. I tried Saint Sebastian's. Someone there would know how to find whoever owned the concession stand, and they in turn could lead me to the girl who worked there. She'd had a clear view of the Cozy Corpse's booth. She was bored and she was at the fair all the time. If anyone had seen Karen late in the day on Sunday, it would most likely have been that girl. But Karen had said that she'd *seen* someone who'd given her the information she thought I'd find so interesting. Karen must have met that person in the book fair. I had to assume that, like most of the dealers, Karen would have stuck close to her booth all day. I hoped that this girl had spotted someone noteworthy.

I kept getting the answering machine at Saint Sebastian's. After repeated messages and no call back, I was ready to try another approach.

I pulled into Saint Sebastian's parking lot in the middle of the afternoon. Several dozen cars were parked neatly on the shady side of the building. I pulled the Saab into one of the few remaining places and got out. The bright afternoon sun had turned the pavement into a cooking surface, and the scent of the now fading lilacs was heavy. I would have preferred not to be returning to the place where I'd found Karen Smith. Anywhere but. Still, Karen needed help and I sure needed information. I was betting that someone here would have to know how to get in touch with the girl at the concession stand. This time I walked around to the front entrance, sticking to the cool lawn, ignoring the "Keep Off the Grass" sign. As usual, there was no one in the office.

The display by the entrance advertised a big payoff.

FIND YOUR TRUE POTENTIAL TODAY!!!

With renowned *career coach Nancilee Cardiff*
1–4 p.m.
Networking reception: 4–5 p.m.

The registration desk had an irritable-looking fortyish woman staring at a broken nail and guarding a few unclaimed name tags. Apparently true potential hadn't been handed out to the hired help. Through the one open door, I could see rows of chairs, arranged classroom style, and rows of nodding heads swallowing the words of a woman with a shiny yellow helmet of hair, a jacket with serious shoulders and a smile that made me want to reach for sunglasses again. More to the point, I could also see that the concession stand was set up in the corner.

"I've been looking forward to this," I said, reaching for the name tag of Nikki Renouf.

"It's almost over. The networking party starts soon."

"Ah yes, that's the part I like best," I said, picking up a binder of materials and waltzing through the door.

I took a seat in the empty last row as close as I could get to the concession stand. Only after I claimed a chair did I realize I was sitting close to where Karen Smith had been found. My stomach constricted at the thought, and I forced myself to keep from staring at the patterned carpet where a dark stain hadn't been completely eliminated. I was surprised it was no longer a crime scene.

The woman, Nancilee Cardiff, I assumed, was reasonably diverting, with her exaggerated eyebrows and blinding teeth. The uncles would think this was a good gig. Nancilee had taken a few buzzwords from popular psychology and motivational pitches and was giving them a workout. She'd found an appreciative audience. I nodded and clapped along with the folks who'd just been separated from their hard-earned cash. From time to time I glanced toward the concession stand. Sooner or later, someone would have to show up.

I was rewarded for my patience—not to mention my nodding, clapping and sneaking in—when a familiar face appeared. I recognized the long dark hair. It was the same girl who'd been there on the weekend. From her draggy posture as she shuffled into the stand, I could tell she wasn't any more in love with the job than she had been the last time I'd seen her. If anything, she was in a real slump. Never mind. She didn't have to love that job. She just needed to answer my questions; she could search for her true potential later.

The minute she headed through a side door into another room, I whipped after her and closed that door behind us. As I should have expected, it was a claustrophobic storage room with towering stacks of supplies. She was reaching for a new batch of paper cups when I made my appearance. She whirled and gasped. I gasped too—at her two black eyes, one of them swollen. I had no idea what she was gasping at until it dawned on me that she was very, very afraid.

Of me.

She held her arms in front of her, classic defense position. And no wonder. Someone had really worked her over. "What do you want?" Her split lip quivered as she faced me down. She had guts to show up for work looking like that. I admired her backbone.

"Don't worry," I said. "I'm Jordan Bingham. I was here the other day and bought a Danish."

Her voice wobbled. "Your name tag says 'Nikki Renouf.' Oh my God, don't hurt me. I don't know anything. I swear! Please. Get away from me."

Just when I thought it couldn't get any worse, she started to cry.

"What happened to you?" I blurted.

"I don't know anything," she wailed. "Why are you pretending to be Nikki Renouf?"

"To get in without paying hundreds of dollars."

"Oh." She got that. I knew she would.

"But you must know what happened to you," I said reasonably.

But reason wasn't going to cut it. "I told you. I don't know anything." Her voice rose even higher. Could they hear her in the next room? I was praying she wouldn't scream. I held my own hands up to show how harmless I was. "Okay. Okay. I am so sorry. I don't want to upset you. A friend of mine was attacked here, and I thought you might know something about who she'd been talking to."

She stared at me. "Why does everybody think I know things? What things?"

"Who is 'everybody'?"

Her jaw dropped. I figured that had to hurt. "I don't know. I told you I don't know anything."

I reached out and gave her a soothing little pat, hoping I was touching a part of her body that didn't ache.

She snuffled. "My world is falling apart."

I managed not to say, "Imagine how Karen Smith feels." I reached for one of the folding chairs that were stacked in the corner and set one up for her. "Sit down. Take a deep breath. Please."

I opened up a chair for myself and sat down too. "Can I get you something? A glass of water?"

It took a while for her to compose herself.

"I hope you can help me. I am very stressed about my friend, Karen Smith. She was working right in front of your concession stand on the weekend at the book fair. She owns the Cozy Corpse. I thought you may have overheard a conversation she had on Sunday afternoon, late."

"Karen Smith? She's that red-haired lady who was right across from me. She was nearly killed. I heard it on the radio."

"Yes."

"But I didn't see that happen. I didn't!"

"I'm not suggesting you saw it. I'm just asking if you saw her talking to anyone late in the afternoon."

"I was having my own problems that night."

"I can see that. Did you have a car accident?"

"No. Somebody came up behind me and threw me to the ground and beat the hell out of me." She started to cry in earnest now. "Don't ask me why. I don't know *why*. It just happened. The cop said it must have been just a random crazy person."

"Where were you? Here? Because maybe it was the same person who attacked Karen."

Her forehead puckered. "How could it be the same person? It wasn't anywhere near Saint Sebastian's. It was in my driveway. I live in Harrison Falls. I don't see how it could be connected."

Play from your strengths, my uncles always say. "Tell me, was it your boyfriend?" I thought she was going to lose it. She shook her head so violently that it must have hurt. She made a gargling noise. "No. No! I don't have a boyfriend. And I don't know who did this, and I don't know why."

The door behind me was wrenched open, and Nancilee Cardiff thrust her bright golden head in. No sign of the high-wattage smile.

"I'm delivering a session here, and you are supposed to be setting up for our networking party, not shrieking your silly head off. You are going to be out of a job if you don't pull yourself together."

"Really?" I said. "That's how you follow your dreams? You bully innocent women who have been attacked and who probably should be in the hospital? Let me at the microphone and I'll give you some comments they won't forget in a hurry." I stood up, knocking over a tower of paper cups.

The bright head snapped back. "Just keep it down and make sure we're ready for our reception." The door closed behind her.

The girl sniffed. "Bitch. Thank you for standing up for me. I deal with plenty of weirdos, but she's been, like, totally impossible to work with."

"Don't worry. I can speak to your boss if you want. Explain." Explain what, I wasn't sure.

She gave a sad smile. "It's my own concession. I own

Yummers. It's not easy trying to source decent products and dealing with horrible people, but I'm still not likely to fire myself."

I felt a bit guilty over my comments about the Danish on my last visit, but I couldn't resist a grin. "At least there's that."

"I guess so. But if she complains to the parish administration, I might lose the concession for the hall. It's a big part of my business. Then I'd really be out of luck."

"I hate to keep coming back to it, but I think someone came by to talk to Karen Sunday afternoon, and you may have seen that person. I believe he is connected with her attack. Do you remember anybody who looked out of place? Suspicious?"

"I see a lot of people. I don't pay much attention anymore. No point asking me."

"Think about it. What are the chances that you and Karen, two women who were at the same book fair on the same afternoon, would both be assaulted on the same night. The two attacks have to be connected."

"It sounds horrible, but I'd be glad if they were connected because then it might make a bit of sense."

"Somebody must think you saw something."

"But I didn't see anything. I keep telling everyone." Her voice rose an octave.

"More likely you saw something that didn't seem important and you wouldn't imagine was important. Close your eyes. Try to remember people coming and going from the Cozy Corpse."

She closed her eyes, although that looked like it might hurt. She kept them closed for a couple of minutes while I waited patiently. Finally she said, "I didn't see anyone unusual. No one who looked dangerous. It was a book fair. Everyone is a little bit, you know, peculiar. They're oddballs and they're nerdy and tweedy, but they're not going to attack someone. They just spend all their money on old books, and some of them walk around wearing clothes that look like they came from a Dumpster. It's stupid, but harmless."

I resisted standing up for the eccentric and Dumpster-dressed regulars. This description was, after all, quite true of Vera Van Alst. I couldn't imagine her bashing anyone over the head, although she could certainly savage a person's feelings.

"So, no one struck you as suspicious or unusual? No bad vibes from anybody?"

She scrunched up her face this time. I flinched just imagining how that must have felt given those injuries. "There was one guy. I've never seen him *here* before. He was in a real intense conversation with her. But it didn't look like he'd hurt her or anything. Or I would have, like, stopped him."

I almost held my breath. "What did he look like?"

She thought back. "Thin, very thin. Not tall. Pale with only a few bits of hair, you know, combed over. Old."

Old? "How old?"

"Really old. Fifty? At least. Maybe even more." She shivered at the dual nightmare of advanced age and comb-over.

"Do you know him?"

"Not his name. But I've seen him around."

"Around here?"

"No. Not at the fair and not in Grandville. I'm pretty sure this guy lives in Harrison Falls too, because I've seen him recently when I was visiting my dad's place. I've seen him all over town."

"All over town?"

"Sure. He's a mailman. He's not my mailman, but I've seen him walking his route. I don't know his name, though."

The door opened again and Nancilee gave us the stink eye. "Now would be good," she said with an unflattering snarl.

The girl flinched, but stood up to go.

"Wait," I said as she squeezed past me, knocking over a package of serviettes. "I need to know—"

Too late. She had hobbled out, and as I followed her, I noticed that people were pointing in my direction. Nancilee began to advance toward me, menace in her every stiletto-heeled step. I said, "How can I reach you. What's your cell number?"

As she rattled off the number, I tapped it into my contact list, while Nancilee gave the impression her hair was about to catch fire. I thrust my business card into the girl's hand.

"Please call me. I'm—"

"Sure. Everyone knows who you are," she said. "You're Jordan whatever, and you work for *that* woman."

The loathing for Vera was unmistakable. Was I the only person in the world, aside from Signora Panetone, and possibly Eddie, who didn't detest Vera Van Alst? For all I knew, her doctor hated her.

I had no time to find out why the Yummers girl did. I dashed out the door one step ahead of the vengeance of Nancilee. I raced across the grass and into the baking oven that was the Saab. I rolled down the window and took off like a shot. I spotted Nancilee glaring at me, hands on her designer hips, as I rocketed off the property.

Of course, I didn't go far. There was still much to find out from the girl at Yummers. I couldn't believe I'd forgotten to ask her name. The sight of her facial injuries must have zapped my brain. I'd make sure to find it out at the start of our next conversation, as soon as that was possible. I just had to find somewhere cool to hide out until the networking reception was over and Nancilee had gone back to Witch Central. I estimated an hour and a half.

The Saab was hot in more ways than one. I used the time to whip back to Harrison Falls with a plan to borrow one of my Uncle Lucky's spare vehicles. The Saab was too much of a statement. As I walked into Uncle Mick's place, I tucked my hair into a ponytail and snatched up a baseball cap, "Sid's Moving and Storage" this time. The Saab could cool off in the garage while I chilled in the air-conditioned interior of Uncle Lucky's car.

My uncles looked on with interest. Uncle Mick was setting the table and getting ready for our family favorite for days when it's too hot to open a tin: KFC with creamy cole slaw *and* macaroni salad. Fries too, but that goes without saying.

Walter was eying his bowl on the floor and gazing at Uncle Lucky with what looked like adoration. One less thing for me to worry about.

I said, "Does every single person in Harrison Falls hate Vera Van Alst?"

Lucky nodded gravely.

Mick said, "Not just Harrison Falls, my girl. Staying for dinner? There's plenty. Got to keep your strength up."

Not to be deflected, I said, "But Vera Van Alst, why? Why this antagonism?"

"And she's such a warm and friendly lady, you mean?"

Lucky snorted at Uncle Mick's words, and scratched Walter's cute and velvety ears.

"Fair enough," I said, "she has all the warmth of a cobra. But she stays in her deteriorating old home and doesn't do anything to bother anyone, except me, perhaps. So why the visceral reactions?"

"Watch it with the hoity-toity words at the table. You know that Lucky doesn't care for pretense."

I let that go even though everyone in my family cares deeply for pretense. "Why does everyone hate her?"

"Not her per se," Mick said. "Sure you won't have just a drumstick?"

"What do you mean, not her *per se*?"

"Well, it's the family, isn't it?"

"Is it?"

"Of course, it is."

"But what family?"

"The Van Alsts, of course. Have you been out in the sun too long?"

"But she's the only Van Alst left, isn't she? So she's the family. So what do people have against *her*?"

"When the business closed, a lot of people lost their jobs. The local economy took a real hit. And we Kellys paid a price too, you know. Didn't we, Lucky?"

There it was. Pretty much the same thing that Lance had said. And pretty much what I'd known all along. I couldn't help feeling that there was more to it than that.

"Vera's paid a price too," I said.

"So how come she got off so easy over there in her mansion with all her servants living the high life when so many people lost everything?"

I couldn't let that go unchallenged. "The high life? Oh please. She's in a wheelchair, practically dressed in rags and never leaves the house. I don't know how easy that is."

I decided not to mention that Vera seemed to be selling off paintings and furniture to keep her collection going and everything seemed to be maintained by one elderly servant and one aging gardener and handyman. Except for the library, my garret was the best part of the whole place. I didn't see any of that creating sympathy.

Lucky shrugged. Uncle Mick rolled his eyes. "You asked me and I'm telling you. That's how people feel. You can't tell people how to feel. The whole reason she has you is that you can go out and meet people and they won't hate you."

"That's no longer completely true," I said.

"Well, they won't hate you because you're Jordan. Everyone likes you."

"Not everyone, but thanks for the vote of confidence, Uncle Mick. Could I borrow a car, Uncle Lucky?"

Mick said, "You know he never refuses you. Which one?"

Sometimes I have to wonder if Lucky would speak for himself if Uncle Mick the Mouth wasn't on the job all the time. Lucky nodded his okay and went back to scratching Walter's ears. The world really was full of surprises.

"One more thing," I said. "I have to run now, but can you check the word on the street about the postal carrier in the Van Alst neighborhood? Eddie something, if that helps."

"Eddie who?"

"No idea. How many postal Eddies can there be? I appreciate anything you turn up. Look for dirt. Bad debts, bad connections, bad habits. I already know about the bad hair."

CHAPTER THIRTEEN

❧❖❧

I FIGURED THAT anyone watching might have seen Lucky driving the Town Car during our sleight of wheels earlier, so I took the Lincoln Navigator that Lucky keeps for large jobs. It's a big vehicle for a big man, but I found it fun to drive and it wouldn't be recognized back at Saint Sebastian's if I ran into Nancilee. Plus it was not registered under any Kelly or Bingham name. Best of all, it had a great air-conditioning system and, of course, the price was right.

I stopped off at the hospital to see how Karen Smith was doing and was shocked to discover they still had her in a drug-induced coma, waiting for the swelling in her brain to come down.

Outside Saint Sebastian's Hall a fast ride later, I watched as the big-smiling networkers gradually pulled away. When only one car remained, I pulled in and ducked through the doors. The girl was lethargically closing up shop at Yummers. I guessed if I had two black eyes, I'd be moving slowly too.

"Give you a hand?" I said.

She gasped.

"Sorry. I shouldn't have pounced like that."

"Yeah, I'm jumpy."

"The attack. I should have been more sensitive."

"Not just the attack. Everything."

"Everything?"

Her lip quivered. "My life is a mess. I am falling apart. My fiancé died and I'm having a lot of trouble dealing with it."

"What? You mean when you were attacked?" No wonder she was terrified.

She shook her head. "Before. It was an accident."

I stared at her. A dead fiancé? What were the chances? Was that too much of a coincidence? Could Alex Fine have been her fiancé?

"I am so sorry." I might have given her a hug, but she looked like she hurt all over. "How awful for you. And him."

She sniffed. I thought back to the newspaper photos of Ashley with Alex. Her face hadn't been that clear. I did remember the shot of the donkey-faced girl with the big teeth. That photographer must have had it in for her because she looked far better in real life. Well, she had before the attack. Of course she was Alex's fiancée. Alex would have frequented this book fair and any others held here at the hall, and she probably worked at all of them. It would have been hard for them to avoid each other. He'd been serious and shy, but it would have been easy for him to talk to the very ordinary girl behind the counter.

I said, "I'm sorry, but I don't think I ever got your name."

She blinked. "Ashley. Ashley Snell."

"You were engaged to Alex Fine."

She started to weep. I felt like a total jerk. I reached over and gave her a hug. "I'm so sorry for your loss."

She sniffed and tried to pull herself together. I waited

until she blew her nose. She still had a quaver in her voice when she asked, "Did you know him?"

"I feel like I did. You probably know I now have his research job."

"With that horrible woman."

"Yes."

"I blame her for what happened to Alex."

I said, "But she wasn't anywhere near the—"

Ashley trembled, turned the color of plaster and nearly missed the chair she sank onto.

Before I could come up with some soothing comment, Ashley straightened her shoulders and said, "She wasn't there, but she pushed Alex to get that stupid thing. She bullied him and she mocked him and she made his life miserable. That's why he took such a chance."

Maybe the answer to what happened to Alex was right here in this room. Alex would have met Karen and many other contacts. Maybe he'd even found the link to Merlin.

I said gently, "What chance did he take exactly?"

Ashley blew her nose again. "Are you serious? He's dead, isn't he?"

That was true.

She said, "He gave his life for whatever was in that computer bag. I told the police, but they didn't listen to me."

"Tell me, Ashley, does the name Merlin mean anything to you?"

"Merlin? How do you know about Merlin?"

I waited until she blew her nose again. It took her a while to compose herself. "Alex said we weren't to say anything about Merlin. To anyone."

"Did *he* say anything to anyone?"

She nodded, obviously trying to keep back a tidal wave of tears. Even though I also felt a flood of sympathy, I hoped those tears would hold off until she finished talking.

"Yes. He did." A distinct wobble in her voice.

"Do you know why? Or who he spoke to?"

"He couldn't tell me."

"Can you take a guess?"

"Alex was very worried about Merlin. I don't want to talk about it."

I tried reassurance. "Well, whoever he is, this Merlin doesn't know we're having this talk."

"I guess not. But he's supposed to be like a magician, isn't he?"

"Despite his reputation, he won't know what we're saying. We're alone here."

"I suppose Merlin the Magician is just in stories. But Alex wanted to buy something from him and he was really afraid that Merlin would change his mind. Merlin is very secretive. So Alex was very careful. I think he was worried that I'd blab it to somebody here at Yummers because I do a lot of events and I see a lot of people. Everyone knows I can't keep a secret. I know it's true. The book people love gossip. It goes like wildfire around here."

I had a vision of the plush patterned carpet catching fire.

"Let me give you a hand closing up."

"Thanks. I don't want to be alone here. It's creepy after what happened with the lady at the Cozy Corpse."

"No kidding. We can get this done in a couple of minutes."

I helped Ashley pack up the refreshments and clean the Yummers counters. "So, was Merlin the reason Alex went to New York City?"

She paused, looking me over as if to confirm she could really trust me. "I think so. He was going to see someone about something important. But of course, being Alex, he wouldn't talk about it. Especially to mouthy me."

"Is there anyone he would have spoken to?"

She paused, frowned. "I don't think so. He didn't work with anyone. He wouldn't have told his parents. He didn't tell me. He didn't really have any close friends around here. I guess the only person who might have known is his boss."

We stared at each other, because we both knew that we were talking about my boss.

She said, "I suppose you could always ask."

"Judging by her behavior, I think he was acting on his own."

"I guess."

"I wonder if, after I spoke to her, Karen Smith made the connection about who might have told Alex about the manuscript. Maybe that's what she was going to tell me."

Ashley's mouth dropped. "But even I didn't know."

"Would Karen have known about Merlin?"

Ashley took a second to consider that. "I suppose, but I don't really think so. I'm not sure she and Alex ever knew each other except for Alex going by her booth. She wasn't always one of the regular vendors here. I got the feeling that the contact knew that Alex was looking for something for Vera Van Alst. I'm sorry I'm not more help about that. If I think of anything, I'll let you know. How would I find you? Oh right. You gave me your card. I'm sorry. I guess I was kind of nasty to you then."

I shrugged. "Don't worry about it. I can see why you were upset. But if you think of anything, please get in touch. Even though you are afraid to mention it, keep in mind that whoever attacked you was most likely the same person who almost killed Karen Smith."

She paled. "That reminds me, what time was she attacked?"

"Around nine o'clock, Sunday night."

Her hand shot to her face. "My attack happened around eight thirty. The police took me to emergency. I think I saw the ambulance bring that lady in. I sat there for about two hours, but they rushed her right by. Is she going to make it? She seemed so nice and harmless."

That made me think. Was Karen Smith harmless? Or was she involved in some way in this whole crazy business? Had someone tried to kill her because she knew something? Or was her part more sinister and dangerous?

"I hope she's going to make it, but there's no way to know. You might not agree, after your attack, but you may have been the lucky one. Perhaps someone was trying to kill you too."

Astonishment spread over her long face. "But why?"

"Perhaps he thought you might have seen something, some transaction between him and Karen. Something that you don't realize is important."

She gasped. "What if he needed to be alone to attack her? I was about to head back to the hall to see if there was anything left to do. I always check the facility when I'm done. The Saint Sebastian's people are really fussy about everything being left perfect. If there are coffee cups or anything, I hear about it. The guy was waiting for me as I got into my car, just by my apartment."

"That makes sense in a twisted way. He also may have wanted to make sure you didn't get back here and find Karen. If she hadn't been found until the next morning, it might have been harder to pinpoint the time when she was attacked."

Ashley shivered.

And she would have died alone, I added to myself.

I said, "If we're right, that means that whoever did it planned both attacks." I thought about what kind of person could have hit Karen on the head and moved her unconscious body, leaving her to die. It would be the same kind of person who could walk up to an unsuspecting girl and belt her in the face. "This is one very dangerous dude."

"I know." She pointed to her black eyes. "What if he's still out there?"

"I'll stay until you're completely packed up, and I'll walk you to your car. But—"

She beat me to the punch. "He knows where I live. He was waiting by my car."

"And were you able to tell the police anything about what he looked like?"

"No. It was all a blur. He wasn't very tall."

"Could it have been a woman?"

She shook her head. "No. He moved like a man, but his head was covered with a hoodie. You know, the police didn't get too excited about what happened to me. They kept insisting that my boyfriend did this. What boyfriend is that? That's why I got so upset when you asked me the same thing. It sounds crazy, but I thought maybe you were an undercover cop or something, trying to get me to spill the beans on my dead fiancé or nonexistent boyfriend."

"Sorry. I didn't know any of that. But the danger is real and you must be connected somehow. Is there somewhere you can go until the police find out what's going on?"

"I'm not too confident about them, but, yeah, I guess I can stay at my dad's."

"Maybe Karen Smith will regain consciousness, and then we'll stand a chance of finding out who is behind this. In the meantime, you have to keep yourself safe. But before I go, can you tell me about the attack? I'm sorry. I know it's hard for you."

"There's nothing to tell. I was in my driveway getting into my car when a man came up behind me and when I turned around, he hit me in the face."

"You said you didn't see his face, but he moved like a man. A young man? A teenager?"

She thought for a minute and shook her head. "No. An older guy. He ran off when a car drove by."

"Did the people in the car see what happened?"

She shook her head. "They didn't stop. I don't even know if they saw what was going on, but I think they scared him off. He might have killed me."

That was true. "Will there be someone around at your dad's place?"

"He's got a pretty flexible schedule. I'll ask him to help

me with opening and closing Yummers for my events. I don't think this guy would start anything in a crowd, do you?"

"Make sure you're not alone. You're lucky to have your dad. I never knew mine. But my uncles are pretty terrific."

"I can't imagine not having my dad. That must be awful. We've had some hard times, but at least we're always there for each other now. We're not alone," she said with a sad smile.

Not like Alex, alone in his grave.

I patted her shoulder. "I'll make sure you get to your car safely."

"Thanks. It feels stupid to be so nervous when it's not even dark out."

"It's kind of isolated in the parking lot."

As we reached her silver Yaris, she glanced over and up at the massive Navigator and back at me. I said, "It's a loaner. My car's in the shop. Don't forget to call me if you remember what was familiar about the guy, or even if you're worried."

She opened her door and said with a smile that looked really painful, "Don't worry. You'll be the first person I call if I see anything suspicious. And I'll make sure the cops take me seriously."

An image of the shambling man coming up behind Ashley chilled my blood. "By the way, did the guy who attacked you have a limp?"

Her eyes widened. "A limp? No. He was kind of slower moving, like an older person."

"Did you actually see him run away?"

She closed her eyes and thought. She opened them and said, "Yes. I did see him. He wasn't running, but he definitely wasn't limping. I'm sure of that. Why?"

"Just trying to get my facts straight. Could it have been the man you saw talking to Karen at the book fair?"

"That mailman?"

I nodded.

She took the time to consider it. "I didn't see him closely and I really didn't see his face, or his hair, but you know, it could have been. He was about the same size, I think. That's not much help, but yes, maybe."

I said, "Ashley, promise you will watch out for this guy, and whatever you do, if you see a smiley blond cop with a tendency to blush, don't trust him."

"You mean that guy who talked to me after I was attacked? The first cop to show up."

What? Now that was just plain wrong. Officer Smiley had talked to her after the attack? Wasn't it way too coincidental that he would show up when Ashley had been injured?

"I didn't realize that he was the officer first on the scene. Did he come after you called 911?"

"No, I was just lucky that he came along on patrol."

"Well, I don't think it was lucky. Kind of the opposite. He's involved somehow. So whatever you do, don't be alone with him and don't go anywhere with him."

Her jaw dropped. "You think the cop is involved?"

"I don't know why or how, but there's something off. Be very, very careful. And can you give me your telephone number?"

"Good idea."

I keyed her number into my phone and watched her drive away. I hoped the next time I saw her, it wouldn't be in the hospital.

Or worse.

CHAPTER FOURTEEN

——※·※——

I PONDERED THE connections between Eddie, Karen and Ashley as I gunned the Navigator and drove ten miles into the rolling green countryside. I checked each property I passed until I located the rambling yellow farmhouse of George Beckwith, the owner of Nevermore and the first dealer I'd spoken to at the book fair. Through the twin miracles of Lance and my iPhone, I had his address. The house seemed to be called Nevermore too. I saw no sign of a shop or an office as I arrived. I did approve of the wide wraparound verandah and the broad lawns.

A beautiful black horse with a white blaze was cantering around a corral on the property. Ducks, geese and a willowy Border collie completed the picture. The collie seemed delighted at my arrival.

George Beckwith did remember me. He seemed surprised to see me showing up at his home unannounced in the evening and not in the least bit happy. This was a beautiful place. I wondered what it would cost to keep it going. More than you'd take in from a rare book business? He ambled along the porch and gestured toward a porch swing, and I sat. He took his place in the wicker rocker beside it. I noted that he neither limped nor shuffled. Damn.

The reproach was obvious, even in his smooth, buttery voice. "I haven't been able to find out anything about the item you were searching for, but I haven't given up. These things take time. You can't push it. You've caught me by surprise. I rarely have clients here and never without an appointment."

I ignored him. "It's urgent and not about a purchase. I have some questions."

As his eyebrows rose, the screen door banged and his wife, a small smiling woman with a cap of silver hair and a slow, stilted walk, arrived with a tray of lemonade, three glasses and a shy smile. She introduced herself as Jeannette. I liked her instantly.

"I don't usually answer questions at home. I'll—" He shot his wife a dirty look as she happily filled the glasses of lemonade. She seemed thrilled to have company besides his majesty. Who could blame her?

"Karen Smith was attacked and left for dead after the book fair. Did you know that?"

The glass hit the floor with a crash. Jeannette's hand flew to her face. "No! That's terrible. Did you know, George?"

From the way he'd turned white, my guess was he hadn't. "We were on the road yesterday and today. We just got home. I haven't even had the news on."

"I imagine you'll hear from the police investigators soon. They'll be interviewing people who were there."

"What do you mean 'people who were there'? Where?"

As Jeannette headed unsteadily through the door to get something to clean up the lemonade, I said, "Karen was hit on the head and left for dead in Saint Sebastian's Hall after the book fair. She was the last person on site."

"In the hall?" His voice was closer to a croak than its usual smooth tone.

"Yes. And I'd like to know if you saw anyone unusual talking to her or arguing with her or even doing business with her. Anyone that struck you as odd. Someone who shuffled perhaps? Or limped?"

The screen door banged behind Jeannette as she returned with a broom and a dustpan and a bucket and mop.

They exchanged glances. She started to sweep up the broken glass and said, "We have lots of older customers, people like us. It's not unusual for someone to have a cane or to move slowly, with all our creaky old bones. Like me, getting close to needing a hip replacement."

I nodded in sympathy but kept on topic. "But did either of you notice her talking to anyone suspicious or out of the ordinary? Someone reported a slight fiftyish man with thin fair hair combed over." I made a gesture to simulate a comb-over.

They both shook their heads.

George said, "Karen was at the diagonal opposite corner. I couldn't really see her that easily from our section."

Jeannette said, "I wasn't at that fair. There was too much to look after here on Sunday, although I love the fairs. It's so nice to see old friends."

I wasn't prepared to let it drop. I turned to George. "Did you get anything to eat at the concession stand? Maybe you noticed her then?"

George said, "I bought a sandwich and some coffee, but I don't recall anything out of the ordinary. Karen's a nice, friendly woman, although I don't know her that well. Jeannette knows her a bit better, but Jeannette wasn't there. There weren't any customers at Karen's booth when I went by. She was reading, and she looked up and smiled. It's hard to imagine anyone attacking her. Or any of the dealers. Was it theft?"

"Doesn't seem that way. I think the person planned it, made sure she was alone and tried to kill her."

George had made no attempt to help his wife clean up the glass and spilled lemonade. "It must have been a robbery attempt. Why else would anyone try to kill a harmless woman like Karen Smith?"

"That's what I'm wondering, and that reminds me, do either of you know anything about a collector or dealer known by the name Merlin?"

"Never heard of him," George snapped.

Jeannette stared blankly.

"I just wondered if he might be the person you contacted after my visit to your booth."

"I have no idea what you're going on about."

I shrugged. "People talk. And they listen. And they pass things on. I wouldn't be at all happy if it turned out your conversation was with this Merlin."

"If that's all," George said in his snootiest British accent, "we're both quite tired after our trip and we need to say good night."

"Fine with me. I have somewhere to be anyway," I said, getting to my feet. I had one piece of information I'd come for. I didn't know if Merlin shuffled or limped, but I knew I'd made George very nervous when I asked him who he'd been talking to.

ON THE COUNTRY road I pulled out my cell and checked with the uncles on the well-being of Walter. I wanted to make a good report to Karen, if and when she opened her eyes. I kept expecting the dog honeymoon to be over. But the uncles were rising to the challenge.

"Pet Universe," Uncle Mick said without a preamble. "Amazing place."

"What?"

"We went right after you left."

"You did?" I said.

"Lucky was quite overwhelmed."

"Huh. What did you get? I've been meaning to pick up some dog food, but I figured that KD would—"

"Couldn't get over the choices of beds, my girl. It's a dog's world, all right."

"I suppose it—"

"We went for a neutral, but a good solid foam base. Washable. We kept the color for the collar and the lead. Red. And the bowls, you know. Little paw prints on them. Can't be using the everyday dishes."

"Of course not." What the—?

Mick's voice lowered. "Your uncle Lucky has gone over the edge with this situation."

"You mean—?"

"Lamb and rice food. Duck and sweet potato. Where will it end?"

"Well," I said, "I'm starting to lose signal, but I'm really glad it's working out for all of you."

Don't ever let anyone tell you that there are no miracles in this bad old world.

IN THE HOSPITAL, I scurried along to the nurses' station, trying to get an update on Karen. Apparently, she was out of danger. Her condition had been upgraded to fair, and she was now in a different room. I was hoping she'd be awake so I could give her the news about Walter and his temporary digs.

As I opened the door to her room, I made an effort to keep my expression cheerful. I had a feeling that I might be upset by the sight of her injuries and whatever new changes had resulted from her treatment.

A surgeon was bending over the bed with a pillow in his hand, his surgical mask still in place. He whirled to face me, and my brain struggled to make sense of the scene. Pillow did not compute. Especially as Karen's hands were pushing frantically against it.

"Hey!" I yelled. "What are you doing?"

Karen made a desperate gasp for breath as he dropped

the pillow and ran for the door, shoving me hard as he went. My head banged against the wall, and I dropped to the floor. I struggled to my feet and rushed out the door, shouting, "Stop that man! He's assaulted a patient!"

Passing staff stared at me with astonishment. The assailant knocked over an IV pole and pushed a gurney sideways across the hallway to impede any chase. But there were no pursuers. It was all too astonishing. The man opened the door to a stairway exit and vanished into it. But not before I'd had time to notice that he had a distinctive limp.

I raced back to Karen's bedside. She was pale and shaking, but alive. She squeezed my hand until it hurt. I waited until her grip loosened a tiny bit.

"The man who tried to hurt you, did you recognize him?" I asked.

"Was it a man? I couldn't see him. I was sleeping, and then I woke up struggling to breathe. Something was blocking my mouth and nose. It was horrible."

I could imagine how horrible it must have been. With a soft squeak of shoes, a pair of nurses entered the room. I said, "Karen, can you think of anyone who would want to hurt you?"

Her eyes were wide. "No one."

"Do you know who attacked you in Saint Sebastian's?"

"The police officer asked me that. I don't remember."

"Well, two pieces of good news," I said. "One, whoever it was failed again. And two, your pooch is having a spa holiday."

I wasn't sure if that last one sunk in.

I found myself displaced quickly as a doctor arrived to check out Karen. I stared suspiciously at everyone who went into the room, but this one appeared to be for real, judging by the reaction of the other medical staff. Karen's assailant had been dressed as a physician. He'd have no trouble passing freely through the corridors of the hospital. Even if there were security cameras, what would they show? A doctor. Big deal. The place was crawling with them.

The one thing I knew for sure: whoever was out to get Karen was really out to get her. He'd taken a big chance making an attempt on her life in a busy hospital. The worst part was that he'd almost succeeded.

I felt desperate to find out the doctor's take on whether this latest attack had harmed her in any way. The attempt to smother her could have been the last straw. But I got nowhere with the medical staff.

I paced in the hallway wondering what to do about that while I waited a ridiculously long time for the police to arrive. I finally decided to wait for them outside where I could at least use my iPhone. I clicked on *Ashley* in my contact list and fidgeted while it rang. No answer. Damn. I really hoped she'd get my message.

"Ashley, there's been another attempt on Karen's life at the hospital. Please take care to keep yourself safe. Call the police if you see anything at all unusual. The attacker was dressed as a doctor, so be vigilant and let me know that you got this message."

Ten minutes later a pair of police officers arrived in a cruiser, and for once I was glad to see them. I identified myself and filled them in on what I'd witnessed. I watched the female officer record it while the other one looked around. I had a quaver in my voice when I said, "She needs a guard at her door. A police officer or at the very least a security guard. Can you arrange it?"

She said, "Not up to us, but we will pass it along. Were you the only person to witness this attempt?"

"The attempt itself, yes. But hospital staff saw the attacker fleeing. Check with security too."

"But we have just your word that this person attacked the patient. We'll have to take statements from the staff on the floor and any other witnesses. Wait here for Detective Zinger."

It didn't take me long to pick up the subtext there. The world is full of whack jobs. "Go ahead and get your statements. I'll wait for you here." I wasn't hopeful. The nurses had seen me run out of Karen's room after I'd stopped the attempt to smother her, but of course, I had no proof of what I'd witnessed.

As the cops moved toward the entrance, I called after them. "The guy ran. Why else would he run if he wasn't up to something?" As I was speaking, I saw a familiar figure emerge from the parking lot, stop and stare at the police and at me. Eddie. That couldn't be a coincidence.

"Excuse me, but I need to talk to that man."

The cops exchanged glances, and then one of them said, "Um, no. You'd better wait here for Detective Zinger."

I said, "But—"

The other one said, "We need you to wait here. Don't leave the area."

"But that's . . ." What could I say? Eddie clearly looked nothing like the man I'd caught trying to smother Karen. But he *was* here, at the hospital, and if he had just walked out now, wouldn't he have been in the building when the latest attempt on Karen's life was happening?

I stayed put, though. These two officers obviously thought I was a loose cannon already. And if I were in their large black boots, I wouldn't have given me the time of day. The question was, what would Agatha do? For sure, she'd have Hercule Poirot or possibly the divine Miss M pursue the Eddie angle. Likely they wouldn't place much stock in police smarts.

It didn't take long for the news of an attack to filter out. Soon a media van pulled up, and a reporter who was eager to talk to anyone and everyone hopped out. The crowd was growing larger, late visitors who'd decided to wait and be part of the drama, staff on smoke breaks on the edge of the property, people in the neighborhood. Who knows why crowds materialize so quickly?

Eddie was long gone well before Detective Zinger was finished putting me through the wringer, rhyme not intended. A certain coincidence was bothering him.

"So let me see if I have this straight," he said, stroking his granite chin and looking through me with his weird X-ray eyes, after he got the bare-bones story. "You found this Karen Smith after the first attack."

"Yes."

"You called it in."

"Correct. You know that. You interviewed me."

He held up his hand to silence me. "Then, you happened to go to her room in the hospital and by a stroke of luck, foil another attempt on her life."

"Exactly."

"You don't find that a bit weird?"

"Of course it's weird. Everything that's going on is bizarre and horrible. But Karen must know something so damaging that someone is willing to kill her to prevent her from talking."

"Talking to whom? About what?"

"Well, I'm pretty sure the person who is trying to kill her believes she knows who he is. I find that interesting, don't you, Detective?"

After a few more desultory questions, including my name, address and telephone number, yet again, he uttered the usual cliché: "Don't leave town."

"I don't live in Grandville, as you know," I said. "You can find me in Harrison Falls."

"You know what I mean."

"Have you put someone in place to make sure Karen Smith is not attacked again?"

He squinted at me.

I said, "Two attempts on her life. We don't want the third one to be the charm. I mentioned it to the other officers."

He moved off and spoke into his cell phone. It was not

my business apparently, although I had raised the warning flag. I waited.

"The hospital administration will place a security guard at her door for the next while. You can rest easy."

"How long?"

"Hard to say, but they won't let anything happen to her."

Oh sure, I thought. Isn't that what they always say just before the next person dies? *Don't worry. We'll take care of you. You're safe with us.*

Before I could make this comment, I spotted another familiar face in the crowd still milling around the front of the hospital.

Well, well. If it wasn't Officer Smiley. In civvies, this time. How long had he been there? That was the question. Like Eddie, he didn't hang around to chat.

EIGHT O'CLOCK WAS looming, and I was conscious that I would barely make it to dinner in time. I squealed into the driveway at the Van Alst house, raced along the endless hallway and took the stairs two at a time. I managed to change into my standby silk shift and hop into a pair of heels. I grabbed my mother's pearls, the always necessary cardigan, and I even stopped long enough in front of the mirror to slap on a bit of lip gloss. The baseball cap hadn't done me any favors, and I had to do something about that, although I was out of time. On the way down the stairs, I managed to walk very fast and twist it into a makeshift updo. I hoped I resembled something human. No time to check.

In the hallway, I was almost knocked over by the same large, ungainly woman I'd seen a few days earlier. She stared at me in alarm and seemed to bolt through the door and off toward the parking area. "Excuse me" would have been good. My family might be crooks, but they had managed to teach me manners.

Although she'd barely arrived ahead of me, Vera Van Alst still glowered from the end of the long table and made a big show of checking her watch.

"Eight on the nose," I breathed as Signora Panetone exploded through the swinging door, bearing a platter with a mountain of gnocchi.

"Eat!"

I was all for it. This chasing around after shadowy crooks and pillow-wielding thugs might not have yielded any answers, but it did make a girl hungry.

"Sure thing," I said as she swooped by and loaded up my plate with feather-light gnocchi in a delicate tomato sauce topped by generous heapings of freshly grated Romano and Parmesan.

"I missed you this morning," I said to Vera. "I hope you are feeling better."

I guessed the grunt meant something: yes or no or kiss my foot. I sampled the gnocchi before I sprung my surprises.

As Vera stared at the tiny bit of food on her plate, occasionally pushing a gnocchi with her Francis I fork, I said, "A couple of interesting developments."

Vera raised an eyebrow.

I had her attention. "Someone tried to kill Karen Smith today."

That earned me a frown.

"Right in the hospital."

Vera pursed her lips.

The signora stopped swooping, put down the platter and crossed herself.

"Whoever did that is dangerous."

Vera stared off at the sideboard where a cat was poised to spring. Damn. I had forgotten my boots.

"And perhaps not only dangerous to Karen Smith. I think he believes she knows who he is. Maybe he thinks you know something too."

"Me?" Vera scowled. "What could I know about him?"

"You tell me. But for the record, last night I saw a dark figure skulking around the house."

"Skulking?" Vera snorted. "Is this fiction? Don't be ridiculous."

I shrugged. "Have it your own way. But I know what I saw. A large man was skulking near the side door."

"As you know, Miss Bingham, we have first-rate security here at the Van Alst house. I do not fear intruders."

"Well, that's reassuring. The security's pretty good at the hospital too. But someone tried to smother her with her pillow."

"I believe that if someone only *attempted* to kill Karen Smith, the security must be more than adequate."

"Wrong. I interrupted the attempt and the attacker ran off. The staff saw nothing and wouldn't have been able to prevent it."

The scowl returned.

"You should take me seriously. Is there something you know about what happened to Karen Smith or Alex Fine? If so, you'd better tell me, because this guy is playing for keeps and you are definitely involved somehow."

I thought I heard the signora mutter, "Madonna!"

Vera merely stared at the table

"By the way," I said loudly, "I noticed Eddie was at the hospital too. Coincidence?"

The signora snatched up the platter and vanished through the swinging door into the kitchen, nicking the frame of the door as she went. I guessed I'd hit a nerve.

There was no dessert for me that night.

AFTER DINNER, I continued to worry. How safe was Karen Smith? How dangerous was this person? I figured two attempts at murder meant he was very dangerous indeed.

How competent would hospital security guards be to deal

with a determined killer? It seemed outside of the normal scope of hospital work. Would they leave the door unguarded for a bathroom break? Could they be fooled by the right person dressed like a resident or a surgeon? This was a hospital in a gentle and civilized community. What were the chances they would be equal to the task?

Then there were the Grandville police. They'd be used to bar fights, stolen vehicles, domestic disturbances, small-potatoes robberies and speeders, plus a range of drug investigations and charges. But this level of violence with no apparent motive? I wasn't convinced they could solve the case, and more to the point, I didn't really trust them to protect Karen Smith. The fact that Officer Smiley was one of their number, even though from the next town, had something to do with that. No question.

Karen Smith seemed to be the key to what was going on. Perhaps in time, she would be able to identify her own attacker, who would most likely be the same person who'd injured Ashley. I was pretty sure that the attacks were connected somehow to Alex Fine, the secretive Merlin and the mystery of the Christie play.

So, what to do? I figured I would have one unlikely ally in this game of wits with the killer, and I needed to see her now. Seconds later I was knocking firmly and purposefully on the door to Vera's suite, in her personal wing on the second floor, having managed not to injure myself stumbling through the dark hallways, and then surviving the clanking elevator.

I didn't intend to alarm her, so I announced myself at the same time. "It's Jordan. I urgently need to talk to you."

She opened the door and glared up at me from her wheelchair. She was still in her day clothes, the same shades of pale mud that she'd worn at dinner a short time earlier. A copy of Christie's *Sad Cypress* lay on her lap. Perhaps she'd actually been reading it, or more likely stroking it.

She said, "You'd better have a good reason for disturbing me in my private quarters, Miss Bingham."

"I need your assistance to ensure that Karen Smith is not murdered. We want to avoid the 'third time's a charm' principle. She's the key to this and you can help."

"But what can I do?" For once, she seemed genuinely astonished.

"I understand you are a major donor to the Grandville hospital."

"This couldn't wait until morning? I do support the hospital, for reasons of my own."

"You have clout with the hospital administration."

"The board of directors," she said with a sniff.

"I should have known. Well, here's the thing. The security there doesn't seem to be up to snuff as I made clear, and I'm not convinced the police are on the ball. But I know a few people who are, and I'd like you to contact a decision maker at the hospital, perhaps the CEO or the chair of the board, and ensure that my people are permitted to watch Karen Smith's door and keep everyone out. They will require access to the room if medical personnel enter. The last villain was dressed as a surgeon."

Vera shivered. "Dressed as a surgeon? May I know who these people are before I put their names forward?"

"Believe me, she'll be in good hands with them." For one thing, they wouldn't be falling for any tricks by Eddie the postman or Officer Smiley, the so-called police officer, or the man with the limp who had been disguised as a surgeon.

"Names?" she said.

I was startled as something black swooped toward me before I could answer.

"No! No! Sleep, sleep!" Well, that was a relief. It was only Signora Panetone, flapping like a deranged crow.

"Sleep! Now! Yes!"

"Go back to bed, Fiammetta. Miss Bingham needs to speak to me without your squawking."

Signora Panetone seemed to melt away into the darkness, muttering, "Sleep now."

As if there'd been no interruptions, Vera Van Alst said, "Names, Miss Bingham?"

There was no avoiding it. "First names: Valentine. Daniel. William. Conrad. Last name, Kelly."

Of course, that would be Uncle Tiny, Uncle Danny, Uncle Billy and Uncle Connie to me. The twins were incommunicado lately, but these four uncles were stalwart, strapping, brave, untrusting and stubborn as anyone of Irish extraction could ever be.

"Tell your celestial contacts that these four men are in your employ for the moment."

"What's that going to cost me?"

"I'll take care of it. But I don't have pull with the hospital. You do."

Of course, my uncles would do it for me in this life-and-death situation. I'd have a chance to return the favor in time. Even so, I thought Vera might have argued in favor of picking up the tab.

"We need to take care of this now. It can't wait until morning."

"And you need to remember what I am paying you to find."

The door closed in my face.

As they say, point taken.

I MADE A call to alert the uncles. The great thing about being the only niece in the family and the daughter of the beloved sister is that your uncles will do whatever ridiculous thing you want. No charge. No guilt trips. No questions asked. Also as they were unencumbered by jobs, they'd most likely be available. I was blessed, no doubt about it. I hoped that their guard shifts at the hospital would be officially approved. Otherwise a plan B would be needed, and that might be a bit more complicated to bring about. Could I count on Vera to care enough to make it happen? I sure hoped so.

In the meantime, I worried about Karen. I was pretty sure that Detective Zinger hadn't really believed me about the latest attempt on her life. I hoped that Karen would be lucid enough to convince him and that the police would take her safety seriously. With luck my uncles would be there in the morning, but what about overnight? I shivered when I thought of someone creeping through the darkened corridors, disguised as a doctor, a nurse, a cleaner, and outwitting the security guard. It was easy to blend into the background in a hospital. And easy to get away, as I'd seen when Karen's assailant vanished as if he'd never existed. Which he had, I reminded myself.

Even my cabbage rose retreat wasn't enough to take my mind off what was going on that night. Neither was the stack of Christie reading. It would have been great to talk to Tiff, but she must have been tied up with some emergency. I reminded myself of the two-hour time difference and decided against leaving a "call me" message.

Talk tomorrow! xoxo

I tossed and turned. The third time I turned on the light, I decided I might as well stay up and try to make sense of things. I figured that's what Agatha Christie would have done, as would her charming creations, Miss Jane Marple and Hercule Poirot. I'd learned a lot from reading Christie's work as well as the many books about her. Could I use any of that to help figure out this tangled mess? I decided, as I'd be awake anyway, to do something about what was bothering me most.

Five minutes later, I was crossing the shadowy parking area. I checked the backseat of the Navigator, locked the doors and drove to the hospital.

"CHECK WITH DETECTIVE Zinger of the Grandville Police if you're worried," I told the young security guard who had the boring job of watching Karen Smith's door while she slept the troubled sleep of the injured and drugged.

I guessed the guard wasn't worried, because she didn't check with anyone. I made myself at home in the visitor's chair by Karen's bed.

"Leave the door open to be on the safe side," I added.

She stared at me. I was glad I'd come. Mickey Mouse could have talked his way past this girl.

The night promised to be longer than most, but I planned on figuring out who was who and what was what in recent events. At least I had Christie in my corner, and I'd brought a notebook along with me.

In the Christie world, things were never what they seemed. Insignificant items, seen in passing, could be very important to the solution. People might not be what they seemed, or they might not be where they should be. Someone might be present who should have been elsewhere, or absent when they should have been present.

And if items weren't where they should be, people were even less so. They might not even be who they said they were. They might not have been doing what they claimed to be doing or what other people thought they'd witnessed. Their relationships might not be what they'd led us to believe. Their connections to other characters would be very surprising when revealed. Even their crimes were not what they were supposed to have been. One crime could be a smoke screen for another. Plus everyone lied. Even villains couldn't be trusted to tell the truth on the page. How unfair was that? No wonder it took a Poirot or a Jane Marple (or occasionally Tommy and Tuppence) to solve these cases.

Certainly the police didn't have a hope. Mind you, fictional detectives usually had the advantage of a closed cast of characters, while I had all of upstate New York—and beyond—to draw on. I knew that if I didn't figure out what

was going on, Karen Smith and Ashley Snell might never
be safe. Other people might be drawn into danger. And if I
didn't make some progress on my task of finding the Christie manuscript, I would be out of a job. Vera had made that
quite clear. That would mean forgetting about returning to
grad school for a while and—worse—leaving my cabbage
rose kingdom.

I sure could have used a sidekick.

As the clock moved slowly, I made a list of everyone I
thought might be involved and recapped what I knew. Of
course, I didn't necessarily know what I didn't know, but
you can make yourself crazy if you think too hard. I had to
work with what I had.

Under the names, I had notes and questions about
motives, connections and general suspicious elements.

Vera Van Alst

She was a bitter, selfish, difficult obsessive. She wasn't one to
pretend otherwise. But what didn't I know about her? How had
she become an invalid? I didn't know, except that it had been
the result of a car accident. I intended to find out. For all I knew
it was one of those missing bits of information that linked *all*
the others. She knew Karen. Had she met Ashley? I made a
note to check. Finally, Alex had been in her employ.

She had nothing to gain from what happened to Karen
Smith and Ashley Snell. Or did she? Was this just an elaborate
shell game with them as the victims and me as the mark?

Karen Smith

What did I really know about her? She would have met Alex
and Ashley at the book fairs. Was she connected in any way
with anyone else? She was seen speaking to Eddie. She had a
collegial relationship with George Beckwith and his wife, Jeannette. What was her connection with the shadowy and possibly
nonexistent Merlin? Someone had tried to murder Karen, twice.

The man with the limp had tried to break into her apartment and her hospital room, but no one had seen him at the fair. Whatever else, Karen was definitely connected to something very bad. Maybe she was at the heart of it.

George and Jeannette Beckwith
The owner of Nevermore and his wife seemed harmless, and she seemed very nice. But he'd been in the same book fair. They knew I was looking for someone. They would also know Karen, Ashley and most likely Alex. He had encountered Vera, who had nothing but contempt for him. Had Eddie talked to George at the fair as well as Karen? He'd denied it, but I knew that everyone can lie. Would they have anything to gain by lying? Was there business enough to support their hobby farm with horses?

Eddie McRae
I knew he was a postie, but what was he doing hanging around in Vera's kitchen? Mooching food? Signora Panetone seemed very fond of him, and Vera didn't want to hear anything bad about him. Why would he have been at the book fair talking to Karen? Had he let something slip? Something about his relationship with Vera or perhaps Alex? Had he waited until Karen was alone and attacked her before she could tell me what she'd learned? Could he have been the person who assaulted Ashley? Perhaps because he knew she'd spotted him talking to Karen?

Had he talked to others? George? What did his warning to me mean? Or had that been a threat? Why had he been at Grandville General Hospital? What was I missing?

Officer Tyler Dekker (Smiley)
He seemed to be a police officer, but he engaged in behaviors that other police officers didn't. He was always near where the action was, just after it had taken place: Karen's attack, the

attempt in the hospital, the assault on Ashley. It was almost as though he'd anticipated these shocking events. Or worse, caused them. I could find no connection between him and Vera, except for me as an intermediary. I had no indication that he'd known Karen or Ashley before, or Alex for that matter. However, it seemed quite likely that he had shown up at Karen's apartment and let himself in, or possibly even broken in. There was something definitely not right about Officer Smiley. He was not who he seemed to be. But who *was* he?

Signora Fiammetta Panetone

Was she a faithful retainer or something else? It was hard to imagine the signora being anything other than a whirling food magician. But what was her relationship with Eddie? She seemed to know everything that was going on. She'd reacted to the talk about Alex and the discussion about the attack on Karen. She had the keys to everything in the Van Alst house. Nothing happened without her knowledge. Did the information stay with her? Or did it get passed on to someone more dangerous?

The man with the limp

I had to keep my eyes open for him in the hospital and elsewhere. Had he been at the book fair? I couldn't place him there, and neither Beckwith nor Ashley had seen him, but I hadn't been watching for a man with a limp. He knew where Karen lived, and he'd showed up there. That meant he'd connected with her earlier, before the attack. Although I had no evidence that he was behind the attack in the hall, there was no doubt he'd tried to smother her in the hospital. Was he working with Merlin? Was *he* Merlin?

Merlin

Real? Not real? Real, but not who he seemed to be? What was he up to? And why?

How dangerous was he? He was connected to Vera indirectly, to Alex, and through Alex, to Ashley. I knew of no connection between him and Karen, but it wouldn't be surprising given the business she was in.

Ashley Snell
Ashley didn't know Vera, but she knew Alex, Karen, George and Jeannette Beckwith, Officer (who is he really?) Smiley, and had seen and observed Eddie at the fair and around town. Alex had revealed information about Merlin to her against his better judgment. She was a person who talked without thinking. Had she blurted out the Merlin connection to someone she shouldn't have?

Alex Fine
Was he what he'd seemed to be—naïve, hardworking, honest, agreeable? Shy. Or something more? He was connected to Vera, Ashley, Karen, and probably George, Eddie, the signora and the mysterious Merlin.

What about his death? What had that been about? With two other attacks, was it really possible that he'd been the victim of a random act of violence by a homeless man? I needed to find out.

The play
The play (possibly nonexistent) was like a person in this whole complicated scenario. Almost everyone had some connection. Vera wanted it. Alex had hunted it. Ashley had found out things she wasn't supposed to know about the seller. The signora probably had overhead talk about it. Eddie most likely had eavesdropped and found out about it. Karen might have had a lead on it. George and Jeannette most likely had heard rumors. Merlin was the kingpin who might or might not be able to provide it (if he was real). How did the man with the limp fit in with the play?

Missing info? Unknown connections?

What else was I missing? What didn't I know? Why couldn't I figure it out? It would have been a good night to be Agatha Christie, but I was Jordan Bingham, perched on an astoundingly hard plastic chair in the hospital, watching a woman sleep. It was not a good night for me.

Karen didn't stir all night, not even when the nurses made their infrequent visits to check vitals. Each of them nodded to me, the caring "niece."

I didn't dare fall asleep.

The security guard did.

CHAPTER FIFTEEN

❦

U NCLE BILLY SHOWED up well before six with an ID tag. He was always an early bird. The security guard was nowhere to be seen. I guessed that Vera had worked her high-status magic for the Kelly contingent.

"Your uncle Danny will be along shortly," he said. "He's always running late, usually from some husband."

I laughed. "Well, I am glad you can take over from security. They seem to be falling down on the job."

Uncle Billy shook his head in disgust at the chair, now vacant, where the guard had been sitting. "In my day, heads would roll for less. Can't trust anyone."

"Not true. I can trust my uncles."

With Karen in good hands and reinforcements on the way, I yawned and headed home to get a bit of sleep.

EVEN THOUGH THE morning sun was streaming through the window, I flaked out the minute I sat on the bed to take off my shoes. My last thought was surprise that no cat had managed to follow me in. Then I keeled over fully clothed. I spent an hour or so dreaming of sprawling hospitals full of policemen who were lost, cats who were burglars and books that were missing. My eyes popped open in the middle of the missing-book dream. What was that about? Something I had noticed and hadn't thought much about? Yes, gaps in the shelves in Vera's collection, books not where they should have been. Had I really noticed that? Or was the dream messing with my brain?

I reached for my notebook and made a note to myself to check that in the morning. By then I was wide awake. It was morning. Seven thirty to be exact. Of course, it had already been morning when I hit the hay.

As the uncles say just before plunging into some risky business, nothing ventured, nothing gained. I had no choice but to head down those dark and endless hallways to Vera's library to check it out. I knew my way around the Van Alst house, but what I didn't know was Eddie McRae's role in all this. Eddie seemed to be quite at home in the house, and there was a chance that either Signora Panetone or Vera might have told him I was suspicious of him. I decided the best time to test my hunch was in broad daylight when everyone was awake and around.

At that point I conked out again.

THE THUNDER OF Signora Panetone banging on my door woke me up. The inevitable cat was dozing on the flowered quilt. I glanced at the clock. Eight a.m.

"Breakfast ready! Vera says hurry! Late, late!"

My iPhone vibrated. A text message from Uncle Tiny let me know that all systems were go and "the boys" were keen. After the world's fastest shower, I slipped into a black cotton scooped-neck tee, a flowered knee-length appliquéd skirt that my mother had bought in San Francisco sometime in the sixties, and a pair of black sandals that would let me run or leap a fence if I had to. Who knew what the day would hold? Each one had been full of surprises lately. I tucked my hair into a fairly neat ponytail and headed for the lion's den. Makeup could wait.

I entered the conservatory, ready to apologize, but Vera tore her eyes from her *New York Times* and held up her hand.

"I have a report that you slept at the hospital last night."

"Didn't sleep. That was the whole idea, to have someone awake and watching to make sure that Karen Smith made it through the night. Unlike Grandville General's so-called security."

"No need to quibble on the wording. My point is, that shouldn't have been necessary. You need your wits about you for this job."

No kidding.

"I didn't have a choice."

"There's always a choice. We could have had someone else spend the night there. You are hardly a bodyguard."

Someone else? Like who? The signora? She seemed to be tearing around twenty hours a day as it was. Eddie? He was part of the problem. Brian? As if maintaining the gardens and the rest of this huge property weren't enough. Vera had a real problem with boundaries in the case of her employees. And why would any of them have been better than me? I was one of her employees too. And I'd already saved Karen's life twice.

I kept these thoughts to myself. I took my place at the table, angling myself as usual for the best view of the side garden. The signora had been waiting impatiently and immediately transferred a small mountain of French toast to my plate. Without asking, she poured on about a cup of maple syrup and then ladled on sliced strawberries. My brain might have been sleepy, but my hand went right for my Francis I silver fork.

But Vera wasn't done with me.

"In future, remember that I pay you to be awake and alert, not walking around like a zombie."

I said, "Thank you for making the arrangements to have the Kellys there keeping an eye on Karen. I'd like to check something in the library this morning. Will that interfere with any of your plans?"

She looked surprised. The small distraction allowed the signora to slip a few more strawberries onto her plate.

The signora said, "No plans. Doctor coming, only doctor. Eat, Vera."

"For the thousandth time, Fiammetta, it's the physio, not the doctor. When have you known a doctor to make a morning call to a person who wasn't at death's door?"

Fiammetta crossed herself and muttered, "Eat," darkly.

"Tell me what it is you're looking for, Miss Bingham."

"I'll know when I find it," I said. "It's just an idea, to do with the play. You'll know the minute I do."

Vera answered with more of her dismissive grunts and turned her attention back to the *Times*.

Breakfast was a quieter affair than usual. At least the garden was gorgeous, with the peony beds in full flower.

I SPENT AN hour in my quarters, with paper in hand, making notes about different ways I could think about recent events. That was an hour wasted. After that, I set off for the library. As I crossed the grand foyer and started down the endless corridor on the east wing, I passed the strange, tall woman with the salt-and-pepper pageboy and the football player's shoulders. She was standing by the elevator, tapping her toe as she waited for it to arrive from the second floor. Of course, that was the answer. No mystery there. This must be Vera's physiotherapist.

She didn't respond to my greeting. Not that I really cared. I had the library on my mind.

Even in the daylight there was a residual spookiness in

the Van Alst corridors. I figured some of those relatives must have had seriously bad karma. I unlocked the library door and then secured it behind me. Not that I expected any of those relatives to leap from their frames and come after me, but better safe than sorry. I started systematically checking the shelves for gaps in the collections.

A half hour later, I had confirmed that the main level seemed fine. I climbed the circular wrought-iron staircase to the mezzanine and continued my search there. That was where the memory of odd spaces had come from, and most likely that memory had triggered my dream. Here and there were small gaps. Titles missing? Or room for growth? The Rex Stout section was there. I could see gaps. My uncles love Nero Wolfe. Well, I think they love Archie Goodwin. Sure enough, there were gaps where I would expect to find titles. More room for growth? A few volumes were not where they should be. But Vera might have had them in her room. I had noted that copy of *Sad Cypress* on her lap when she opened the door the night before. But the only gaps were on the mezzanine. What was one of the Nero Wolfe titles my uncles enjoyed? I recalled *The Second Confession*. Was there a copy of that here? There wasn't. I tried to remember another Rex Stout title and finally came up with *Black Orchids*. No sign of that either. What were the chances that Vera didn't have these? I kept going, slowly and meticulously, noting spaces that didn't seem right. Vera must have an inventory of her collection. Where was that? I was surprised I didn't know. I was falling down on the job. But I would ask, and I would return with it and compare it to the shelves on the mezzanine. I felt confident that Vera hadn't taken any of those books away herself.

I had no way of knowing how mobile Vera might be without her wheelchair, but I figured those stairs would be very difficult for her. If I were going to pinch books, which despite my criminal pedigree I would never do, I'd pick a spot where they wouldn't be discovered. The question was, who had taken them? I hadn't. What about Alex? He'd worked for Vera. He could have had a sideline, selling duplicates or poorer copies when better ones were acquired. Or perhaps selling them and substituting cheaper copies. Would she have ever discovered what had happened?

This didn't line up with what I knew about Alex, but I had to keep the possibility in mind.

And what about Eddie? How hard would it be for him to get his mitts on a copy of the key and to find out the access code? He seemed to have the run of the house. If he could get into the library, he could get out with something of value. Piece of cake if you asked me. And Eddie had been seen talking to Karen not long before she was attacked. That could not be a coincidence. Did they have a business relationship? Eddie seemed a likely candidate. I couldn't imagine Signora Panetone stealing books. Where would she ever find the time? She seemed totally devoted to Vera. If money was her motivation, she could have been making a fortune running her own restaurant rather than shouting at Vera to eat three times a day and, as far as I could tell, seven days a week. Was she connected to anyone who might not feel as loyal? Someone who could take advantage of her position? She couldn't have just materialized at the Van Alst house out of nowhere. I couldn't discount some unknown Panetone connection, even though Eddie seemed like the prime suspect. I had an idea of how to find out.

It suddenly crossed my mind that if Eddie had an access key to the library and trapped me there, I wouldn't have a hope here in the east wing. The library was at the farthest end of the wing. It was as far as you could get from the kitchen and the conservatory, where Vera would probably be if her physio appointment was over. The library windows had been covered up, so there wouldn't be any way to attract the attention of the gardener. No one would hear a sound, and most likely no one would ever see Eddie coming or going. The second attempt on Karen's life had been in a busy hospital in the early evening.

I had good reason to feel edgy. I picked up the small bronze of the naked man reading. I loved that little bronze, and now there was another good reason to. I gripped it tight. If anyone tried to get me, they were going to have an unexpected fight on their hands. There were benefits to being raised by Kellys. Rolling over and playing dead wasn't in our DNA.

ON MY WAY back to my own quarters, still clutching the bronze statue and fighting the urge to look over my shoulder in case Eddie was about to clobber me, I spotted Vera in the conservatory. She must have finished her physiotherapy session. Judging by her expression, it hadn't helped much. She was glaring at the *New York Times*, ignoring the spectacular garden behind her. I felt a jolt of the signora's excellent coffee would help me stay awake, and there was a pot sitting in front of Vera. I decided to join her. Sometimes good espresso is worth a sacrifice.

The signora appeared as if by magic with another cup and saucer for me.

I was somewhat distracted by the smell of the fresh baked bread that arrived with her. Once again, I wondered when or if Signora Panetone slept.

Vera glanced up over her espresso and raised one eyebrow. When I looked down and saw the statue in my hand, I had to think fast.

I met Vera's gimlet-eyed gaze. "I'm afraid I've fallen a bit in love with this little bronze, and I wanted to find out about it." I resisted apologizing for carrying it out of the library, or even asking permission. "Who is the sculptor? I can't really read the artist's signature."

"I have no idea. If he wasn't holding that book, he

wouldn't be in the library. It's just something my father picked up. He was the one with the fondness for bronzes. I never really cared for them."

"Really? But they're so beautiful. When they're done well, and this one is."

"If you say so. I can't get excited over it. My father got to know a lot of sculptors. I guess they could smell a patsy."

I hadn't noticed many bronzes or other statues in any of the grand rooms around the house. Perhaps Vera had chosen to sell them off.

"Well, this one is lovely," I said.

"Is it? I suppose you want it for your quarters."

I barely managed not to stutter out a "w-w-what," which would have diminished me in Vera's eyes for sure. "It belongs with your book collection."

She waved a hand. "Bronzes always make my skin crawl. Take it. The offer stands only while you're in my employ, it goes without saying."

"Naturally. Thank you."

"You hungry?" Signora Panetone pounced again.

I blinked. "Thanks, but I ate a lot of that French toast. Very good with the strawberries and maple syrup," I mentioned in case she had forgotten heaping my plate an hour earlier.

"More coffee would be good," I added. That got the right response. I watched her carefully as she motored through the door from the kitchen. No sign of Eddie, but he may have learned to stay out of my line of sight.

The conservatory was quiet while I sipped my coffee and Vera ignored her plate, as usual. Outside the window, I could see and hear the gardener on the lawn tractor. The sight of the magnificent peonies and smell of cut grass added to the moment. If there hadn't been a murderer about, life would have been just about perfect.

"So," I said after my third cup, "do you house some of the books from the collection elsewhere?"

She scowled. I was used to that and composed my own expression to reflect pleasant inquiry.

She said, "I do not. Why would you ask?"

"I thought I saw some gaps on the mezzanine, just a few, but I could tell that something had been taken. Was—"

A timid person could start to become very nervous around now. "No."

"No? But I'm sure—"

"I haven't taken anything from the mezzanine or the main level for that matter, except the one book I am reading. *Sad Cypress*. I am going through my Christie collection again. It's not the best copy, but it's still lovely. But that's it."

"And you haven't decided to sell any? That would explain it."

"Have you taken leave of your senses? *Decimate my collection?*"

We stared at each other. "I wasn't suggesting that you were decimating your collection, only that you may have replaced some copies with better ones. Or perhaps some were elsewhere to be, oh, I don't know, appraised or repaired."

"Never." Her espresso cup jumped as she banged the table to emphasize the neverness.

"Good to know," I said.

"What were you really doing in the library?"

I managed a look of surprise. "I was looking for a couple of Christie novels that I seemed to have missed. She sure did churn them out."

"Did you find them?"

"Coffee!" The signora stormed through the door from the kitchen to the conservatory and topped up my cup for a fourth time. I might never sleep again. She swooped out again, probably to brew another vat.

Finally I said, "What I found was holes, gaps on shelves. So I wondered if someone had taken a number of volumes for some reason. Or if the gaps were supposed to be there."

"What shelves?"

"I was looking in the Nero Wolfe books. I noticed no copy of *Black Orchids* or *The Second Confession*, two titles I know. Do you own copies?"

She paled. Her scowl deepened, although I wouldn't have thought it possible. "It would have to be someone with an entry code."

"I suppose so. Who has the entry code?" I thought I knew the answer.

"You do."

"And you can assume I didn't take them because *I* just brought the matter to your attention and *you* had been unaware of it."

"Could be a ploy to throw me off."

I sighed to make my point. "Could be, but isn't."

"If you think I don't know about your unsavory connections, you have underestimated me."

"And you shouldn't underestimate me. I am not unsavory and haven't taken any of your books. If I had, how long would it take for you to discover them missing from the mezzanine? There's lots of very stealable stuff in this house. So lucky for you, I'm on the up-and-up. Now, who else has the entry code?"

She didn't even blink at my audacious response.

"I do, of course. *You* do."

"Alex?"

"Alex did. Keys to the house and the code to the library."

"Did you get the key back, after he died?"

She frowned. "I didn't. I assumed it was destroyed when he was killed. It's not much good without the alarm code. Am I supposed to worry that someone will get in and start plundering my collection?"

"I think there's already been some plundering."

"So it would seem."

I hesitated. "Do you think it was possible that Alex might have taken some of the books?"

"A few months ago, I would have said no uncategorically. Now, who's to say? Things are not as they seem."

"You're telling me," I muttered.

"There's no one else."

"The signora?"

"Fiammetta would never, never, never take anything from me. She's been with my family since I was born. My parents brought her over from her dirt-poor Italian village in 1956."

"But if she has keys and the code, then perhaps someone else could get access."

"I doubt that."

"Does she have family? Friends who might not be quite as devoted to you?"

She raised an eyebrow. I could see it had her thinking. "No," she said. "But regardless, the signora and our gardener, Brian, who has been with us for more than thirty years, have keys to the house and the house code; however, neither one has ever had the access code to the library. It's me, you and Alex. That's it."

"What about Eddie?"

"Fiammetta lets him in and treats him like a pet. Eddie doesn't even have a key or the house code, let alone the library access."

"He's here all the time, and I wonder why he was so interested in Karen Smith and in what I'm doing."

Vera's nostrils flared slightly, and she pointed to the door. "I have nothing to worry about from Eddie. This conversation is at an end."

I left, but I knew my words had had an impact. With luck, her faith in Eddie might take a bit of a slam.

I WASN'T IN the mood for tragedy, but I had no choice. Alex's death was really bothering me. I got into Uncle Lucky's Navigator and drove out to see Alex's parents. I didn't expect it to be easy, and I was right.

I kept an eye out for Officer Smiley as I drove, but he'd been keeping a low profile lately. Hopefully, that was good.

At the Fines' house, the garden looked even more neglected, too much for the Fines to cope with in the wake of Alex's death.

I had a photo and a series of questions.

The grief was no less intense than on my previous visit. I felt it seeping into my bones from the minute I walked through the front door. The Fines were oddly pleased to see me. The Pirouette cookies were produced. Tea too.

"I have some questions for you. I am very sorry to disturb you again."

Mr. Fine said, "We're happy to see you."

Mrs. Fine added, "It's lucky you caught us. We are leaving to spend a week with my brother in Ithaca. Please come in."

"First of all, do you still have Alex's keys to the Van Alst house?" I didn't mention the library, in case that spooked them. Vera might have thought the keys were unimportant, but I figured a determined person could find a way to get the code. All it might take was a carefully hidden small camera, the type they use to steal credit card information in stores. Not that I have any way of knowing about those.

Mr. Fine bristled just slightly. "The Van Alst key was in his personal effects. We would never keep something like that."

Mrs. Fine said, "Everything went back to his . . . employer. They would have been in that box."

"I know you wouldn't, but I wondered if they might have been tucked somewhere and been missed."

His forehead furrowed. "Doesn't your employer have them?"

"She doesn't." Of course, I didn't necessarily believe Vera about anything, including who had keys, but I thought she'd been sincere.

Mrs. Fine bit her lip. She glanced at her husband. "I don't remember putting that key in the box. Do you?"

"Not specifically, but everything to do with that job went into the box."

Alex's mother said, "We weren't thinking very clearly."

Her husband added, "And we weren't looking for keys."

They exchanged glances and shrugged at the same moment. "It's possible they're still here," Mr. Fine said. "Such a small item. Do you want to have a look in his room? It's still difficult for us."

Once again I found myself in Alex Fine's boyish room. I don't know what I thought I could find that I hadn't the first time, but it was worth the try. I checked here and there, sliding my hands behind cushions, sticking my nose under the bed, checking behind books on the shelf. His clothes were still hanging in the closet, and I checked the pockets, but no keys. I stopped to glance at the photos on the wall, Alex and other young boys fishing. Alex at Black Pine Summer Camp looking very solemn with a group of four young friends. Alex still serious at his college graduation, arm in arm with a grinning blond buddy a good eight inches taller than he was. Their mortarboards were tipped at ridiculous angles over their faces. A solemn but happy moment. Then there were the photo-booth shots of Alex with Ashley, her smiling face turned toward his. In happier times, as they say. Who would want to damage these two harmless young people? Would Ashley be dead soon too if I didn't figure out what was going on?

Back downstairs, I told the Fines that there were no keys to be found. They seemed relieved, as if I'd suspected them of incompetent packing or keynapping.

"Miss Van Alst asked specifically for the keys when you returned the stuff to her?"

"We didn't give them directly to her. We've never met her. She didn't even come to the funeral. Sent flowers. What do you think of that? His own employer."

Tough one. I couldn't see Vera faking sensitivity for the length of a funeral. So perhaps it was just as well. "That must have been hard for you. But she has many health issues. She's confined to a wheelchair, and as far as I can tell, she never leaves the house."

Mrs. Fine said, "Humph." I was inclined to agree with her.

"So you didn't even see her when you took Alex's things from his apartment?"

"No. Signora Panetone met us. We'd heard a lot about her. Alex used to do very funny imitations of her."

"Did you see Miss Van Alst when you dropped the box off?"

"We didn't drop it off. The box was picked up."

Well, Vera wouldn't have picked it up.

I raised my eyebrows inquiringly.

"She sent someone to get it. A staff member, I suppose."

That was news to me and also a good segue into my question. I'd taken the time to print out the photo I'd shot of Eddie in the driveway. "This man?" I asked, flashing the photo and trying not to sound triumphant.

They squinted at the shot and shook their heads in unison. "No. Not him."

That came as a surprise. I thought hard. "Was it the little Italian lady, Signora Panetone?" I was distracted by the image of the signora veering through the countryside shouting, "Stop! Stop! You stop! Eat!" No, that didn't make sense. Maybe it had been Brian. He did everything else for Vera. "Who did pick it up?"

"He didn't give his name. He said Miss Van Alst had sent him to pick it up, and we'd already had a call from her to tell us to have it ready right away. *Without delay.*"

A couple of possibilities occurred to me. This sounded uncaring even for Vera. It made me wonder. Perhaps Vera hadn't been behind getting the box.

"I understand. And you're sure the call came from Miss Van Alst."

"We have caller ID, and it showed 'V Van Alst.'"

So much for those ideas.

"What did he look like? Old? Young?"

"Middle-aged, I guess. Fiftyish. A fairly big man. That's all."

I said, "Glasses?"

They shook their heads.

"Hair color?"

"Sandy. Brown with gray. Just kind of ordinary."

I had an idea. "By any chance, did he have a limp?"

She said, "He did, now that you mention it."

Well, now we were getting somewhere. If only I could figure out where.

Mr. Fine said, "These questions, it makes us wonder."

Mrs. Fine nodded. "There's something funny going on. In your opinion, is it all to do with Alex's death?"

I took a breath. "Some events have made me wonder what really happened to Alex."

They both zeroed in on me. "What type of events?" Mr. Fine asked.

I explained about the attempts on Karen Smith and Ashley and watched as Mrs. Fine gasped. "Who could be doing these things? It couldn't be that same homeless man who pushed Alex to his death."

I said, "I don't know, but it seems that there must be a connection. I understand that the police never found that homeless man."

Mr. Fine said, sadly, "No. We hear from the detective in charge of the investigation every now and then, but they have no new leads. We have tried to feel compassion for this man. Many of these people are seriously mentally disturbed. They don't know what they're doing."

Mrs. Fine added, "But it was hard to believe that Alex could have fallen in that way. He was just so cautious. And I know he would have been wary of a person like that . . ."

Alex's father took up when she trailed off. "He would never have stood so close to the edge in the first place. It just wasn't like him."

She whispered, "Not like Alex at all."

Her husband said, "You understand that we could never bear to watch any of the images after the first time."

I sure did.

I COULD STILL feel their sorrow clinging to me as I drove from Darby back to Harrison Falls. They had hugged me and promised to do anything to help. I just couldn't think of what they could do.

I supposed the drive was pleasant, but I couldn't really tell. My mind was on the strange situation. Someone had arranged to get Alex's things. That someone may or may not have been Vera. Vera hadn't told me, although that didn't necessarily mean anything. The person who'd picked up the box sounded like the large, limping man I'd seen by Karen's apartment, but was definitely not the same person who'd attacked Ashley. Were there two people working together? Was that why things didn't add up? Was Eddie one of them? Eddie seemed to have the run of the kitchen area. Could he have pretended to be Vera with her gravelly voice? The Fines had never met Vera, and they wouldn't know that she had such a distinctive way of talking.

I pulled over and gave the Fines a call. A bit soon, but after all, they had said anything they could do.

"Vera Van Alst's voice, can you describe it?"

A pause. "Just a woman's voice, nothing out of the ordinary."

I remembered how I'd reacted to Vera's voice in our first meeting. It had taken a lot of getting used to. "So not like crunching gravel?"

"What?" Mrs. Fine sounded startled.

I amended that. "Not deep? Gravelly?"

"No. Just a woman's voice. A bit muffled, I suppose, like she had a cold, but not deep. And not gravelly."

And, therefore, not Vera Van Alst.

"Could it have been a man pretending to be Miss Van Alst?"

She paused for a few seconds. "I suppose."

Interesting.

IT CROSSED MY mind that Uncle Lucky might like to get his Navigator back. He was unlikely to squeeze himself into the Saab, and he tended to get bored with the Town Car. I planned to return the SUV after a trip to the hospital in Grandville. I dropped in to see how Karen was doing and found that nurses and residents alike were quite enchanted by Uncle Danny. People say he can charm the pants off . . . I mean, charm the birds out of the trees. He's the most Irish-looking of us all, all wiry red hair and bright blue eyes, an alarming mustache and a blarneyish tongue. He attributes that coloring to a Viking ancestor named Olaf who he claims made a splash in Dublin round about the ninth century. If you buy him a drink, he'll tell you some tales about Olaf. I'd advise any mesmerized listeners to hang on to their wallets.

Danny was happily seated in a very comfortable chair outside Karen's door, playing solitaire and no doubt about to tempt the unwary into a costly game of Texas Hold 'Em. Someone had provided him with an iced cappuccino and a glazed double-chocolate doughnut. I noticed members of the female staff swaying their hips a bit more than I remembered them doing previously. And, in fact, there seemed to be more walking by than usual as well.

Despite this amusing scene, if you were a villain planning something, it would be wise not to underestimate Danny.

Even though he's a hugger and a kisser and that mustache tickles.

"Thank you so much for doing this, Uncle Danny. I know you're busy." Of course, none of my uncles is ever really "busy"; they just have degrees of availability.

"Glad to. Nice place. Good food. Pretty ladies."

I had to grin. "And Karen? Have you heard anything about her prognosis?"

"Pretty lady doc says that your friend is stable and they are thinking that guarded optimism is the phrase."

"That's a relief. Are you okay here on your own? I plan to stir the waters a bit."

Uncle Danny inclined his head toward what looked like an orderly checking a medical instruction, but those hairy forearms and the Celtic cross tattoo should have been my first clue that Uncle Billy wasn't far. In the unlikely event that someone blindsided Uncle Danny, Billy would bring that someone a little closer to his maker. Karen was in four good hands. I loved those guys. I figured Danny's early career choices of riding rodeo in Alberta and later wrestling would pay off in a tight situation. Billy was the family athlete: shot put, javelin, you name it. There wasn't an item that he couldn't heave through the air with mind-popping accuracy.

"We'll manage twelve hours each, and then the relief team shows up. Course, it's more likely that someone will pull something when things are quiet. Lots of traffic here."

"Has anyone tried to get into her room?"

"Sure thing. Half dozen. I stay with them and check them out first. Billy watches the hall. A stethoscope could fool nearly anyone, gotta admit it. But they've all been who they said they were. Billy and I work well together."

That reminded me. They weren't the only people who might be working together. "Okay. Here's a picture of a guy to watch out for." I handed over the print of Eddie McRae. "But like you two, he may be part of a team. The other player is a big guy, limps, sometimes more than other times, and may be wearing a baseball cap. Pass this on to our relief team when they get here, please."

The relief team would be Uncles Tiny and Connie. They made Danny and Billy look like a pair of rookie candy stripers.

I figured if we didn't want to spend the rest of our lives worrying, it was time to take action.

I TOOK A quick detour to get a dog toy for Walter in the Poocherie, a specialty dog store in downtown Harrison Falls. I picked up a giant jar of gummy bears for Walter's caretakers at the Sweet Spot, the candy store in a little row of boutiques that occupied our defunct department store. Harrison Falls was redefining itself after the slam that the Van Alst Shoes failure had inflicted and building a new life fleecing, I mean *attracting*, tourists.

Five minutes later, I parked the Navigator in its usual place and headed off to see how all that dog sitting was working out.

The first thing I noticed was that Walter was parked on the sofa, bug-eyed with contentment. I shook my head in case I was hallucinating. He looked quite comfortable on that heritage quilt. I'd been hoping that would come to me eventually, but I wasn't sure I wanted it now. He welcomed me with his ragged smoker's bark, and Uncle Mick popped out of the kitchen. He had a can opener in one hand and a can of duck and sweet potato dog food in the other. It's a dog's life all right.

"Oh, and about your Eddie," Uncle Mick said.

"Not my Eddie, but what about him?"

"Nothing. Nada. Zip."

"Really?"

"I don't think the guy ever had so much as a parking ticket." Obviously, my uncle felt this was a character flaw.

"Did you find out anything about him?"

Mick shrugged and spooned dog food into the designer dish with the white paws on the red background. It would take more than that to make the duck and sweet potato goop look good, but Walter's curly tail came to life.

"Grew up in Harrison Falls. Went to school here. Never left."

"That's it?"

"Works as a postal carrier. Quiet, close to retirement, no job problems, nothing on his routes, no complaints."

I shrugged in disappointment.

"Supposed to have a thing for Vera Van Alst."

"What?"

"No accounting for taste," Mick said, setting down the dog food for Walter. "Since they were kids is what I heard."

CHAPTER SIXTEEN

—⧫—

I FOUND VERA in the library, a cool sanctuary on a warm day. I used my code to get in. She seemed to wear a ratty dung-colored sweater no matter what day it was. She was stroking the dust jacket of a volume. I couldn't make out the title.

"You have disturbed the sanctuary of my collection with your tale of missing volumes. Now I think that a full inventory will be required before I can rest easy."

I didn't care if she could rest easy. Something terrible was going on, and it was worse than missing books.

"Seems Alex's parents don't remember whether his keys were in the box you insisted on having returned."

Made her blink.

In her normal gravelly voice she said, "I made no such request."

"I realize that, but someone did, a woman, from this number."

She frowned. "But except for you and Fiammetta and me, there is no woman in the house. I didn't do it."

"I didn't think it was you."

"Fiammetta would be very distinctive."

My heart wasn't in it, but I had to ask. "Could she possibly fake it?"

"I doubt it very much. She learned English as a young adult when she came from Italy to work for my family. She'll never lose that accent. Did she insist that they eat?"

I chuckled. "It couldn't have been the signora, and I know it wasn't me. Do you want to talk to the Fine family to confirm this?"

For the first time, I saw a flicker of alarm cross her features.

"I do not care to," she said, as if I hadn't figured that out.

"Then you'll have to take my word for it. All this stuff is connected. I bet the missing books are part of it too, so that makes it part of my job. I have to figure out what's been going on. By the way, Karen Smith is still in danger, although she's improving and is expected to survive."

I left her to think about that, and headed toward the kitchen pretending to want some lunch. I walked through the dining room and banged on the swinging door. Signora Panetone popped her head out.

"Sorry to bother you," I said, still standing in the dining room, "but I'm awfully hungry. Any chance of a sandwich or something?"

"You eat soup!" she shouted. "Good soup. *Carne in brodo.* Go to conservatory. I meet you with soup."

"Sure thing," I said, hoping that Eddie was listening. "Hold on, my phone's vibrating. I have to take this call. You need to heat the soup anyway, no?"

"All ready! Soup is ready now!"

I held up my finger and took the imaginary call.

"Hello?

"What?

"Great news! Are you sure?

"That's wonderful. Thanks for letting me know, Doctor."

I snapped the phone shut.

Signora Panetone said, "Is good? Good news?"

"Very good, Signora. My friend Karen is going to be all right."

"Going home? I send soup!"

"No, no, not yet. She'll have to stay in the hospital for quite a while, but she's conscious, awake."

"Good, good. You go, I come."

I went and made myself comfortable in the conservatory. Large fans made a little breeze, and the whirr of the wheel-chair approaching told me that Vera must have decided to join me. *Carne in brodo* turned out to be meatballs in broth with, naturally, freshly grated Parmesan. Soup and fragrant fresh bread was more than fine with me.

Vera parked herself on her regular side of the table and produced her best scowl. She took a deep breath before saying, "I am sorry about what has happened to Miss Smith. I have no idea why she was attacked."

"And Alex?"

For once she didn't meet my eyes. "I suppose I wanted to think that he was simply careless and stupid. He was an odd young man. Very reserved. Hard to warm to."

Hard to warm to?

I couldn't imagine Vera really warming to anyone. She sure hadn't warmed to me.

"He was secretive." Talk about the pot calling the kettle black, but never mind that.

"Secretive how?"

A flash of the familiar Vera. "In a secretive way, of course." She stopped, caught herself. "I'm sorry. He kept things from me. He liked to have information that other people didn't. He wasn't good at hiding that. You, for instance, are much more subtle."

"Funny," I said, "and all along I've thought you were keeping things from me. Which you were, naturally."

"I was."

"And I hope we can get past that and put an end to whatever is going on. But you'll have to level with me."

"Now I need to accept that boy must have been murdered." She shivered, despite the sweater and the warmth of the conservatory.

"Exactly, by someone posing as a homeless man, who then stole his laptop. And why would someone murder him?" I asked.

"I don't know."

I leaned forward and said, "I think it's time you told me the truth. Enough people have suffered. I need to know why."

At this rate, I'd be looking for a new job before dinner.

"Miss Bingham, may I remind you that it's what *you* need to tell *me* that counts."

"Miss Van Alst, you're the one with the missing information."

"Isn't that what I pay you for? To find out things?"

"Books, yes. Research, yes. But I didn't sign on to let people be killed. Was that your intention?"

Her head snapped back and she glared at me. "Of course not. What do you take me for?"

I waited.

Finally she said, "Alex said he'd found the manuscript. Found the play. He said it was called *When She Was Gone*."

I'd suspected, but I should have known she'd been keeping something key from me. "Found it? Where?"

"In New York City."

It was quite a distance from the spa at Harrogate to Manhattan, but not impossible. "How?"

"Through an intermediary."

"Let me guess. The intermediary was Merlin."

"Yes. Merlin."

"And do you know where they were to meet?"

"He didn't tell me. He needed the money to acquire the play. I arranged for it."

"He took his fiancée when he went to the city."

"Stupid. Lucky she wasn't killed too. He didn't mention that he was planning that."

"You're right, Ashley may have been lucky, but someone's been trying to make up for that. And by the way, she doesn't really know anything about Merlin. If he even exists."

Vera shrugged, tired out by all this truthfulness. "Maybe he doesn't."

"Exactly. There's something not quite right about the whole story."

"My money's gone."

"Ashley didn't mention any money. Just that Alex was going to make the arrangements."

"I told you Alex was secretive. From what I've heard, that girl is quite a talker. He wouldn't have told her. He wouldn't have wanted her to blab."

I almost grinned. "Blab" was not a word I'd expect to hear from Vera. But I agreed.

She said, "If he hadn't needed to *get* that money from me, he wouldn't have told me anything either." She managed a small bitter smile.

Vera was right. Ashley wasn't the sharpest knife and she would have let it slip to some customer without imagining any consequences. Word would have spread like wildfire. Had she done that without knowing what she was saying?

She must have known something without realizing the significance. Or someone thought so. My guess was that person was worried Ashley would remember a conversation about Alex's project and recall a face or a name.

"If Alex was murdered to get the money, then it must have been a fair amount. How much was involved?"

I waited. I didn't see any value in letting her off the hook. She glared at me.

I said, "I assume you'd like to see this person stopped before anyone is wiped out."

"Of course. What do you think I am? Some kind of monster?"

The answer that came to my mind was "a self-centered, antisocial, obsessive collector." But most likely not a monster. "I think you were thinking about the object of your desire and it blinded you to what was going on."

"Someone must have found out, even though Alex was so secretive. But who could have known?" she said.

"Whoever was meeting with Alex to sell the manuscript."

"Merlin. Of course. He got to keep it all," Vera said. "My money and my play."

I interjected, "Or there never was a manuscript and he was after the money anyway. He just had to kill Alex to get his hands on it. If Merlin knew when and how Alex was traveling, he could have intercepted him and pushed him onto the tracks."

"I preferred to believe it was an attack by a deranged homeless person." Then Vera muttered, "Unless Alex was in on the scam all along."

I shook my head. "I think there was more to Alex. His parents believed he was a strong and reliable person."

Vera's face was gray and drawn, her gravelly voice softened. "I am afraid you may be right."

Could it be that she accepted some responsibility? In fairness, Vera hadn't pushed Alex onto the tracks, but perhaps she had mentally pushed him into something shady and perilous. We sat in silence. I was thinking about what had happened to the money, to Alex, to Karen and to Ashley and whether lily-white Eddie McRae was involved in any of it. I assumed that Vera was thinking the same kind of thoughts.

Signora Panetone crept forward, the large tureen at the ready. "Soup!" she said, a bit of hope in her voice.

Vera waved her away.

Even I wasn't hungry anymore.

I CALLED ASHLEY'S cell. "Are you all right?"

"I'm okay. I'm going to have to go to work, though. I can't hide out at my dad's forever."

"Is he with you?"

"Yes. I'm all right when he's around."

"Can he watch out for you at the concession? Is he strong enough to protect you?"

She hesitated. "He has his own job. I don't want him to lose it."

I was hoping to find the permanent solution to Ashley's problem. But I needed to know she was safe for the moment. "It won't be forever. Promise me you won't go anywhere alone."

"There's an antique fair today. There are tons of people. Dad can get away to help me set up and close down."

"I don't know if that is enough, Ashley. I've learned something new about Alex's death."

I heard her sharp intake of breath. "What? What could you have learned about Alex's death?" Her voice cracked. "I was there when—"

I waited until she stopped sobbing. She said, "Tell me. I want to know what you've learned."

"Possibly the reason why Alex was killed."

"Reason? Crazy homeless people don't have reasons. It's the voices in their heads. That's what everyone keeps telling me. They can't help it."

I waited again while Ashley sobbed. After a while she said, "The therapist says it's better if I can learn to forgive. But I will never forgive him."

"I'm not so sure that he was crazy. Maybe he just looked like a street person. There may have been method in his madness."

I wondered if she'd understood. I heard nothing but silence. I blundered on. "There was a lot of money, Ashley. Alex planned to give it to the person who said he had the manuscript. I guess that was Merlin."

"But Alex didn't have any money. Vera hardly paid him anything."

"Believe me, Miss Van Alst provided the money for this sale."

"Oh my God. Why wouldn't he say? Wait, I know why. He worried about everything. He would have been so afraid that I would tell someone."

Again, I gave her time to calm herself down. Finally she said with a quavery voice, "I have a hard time keeping my mouth closed. We were like opposites. If I'd been Alex, I wouldn't have told me either."

I said, "The person who took the money may believe that you can identify him or put two and two together."

"You mean that's why the guy came after me?"

"I believe so."

"He'll keep trying."

"Yes.

"When I tell my dad this, he might be able to get the day off. Hang on."

I hung on.

Ashley was breathless when she came back on the phone. "No worries. He'll let his boss know. We'll stick together. We are quite a team."

Even with all my uncles, I'd always wondered what it would be like to have a dad. Despite everything, Ashley had some good luck in her life. I said, "I have to ask you to keep thinking. There may be some tiny memory in the back of your mind that will give us a clue as to Merlin's identity."

"All right. I'll try, but I really don't think I know anything."

I made Ashley promise not to go anywhere without her father, not even to the corner. "Remember, last time was right in your driveway. And if he found you, he could find your father."

"Thank you so much for all this, Jordan. I hope we can stop him before anything else happens to anyone else, even you."

"Stay safe."

*   *   *

I KEPT THINKING about what I'd said to Ashley about tiny memories. Something was nagging at the back of my own head. Some detail I'd seen in Alex's room. One of those pictures? I kicked myself for not taking the time to study them. I'd had keys and access codes on my brain. Mind you, none of them seemed to have anything to do with Alex's death. I'd stared long and hard at the one of Alex and Ashley. All I got was a guarded slightly awkward man in love and a donkey-faced girl who'd found the man of her dreams. Briefly.

The photos I hadn't studied were the ones when he was a child and the shot of his graduation. There was something about them. I gave his parents a call to plead for one last trip to interrupt their lives. No answer. They'd probably already left to visit the brother in Ithaca.

Damn.

I left a message and kept going. I had an idea who might have an answer. I really didn't want to use my breaking-and-entering tools on the Fines' house.

AS I HUNTED for Lance in the library, the colorful displays of grinning kids surrounded by books caught my eye. It reminded me how much I'd enjoyed the library's summer reading program when I was younger. I'd met the first people I had something in common with, not including my larcenous relatives. I was still in touch with those friends even though we were scattered across the country now.

The boys in the photos on Alex's wall must have been important to him in the same way. If I could track down one of the kids in the photos, I might be able to get some insights into Alex.

Lucky me. Mr. Eye Candy Librarian was on duty. Lance grinned as I walked in.

"I'm looking for a summer camp. Say, Black Pine. Especially photos." I didn't mention our meeting at the Café Hudson, although I'd sure thought about it. "Plus I need to talk to someone who was involved with Black Pine Camp fifteen to twenty years ago and who might remember Alex Fine."

"Hello to you too, beautiful lady."

"Sorry. Kind of caught up in some bad stuff right now."

"No kidding. I've heard that bookseller, Karen Smith, is still in bad shape."

"She is improving. But there's been another attempt on her life." I didn't bother to mention my various uncles keeping watch. They're just too hard to explain quickly. Especially to a man you are thinking about getting involved with.

"Another attempt on her life? But she's in the hospital, isn't she?"

"She is and she was attacked right in her room."

"But you're here looking for information on Alex Fine and summer camp. So do you think there's a connection between Alex and Karen?"

"I am pretty sure there is one. They moved in the same book circles."

"And the connection with the summer camp?"

"That's a stretch. I doubt it has anything to do with Karen. But I need to pursue all angles."

"You do know there are all kinds of privacy issues to do with kids."

"I realize that, but we need a way to get past it. There's a picture at Alex's parents' house that has me wondering, but they've left on a little trip. I don't want to wait until they get back." And I don't want to have to break in.

"I hear you. We may have some photos here. We have a lot of vertical file material on summer camps, and Black Pine is very big in this area. Give me a couple of minutes."

I kept myself busy checking for any Christie reference books I hadn't found yet, while Lance went off on the hunt.

He returned with a stack of files and handed them off to me. I spent the next half hour finding out more than I wanted to about summer camp. Everything but what I needed to know.

"Jordan?"

I jumped. "Lance, don't sneak up like that."

He put a soothing hand on my arm. "Sorry. Didn't mean to alarm you. By any chance did you check out Black Pine on Facebook?"

"Me? With my two friends, one of whom is my uncle? I'm never on Facebook, and I doubt that Alex Fine was the type to be on it either."

"Doesn't matter. Black Pine will probably have a page, and I bet there will be tons of photos going way back."

"I'm on it."

Sure enough, Black Pine Summer Camp was there. I found not only the current crop of lucky kids but also pictures from the past. I clicked into albums for the years that Alex would likely have been there. Jackpot. I spotted Alex before too long in a photo that must have been taken at the same time as the framed shot in his bedroom. He was wearing the same T-shirt. I held my breath as I moved the cursor over the images of the boys. Alex Fine. Tommy Bradley. Lorenzo Gomez. And the blond boy whose picture had belatedly made my spider senses tingle. No question about it, that boy was Tyler Dekker.

Officer Smiley.

The same Officer Smiley who'd been showing up all over town as I tried to find out about Alex Fine, Karen Smith, Ashley Snell, Merlin, the mysterious and possibly nonexistent play and now, the money. He'd been *lurking*, there was no other word for it, outside Sal's office when I'd gone to get help. He obviously had known Alex long before he'd arrived to work in Harrison Falls. Yet he'd never mentioned that, although he must have realized I now had Alex's job. Did he have some kind of hold over Alex? I found my heart beating a bit faster. What did it mean? No doubt Agatha

Christie would have lifted an eyebrow to signal that people are often not who or what you think they are.

Who and what was Tyler Dekker?

"Well?" said Lance with a flirtatious grin. "Any luck?"

"I have a name, and now I need to find out what the relationship was between this person and Alex."

He grinned. "Lucky lady. I have a contact for you."

"The director?"

"Better. The camp nurse. She was a school nurse but did the camp in summer. She's retired, but she's a regular here, and she has a mind like a steel trap. What she doesn't remember is not worth remembering." He scribbled a name, address and a phone number on a piece of paper and handed it to me. "I took the liberty of calling her to tell her she might be hearing from you. Hope that's all right."

"You're the best, Lance. I won't forget this. I owe you."

"All part of the service," he said, "but if you're feeling particularly grateful, you could always meet me for a drink after work one of these days."

"Sure thing. Let's make a plan as soon as life settles down." The women in Harrison Falls would be wild with jealousy, but I wouldn't say no to that.

"By the way, who is it you think might be connected to Alex?"

"I don't want to say."

"Right. Because I'm such a blabbermouth. Everyone knows about us librarians with our megaphones, bellowing secrets."

I laughed out loud. "Because I don't know if I'm right. But if I am, you'll be the second person to know, after Jordan Bingham. Trust me."

FIVE MINUTES LATER, I pulled up in front of Betty Leclair's crisp well-maintained sixties-style bungalow. It turned out to be quite close to the library and not all that far from Uncle Mick's shop. As usual, the scent of the freshly cut grass improved my mood.

Betty Leclair opened the front door and waved before I got out of the car. She was a sturdy woman with a deep tan that set off her silver buzz cut. She seemed even more impatient than I was. She was sporting a fuchsia golf shirt and plaid Bermudas, and she had the kind of build that indicated she was serious about exercise as well as lawn mowing. Tennis? Golf? Maybe she was late for a tee-off.

"How about the backyard?" she said. "Better than inside. I made some lemonade."

The lemonade was waiting, and we sat in Muskoka chairs with comfy cushions on a small deck in the only sunny part of her oversized shady lot. The trees were festooned with bird feeders. I would have liked to check out the mysterious garden with its ferns and hostas, but I was not there on a social call.

"So," she said when she'd poured me a frosty glass of lemonade, "what about Alexander Fine?"

"I am trying to find out about another boy who seemed to be close to him and who may know something about his death."

"You don't have his name?"

Here's where I got a bit evasive. "I think it was Tyler Dekker, but I need to confirm that. I am hoping you'll remember."

"I remember Alex well. He was quiet. Intense. Serious. I saw him quite often."

"Was he sick?"

"Accident prone, more like it. Or so it seemed at the time. Alex was always getting sunburned, scraped, or falling down or getting hit by stray objects. We were a bit less aware of things then, I'm afraid."

"Things?"

"Bullying."

I'd been afraid of that.

She said, "He never seemed to be able to stand up for himself, and bullies can sniff that out. I wish I'd been more aware. He was a nice little fellow, and he could have used our intervention."

"And Tyler Dekker was the bully?" I wondered how any human being could present such a misleading picture of himself.

She sloshed her lemonade. "No. Of course not. Tyler was Alex's protector. He was about the same age, but he was so much bigger than Alex, he seemed older. Once he arrived, Alex stopped getting hurt."

"Huh. So you're saying he looked after Alex?"

"Tyler made a big difference to Alex, and he flourished after that. Of course, he was never going to be a big-talking extrovert or anything, but he did well in the programs and proved himself quite athletic."

"And would Alex have trusted Tyler Dekker?"

"Absolutely. With his life, I imagine."

"You may not know the answer, but was Tyler Dekker from Harrison Falls?"

"I don't remember exactly where he was from, but Black Pine had kids from all over the state and beyond. But you know something? He's here now. He's even been by to say hello. He's a police officer. Would you like me to introduce you?"

"Thanks. I believe I have already met him. I just didn't know about the connection, so I didn't ask him about Alex."

She shook her head sadly. "It's such a shame that Tyler wasn't around to save Alex from that tragic death."

I nodded in agreement, but I couldn't help thinking that maybe she was looking at it the wrong way. Perhaps Alex had touched base with his old friend, and maybe that was the worst mistake he could have made. Miss Marple would have pointed a knitting needle at the police officer who wasn't quite what he pretended to be. I didn't want to share that thought with Betty Leclair, though. She'd been really kind to me and had obviously cared about both the boys.

She was eager to get off to her game, and I needed to leave too. As I got into the Saab, my mind was racing. Had Tyler Dekker known about the sale of the manuscript? Given his job as a police officer, people would have trusted him. Was he involved in the theft of the money? Did he know about Merlin? Or worse, was *he* Merlin?

Alex would have trusted him with his life.

Maybe that had been his fatal mistake.

CHAPTER SEVENTEEN

※◆※

I WAVED TO Betty as she pulled away in her Volvo. I headed in the opposite direction, to Grandville and the hospital.

I found Uncle Danny sitting outside Karen's room, reading a dog-eared Danielle Steel novel while Billy lounged in a chair on the opposite side of the corridor. Billy appeared to be working on wiggling his ears. The uncles have a great capacity to wait and not be driven wild by boredom. I don't like to ask how they honed that skill.

"How is she?" I asked.

"Hanging in there. The girls tell me that it's looking a bit better." Nurses were always "girls" to Uncle Danny, and they didn't seem to be too bothered by it. I think it's that curly hair and the bad-boy pheromones.

"Any sign of a would-be intruder?"

"Nope. Well, Billy thinks there might have been, but I didn't see anything. You know he's the one with the imagination."

I headed down to Billy, who was now apparently studying patterns in the ceiling tiles.

"Possible intruder?"

"You ask me, something wasn't right. But some people demand an unreasonable standard of proof." He nodded his head in the direction of Danny.

"That a yes?"

"It's a maybe. Saw a lady acting strange."

"Strange?"

"Walking head down toward the room. She sees Danny and she turns around. I get up to intercept her and she's off like a rabbit."

"A woman?"

"Yep."

"What did she look like?"

"Hard to tell. A platinum blonde. She had a scarf on, and she was wearing sunglasses."

"Sunglasses. Inside? Is that what alarmed you?"

"Don't really need them in this place. Same with the scarf. Not nearly enough light and no wind at all. Obvious she didn't want anyone to recognize her."

"Did you go after her?"

"She was fast, must have been expecting trouble. She shoved an empty wheelchair in front of me and gave me the slip. I started after her but figured maybe she was a decoy and I'd be leaving Danny on his own. That old trick."

"Right. But no one else came by or tried anything?"

"Really quiet. Maybe I should have gone after her, but there's me thinking it was a diversion to draw us away."

I had another idea. I'd been trying to think in Agatha's way, that is, things not being what they seemed at first. "Crazy question, Uncle Billy."

"Shoot." I can always count on Uncle Billy and his crooked grin.

"Could she have been a man?"

He frowned in concentration.

I added, "Wearing high heels and a skirt? And a wig? Wouldn't be the first time in the history of the world."

He nodded. "People make a living at it. She was a good height for a girl. Could have been a man, I guess. No beer belly."

Eddie McRae was slight, with narrow shoulders and no more than five eight. Could he manage to disguise himself as a woman? Could he fool anyone if he did? He was a postal carrier. He'd be fit, even though he wasn't young. He'd be strong. His legs would be toned. The sunglasses and scarf would disguise the fact that he was no beauty. Unless . . .

"Wait a minute! Did she have a limp?"

Uncle Billy chuckled. "She didn't, but I do after being slammed with that wheelchair."

I wondered if it would be possible for the man with the limp to fool anyone into thinking he was a woman. Then there was Officer Smiley; he was blond. Could he disguise himself that way and fool anyone? Too tall?

At least we knew that there was good reason to keep the uncles on alert. Tiny and Connie would be warned too. There were way too many questions. And not enough answers. One thing I knew for sure: someone wasn't ready to give up on silencing Karen Smith yet. I'd stirred the pot all right, but missed when it came to a boil.

EVEN IF YOU don't know what to do exactly, you have to keep going. That's another Kelly mantra. There seemed no way to discover who the woman with the scarf and the man with the limp were, but there was something I could try to find out and that was, just what was Officer Smiley up to? It was a good idea to confront him before he ran into Betty.

I figured if he was on duty that afternoon, there was a chance he'd be where he was supposed to be, that is, Harrison Falls. It was a nice safe time of day in a nicely populated area.

But just to be on the safest of sides, I conscripted Uncle Lucky. He loved to come along any time I had a plan. And he never bored me with idle chitchat. This time he took the Navigator. The Saab's not his style. Walter came along for the ride.

An added bonus of having relatives like mine was that they could easily figure out where the police were at any given moment. That's why they were walking free.

After checking out the nearest Stewart's and coming up empty (except for vanilla hazelnut coffee for me and Uncle Lucky and a maple-glazed doughnut for Walter), we went by the stoplight at Henry and Bridge, where cruisers are known to hide behind the spreading oak tree near the corner. No joy.

But we struck pay dirt shortly after when we found Officer Smiley idling in his black-and-white on South Street near the roundabout, always a good source of revenue for the town, according to my relatives, who do not care to pay extra taxes in the form of tickets. I hopped out and approached from the rear. I leaned in his window and watched him jump. Of course, I could afford that because Uncle Lucky and Walter were across the street watching. No one would ever call them overly subtle.

"We need to talk."

His neck flushed. "Hop in."

I grinned. "How about you hop out."

He got out of the car. How he'd gotten through the police academy was beyond me. The man lacked basic authoritarian-cop tendencies. Or else he was pretending he did.

He was smiling as he unbent and looked down at me.

I said, "It's not a friendly visit. I need to know what your recent relationship was with Alex Fine."

He wasn't very good at scowling, although he made a halfhearted attempt. "I don't have one."

"Not now, because he's dead, but you definitely had one. You deliberately didn't mention anything about knowing him, although you had plenty of chances. I have proof that you knew him, that you were friends at camp. So I want to know about this year. The year Alex died."

He recoiled. "I didn't see Alex this year."

"Pull the other one. You're lousy at lying. Your color gives you away." As I'd noted before, he seemed born to blush.

He said, blushing a bit more, "I know that, but it's the truth. Alex and I met at summer camp. Black Pine. And we stayed in touch for quite a while, even went to Ithaca College at the same time, although we didn't see each other as much then. Then we drifted apart. I hadn't seen him in about two years when he died. You can believe what you want, but that is true."

"But you're here. In Harrison Falls where Alex lived. You're telling me there's no connection?"

"There's a connection all right. I wasn't here before Alex died, but I am here *because* he died."

"What's that supposed to mean?"

"Not long before he was pushed in front of that train, he contacted me about something he needed to talk about. I was busy at work and I was helping my brother build a house, so I didn't get back to him right away. I meant to, you know how it is. About a week went by and he called again and left a message. I was working nights and didn't even get his message until the next afternoon. When I called him back, it was too late. He was dead."

Good cover.

"Nice," I said.

He flushed again. "I felt responsible. He wanted to tell me about something he was involved in, something criminal perhaps or dangerous, and I let him down."

"Dangerous is the right word. So you're saying you got a job in Harrison Falls because Alex died?"

"A couple of weeks after, a job came up. I applied and here I am."

"Huh. And your connection to Karen Smith would be?"

"She's a crime victim too."

"But not in our town and somehow your new job doesn't entitle you to break into her apartment."

"The same can be said for you."

"I'm not a cop."

"And I'm not a crook."

"Well, *I'm* certainly not a crook."

"Really?"

"Really." I could feel my own neck getting red. It must have been contagious. I needed to steer clear of this guy once I got my information.

"Then you must be the only person in your family who isn't."

"My family is none of your business, and they have nothing to do with this."

"What about the hulk in the Navigator?"

"He's here to make sure that nothing happens to me."

I thought those blue eyes would pop.

"What could happen to you?" he said, looming over me, his hands on his hips. "You're talking to a cop."

"That's right. A cop who had a connection to Alex Fine and Karen Smith. Did you have a connection to Ashley too? Oh right. Of course you did. She was Alex's fiancée. You would have known that. You'd probably even met her. No problem to find out where she lived. So let's tally that up: one of those people is dead, one may not live, and the other was horribly beaten. Coincidence?" I may have raised my voice just a bit. A couple of teenage girls scurried to the other side of the street before they reached us.

He said, "How about my take on it? Alex is killed and then his job becomes available to a woman who is a member of a family of well-known con artists. Karen meets this woman and then is bludgeoned and left for dead, coincidentally found by the same woman. This woman talks her way into Karen's apartment on spurious grounds. But wait, Ashley talks to the same woman, and Ashley is attacked."

I didn't like to turn, but I had the impression that people were gathering on the opposite sidewalk to watch the proceedings. The large blushing policeman yelling at the innocent young woman—at least that's what I hoped they were thinking. Luckily, I had taken the time to dress decently.

"You think I wanted the job with Vera Van Alst because I am a crook?"

"If the shoe fits."

"The shoes are vintage and I came by them honestly, which is the same way I got my job. I think Vera is the victim of some dangerous criminal, and as it's not me, it must be you." Even I could see the flaw in that logic, but he'd really made me mad bringing my family into it and then questioning my honesty. "Someone got away with the money that Vera gave to Alex to negotiate for the Christie play. Who was in a better position to do that than his old friend?"

He blinked. "Vera gave Alex money? For a play? That's what this is about?"

"As if you didn't know. I have a pretty good idea who got away with that. Someone Alex trusted. Maybe you're Merlin."

"I don't know any Merlin, and I didn't know about the money. For a play? What kind of play? This changes things."

"Oh, it changes things all right." If I didn't know better I would have sworn this was news to him. But as they say, never kid a kidder, and I came from a family that could lie like rugs. "An unknown play by Agatha Christie. Probably one that might shed light on her mysterious disappearance in 1926."

"That doesn't even make sense. Wait a minute. How much money?"

"Why should I answer your questions? You've done nothing but evade mine."

"Because I am a police officer."

"And I'm a citizen. There are lots of witnesses who have just observed you harassing me. So if you're thinking that you can sneak up and attack me, you can forget it. The Kellys are watching."

This time he turned pale instead of red. "Attack you?"

"Don't even think about it."

"I'm not thinking about it. How could you even suggest such a thing? I don't attack people. I help them. I am the good guy."

"Oh, spare me. And stay away from Karen Smith. We have people watching her."

His mouth hung open.

I tossed my last grenade. "Who is the man with the limp? Are you working with him?"

"The man with the limp?"

"You heard me. Is he your confederate? Did you just pretend to chase him?"

"Outside Karen Smith's place? That guy."

"The same psycho who tried to get into her room in the hospital."

"I can't believe you are saying these things."

Really, he could have had a career on Broadway. I started to wonder if he was telling the truth. But nobody could be that innocent. He was just born with the look.

A squawking sound came from his patrol car. He turned and headed to the car, shaking his head. It was too bad Smiley was probably a thief and a murderer, because he was so damn cute. A girl's got to protect herself from dangerous cuteness. I was pretty sure that Uncle Lucky had it all on video.

Who knows why I called after him? "Don't leave town."

He stopped and straightened up, but kept going.

I WAVED TO Uncle Lucky and headed home, not wishing to miss a meal at the Van Alsts' for obvious reasons. Lucky went back to grilled cheese sandwiches (processed orange cheese only, please) and canned tomato soup before he and

Uncle Mick, and Walter of course, set out for Albany and some unspecified business meeting. It's always better not to know.

I seemed to be developing a habit of arriving just in time for meals. Vera was already installed at the dining room table, glowering and looking like she didn't plan to say a word to me.

Not a problem from my point of view.

The signora was set to swoop as soon as I sat down. There was something magic about all that.

It started off simply with a minestrone soup that was like nothing I'd ever had before. Then out of the blue, lasagna arrived, and when I say "lasagna," I mean a massive red-enameled casserole with enough in it for a platoon of soldiers, instead of one woman with a healthy appetite and another who seemed to live on the scent of books. Not that I was complaining. I did wonder where all the leftovers went. Had I known that lasagna like this was in the wings, I might have been a bit more careful about how much minestrone I inhaled.

"Eat!" Signora shouted. "You eat. No, no, eat!"

"Just watch me," I said.

Vera made three attempts to wave her away and in the end accepted a serving about the size of a playing card. She poked at it idly with her Francis I fork.

"Interesting day today," I said, giving myself a little time to rest and make room before finishing.

"Eat!"

"Don't worry, I will."

"No, no, eat now."

Vera growled, "Fiammetta, stop that. Let her speak. Do you think you're feeding the bears in the zoo?"

It was always a bit zoo-like in the Van Alst establishment, but who was I to fuss?

"Interesting in what way?"

"There's a police officer in town who knew Alex. He'd known him for years."

"Enlighten me. Why is this of interest? Surely Alex Fine knew many people."

"Well, this police officer has been following me, was in the vicinity of Karen Smith's attack and must have known about the fiancée, Ashley Snell. He showed up after her attack too. He just moved to Harrison Falls, and everywhere I go to check things out, poof, there he is."

Vera shrugged and gave her rectangle of lasagna a sharp poke with the fork.

I said, "His name is Tyler Dekker. Do you know him by any chance?"

"No. I don't know any policemen. Why would I?"

"I told him I was on to him today. He knows what's going on, and he may even be a part of it." Of course, I suppressed my niggling hope that Tyler Dekker was telling the truth.

"Was confronting the police an intelligent course of action?"

"I needed him to know that I was watching him and other people were too."

"Seems unwise."

Signora Panetone took advantage of the conversation to slap down an extra piece of lasagna on my plate, although I hadn't fully worked out a strategy to finish what I already had. As she approached the other end of the table, Vera yanked her own plate out of the way.

"Very unwise," she added, managing to look down the long table and straight into my eyes.

Signora Panetone apparently admitted defeat and headed for the swinging door with the red casserole dish.

"In my opinion, it was worth it to see if he'd blurt out anything about the man with the limp."

The signora paused in the doorway, weighed down by the lasagna. The door stayed open long enough for me to get a good look at Eddie, positioned just inside the door and leaning forward. He had obviously been listening to every word.

"Man with the limp?" Vera frowned. "Who is that?"

"I don't know, but I intend to find out."

"Why do you mention him at all? Is he important?"

"I saw a man with a limp trying to break in to Karen Smith's place, and he later got into her room and tried to finish her off. No one else seems to know anything about him."

For some reason, conversation lagged from then on, although the signora livened things up for me by swooshing through the swinging door yet again to present us with an airy sponge cake dusted lightly with icing sugar. She followed that with a fragrant espresso. Vera managed to avoid eating the cake, although she did move it around on her dessert plate.

As for me, I didn't know when my life would revert to Alphaghetti and grape Jell-O, so I ate up with enthusiasm.

After dinner, as conversation with Vera seemed even more impossible than usual, I hurried back to my room, attempting to get there before the cat did. As I reached the stairs, something furry brushed past me. I remained calm. In fact, I was proud of myself that I didn't scream. I was getting used to that sneaky Jekyll and Hyde cat. My moment of proud calm didn't last long. Someone cleared his throat, and I felt a hand land on my shoulder. I whirled and screamed enough to make up for at least twenty sneaky cat attacks. I shrank back against the wall, my mind racing. I'd never make it up the stairs with him right next to me. What could I use as a weapon? My shoe? My head?

I knew from my self-defense training (the Kelly School of Anything Goes) that if you hit someone's nose hard with the top of your skull, you can break their nose. It was my only choice. Plus of course, I was still screaming. I couldn't believe that neither Vera nor the signora could hear me. I hoped someone was calling 911.

Maybe this guy was going to kill me, but he was going to have a serious souvenir of his action.

I pulled back, preparing to lunge forward and give him

a major nose job. But that was going to be tricky. Eddie was cowering, one hand covering his mouth, his other arm shielding his eyes. I couldn't help but note that his nose would still have been an easy target.

He pleaded, "Please don't hurt me! Please stop shouting."

Hang on. This was all wrong.

"I'm not shouting. I'm screaming. It's not the same thing at all. And I have a right to." I felt quite insulted.

He lowered his hand. "What do you mean you have a right to? Why were you screaming?"

"Why do you think?"

He goggled at me.

I said, "How about this for a reason: because *you* sneaked up behind me and touched my shoulder. Because a man has been killed and two women have been attacked, and seriously injured. That's why."

His jaw dropped. His arms did too. Really, the man was a walking cliché. "But you can't think that I wanted to hurt you?"

"What else would I think? All the victims seem to have some connection with you."

"But I wanted to warn you."

"Warn me about what? Is that a threat?"

"No! Not a threat. But you mentioned a man with a limp."

"Big deal. I already know he's dangerous."

"More than that—"

"No, no, no, Eddie, no! No talking! You come. Come now. Stop, stop, stop. Come." The signora managed to get in between the two of us. She shook her finger in my face. "No police, no! Go away! Come, Eddie!"

Eddie said, "But—"

He was no match for the signora, who managed to drown out whatever he was trying to say to me as she hustled him down the endless hallway.

I heard him call out "careful!" and "here." The rest was lost in a sea of "No, no, no! Come, Eddie!"

It would have been comic if it wasn't so serious. Signora Panetone did have the advantage over Eddie as she could grab him by the ear, but he could hardly manhandle an elderly woman without being a beast. It was a smart play on her part. And it confirmed the conclusion I'd finally reached. Eddie wasn't going to hit any woman. Or probably any man either.

That was too bad because I'd really liked the Eddie theory. I had no attachment to the man, and it seemed to work beautifully. Right down to the bit where Eddie mentioned the man with the limp.

After my rush of adrenaline, my knees felt wobbly. I looked up the stairs and saw the cat. It seemed to be gloating.

I had no choice. I had to find out why I was being warned about the man with the limp. I already knew he was dangerous. And if Eddie had been listening, which he had been, then he was aware that I knew that.

I raced down the hallway after them, but Signora Panetone had disappeared through one of the doors. I figured they were headed for the kitchen. Rather than get lost in the labyrinth that was the Van Alst house, I took my usual route to the dining room and went straight to the swinging door, through the butler's pantry and into the kitchen. I expected to find them on the other side, but there was nothing but the huge old-fashioned kitchen with the eight-burner gas stove and the acre of ancient marble countertops. The evening's dishes were still stacked by the sink, and the lasagna sat cooling on the vast harvest table in the middle of the room.

No Signora.

No Eddie.

No answers.

CHAPTER EIGHTEEN

—◆—

WELL, I FIGURED the signora must have rooms somewhere. She couldn't be in that kitchen twenty-four/seven, even though I sometimes wondered. I spotted a door on the far side of the room and headed for it.

Closed.

I turned the knob. Locked.

I banged and shouted.

"Signora! I need to talk to Eddie. I won't hurt him. I won't call the police. You need to open the door. I have to know who the man with the limp is."

"You go now! No Eddie. Eddie's go home."

I gave up on that approach. I headed through the kitchen door to the side entrance near the signora's vegetable patch, a practical corner on the ornamental grounds.

If I'd calculated correctly, I figured I knew which window belonged to the signora's hideout. The window was slightly open. I looked around for a ladder or something to climb on. No joy.

If you have a huge house full of valuable artifacts, it's wise not to keep ladders around. Vera would have made sure of that. I threw a few decorative river rocks at the window, to no effect. I shouted, "I know you're in there." That didn't work either. Unsurprisingly.

I considered my options. I could go get my lock picks. You can run, Signora and Eddie, I thought, but you cannot hide. You don't know the Kelly side of me. And you *will* answer my perfectly reasonable questions.

On the way, I realized that Vera had also reacted to the talk of the man with the limp. It hit me. They all knew who this was! I wouldn't have been surprised if the damn cat knew.

I took a turn on the endless corridor and walked to the elevator. On the second floor, I made tracks to Vera's room. I knocked, called and knocked again.

Silence.

Vera was my employer, and I decided that throwing rocks at her second-floor window and/or shouting would not be in my best interest, no matter what she knew.

I did keep an eye out (including checking over my shoulder) on the way back to my own room. I watched for a sneaky cat seeking official access to my cabbage rose garret. This time, I got there without incident.

My bed beckoned to me, welcoming, cozy and safe. I made myself comfortable and lay there thinking. The arrival of a smug cat, tail twitching triumphantly, didn't shake my concentration. I needed to figure this out. Agatha would not be proud of me so far.

But who else could this limping man be? Someone connected with the house, with Vera, with the signora and with Eddie. And apparently with me. There was simply no one else around. I had accepted that Eddie might not be our villain. Even stretching my imagination to the fullest, there was no chance that the signora could ever have been ten inches taller and much less round.

Agatha would suggest that nothing should be taken for granted. Vera? If Vera could walk, would she limp? Perhaps. Would she be able to get into the hospital and try to smother Karen Smith? Could she run?

I closed my eyes to try to picture this. It didn't matter whether she could run or not, Vera was probably no more than five four, with narrow shoulders. She might be mentally strong, but I had seen her thin arms. I felt strangely relieved in deciding that she wasn't the killer, but it was still a worry knowing that she was aware of who he was. So who was he? It wasn't like a bazillion people were in and out of the Van Alst house. It wasn't like the physio could have done it.

I stopped. She was tall with broad shoulders, big hands. She had access to the house. It wouldn't be much of a stretch for her to get her hands on the key and the code. She was in and out of Vera's bedroom. She would have known, or at least seen, Alex. She'd been standing still the two times I'd seen her. Did she walk with a limp? Vera and the signora would both know her. Would Vera and the signora try to protect her? Would Eddie warn me about her?

I wasn't going to hunt for the signora this time. Vera would know.

I TOOK THE creaky elevator back to the second floor and walked briskly to Vera's bedroom door. I knocked, trying to sound businesslike and confident. "I'm not going away until you answer. Don't make me call the police."

What an insane bluff from one of the Kelly clan. When the door finally opened, Vera glared at me. There are worse things.

"Your physio," I began.

She narrowed her eyes. "Miss Orsini. What about her?"

"Does she have a limp?"

"Have you taken leave of your senses, Miss Bingham?"

"Maybe, but I need to know. Does she?"   ___

"Why are you asking?"

"Because she's the size of the man I saw. Big shoulders. Because she has the run of the place, she would have known Alex, and if she has a limp, then I have to warn you that she's dangerous. Very dangerous. I know you and the signora reacted when I mentioned the limp, and I need to know if it is this person."

"Sorry to disappoint. Miss Orsini may not be Miss Congeniality, but I know she's not your man with the limp. Let it go, Miss Bingham."

The door closed in my face. Not for the first time either. I loved that Vera would actually refer to someone else as "not Miss Congeniality." On the bright side, she hadn't fired me for banging on her bedroom door. I felt like firing myself, though. I had practically accused a woman of committing some horrible crimes based on some very flimsy evidence. So much for innocent until proven guilty. Maybe the full moon had made me crazy. But even if it had, shame on me.

THE CAT APPEARED out of nowhere. At least it was in an affectionate Dr. Jekyll frame of mind and not an ankle-destroying Mr. Hyde mood this visit. It seemed to raise an eyebrow, before curling up on the flowered duvet and licking its front paw.

I lay in bed envisioning psychotic attackers, stalker cops and felines who could turn evil at any second. I'd checked and rechecked each bolt, latch and window, but if the cat could get in, could a person? I let myself hope that Tiff would have a moment to reassure me. I could still see Ashley's bruised face and swollen eye. I did not want to be next. I tucked myself into my bed. Somehow I felt safer there with my view of all entry points, although I doubted a woman armed with a feather duvet had ever stopped an armed intruder. Luckily, I remembered the bronze figure. I got up and brought it over to my bed. First I sat it on my little side table. Then I rethought that. It could be used against me, so under my pile of pillows it went.

"Hey, you." Tiff was peppy, then turned serious as I filled her in.

"A girl attacked? An attempted murder in a *hospital*? I think it's really time to go stay with the charming uncles, Jordan." I knew she would say that.

"Come on, Tiff. How could I leave Vera and Fiammetta alone if I thought it was too dangerous to stay here? They're a lot more vulnerable than I am."

I ignored the crazy-making full moon. The wind picked up outside; a spooky low moan pushed past the window sills, rustling papers at my bedside. Notes fluttered around the apartment like small paper ghosts, upping the heebie-jeebie factor considerably.

"You are not safe. And your crazy boss is doing nothing to help. Get someone to ride shotgun, but get the hell out of there."

I put on a brave face, even if she couldn't see it. "Tiff, I feel a lot safer here behind locked doors in a house with a first-rate security system. Anyway, Mick and Lucky and Walter are in Albany tonight, so they wouldn't be much help, and the others are guarding Karen. I just want to decompress, and I need you to tell me it's all going to turn out fine in the end. Can you do that without relocating me?"

Tiff laughed. "Of course. I was just being my usual safety inspector to the world. But I do wonder about this job, Jordan. Maybe it's not worth all the stress. To be honest, I'm not quite sure what you are being employed to do, other than eat and find injured people."

"Don't forget being belittled by the boss and pestering the recently bereaved."

"Wait, what was that last one?"

Something caught my eye in the far corner. Was the wallpaper flapping at that uneven seam? Ignoring Tiff as she threw questions at me, I gingerly got out of my safe bed. The wallpaper rustled above the small walnut dresser, drawing me into the dim corner. The pattern was not only mismatched in that spot, but something about the beige curly stem of that rose was off. Why hadn't I found a lamp for that dresser? Using my iPhone screen to light the way, I inched forward. The curlicue in question slipped away into the wall. For a split second terror raised my hair at the roots.

Then I realized what was actually going on.

"Tiff, I'm going to have to let you go. I think I've finally figured out how that cat keeps getting into my place." That cat made a *murp* of protest. Before Tiff could say another word, I hung up. The walnut dresser was stuffed with my belongings and had been heavy enough empty. I struggled to move it out of the way. Next I reached to pull at the paper. Beneath the heavyweight cabbage rose paper I found a space. I made tracks to the sitting area and repositioned my reading lamp to get a better look. Not good enough. I pulled the lamp closer and angled it so I could see. Then I stuck my head into the space. What the heck? I figured the space must have been a closet at one time. But why would anyone paper over a closet door? It wasn't like there was any storage in this apartment. Of course, there was probably tons of storage throughout the rest of the third floor, so it wasn't really an issue. I peered into the dim interior. What kind of closet had ropes and a pulley? It finally dawned on me that I was staring at the platform of an old dumbwaiter. With a Siamese cat hunkered on it. But, hang on a minute, wasn't the cat on the bed?

The next sensation—following astonishment—was pain. This cat reached out and raked my nose with its claws. I yelped and sat back, holding my nose as the mean scratchy cat stalked toward the bed and its sweetly purring twin leapt down and headed over to me. It sashayed into the dumbwaiter and disappeared to somewhere. But where? The dumbwaiter hadn't moved. The cat was gone. I leaned forward, worried about setting the mechanism going and plunging into the bowels of the building. No one would ever find my body.

I clung to the back leg of the dresser as I checked up and down. My eyes were getting used to the darn cat-free space. I could make out a dark shape in the farthest reaches. A cardboard box. I reached over and pulled it out.

"How very Nancy Drew," I said out loud. I peered back into the dumbwaiter space. I saw the swish of a tail as the cat made its way to the other side and out. What was over there? Just attic storage, I figured, easily accessible to felines who deigned to go anywhere they wanted and especially where they weren't wanted.

I carted the box back to the Lucite coffee table. The cat (Mr. Hyde) followed, looking dangerous. It hopped up on the club chair. "Stay away," I said. "I will defend myself." Once you start talking out loud to small mean animals, there's no turning back. I grabbed a tissue to dab at my nose, which was bleeding freely. I checked the mirror. I didn't have a bandage, but a ragged bit of tissue seemed to stem the bleeding. Not my best look, for sure, but the least of my problems.

The box contained three black notebooks, and several volumes that looked like they might be first editions from Vera's private collection. There was also a small lunch box. I opened that to find Ulysses S. Grant gazing up at me. Well, more than one Ulysses S. Grant. Hundreds of him. In stacks. My guess was this was Vera's substantial amount of money. What else would explain it? Alex must have hidden it in the dumbwaiter.

I didn't count the money. I didn't even touch it. I got another tissue to wipe any trace of my fingerprints from the top of the box and the sides of the dumbwaiter.

"I was really not expecting that," I said to the cat. Sweat prickled the back of my neck.

The cat said nothing.

That stack of notes was supposed to be missing. Vera thought her money was gone, perhaps carried off by a deranged man in a subway station. I stared at them. There was more than enough to fund my education. No one would ever know that Alex had hidden that cash here, and if anyone did, it would be impossible to prove. I had no doubt that I would get away with using this money for my quite worthy plans. My uncles would be proud of me.

The cat watched.

I shook my head. I had decided when I first went off to college that I wouldn't follow in the family footsteps. Here was the test of that commitment.

I turned to the cat and said, "So close and yet so far away. But life's like that."

Because it felt good to be sharing this decision with another creature, even one that had raked my nose. I added, "And here's a bit more treasure. I bet these little beauties are Alex's notebooks."

There was a small fortune and several very rare books, but to me the notebooks were the real gold. I just wanted some information, and for reasons I cannot divulge, this was not the first time I'd been in the room when bags of cash were dumped from a sack.

Notebooks one and two were brimming with research, and tucked between the pages were many folded, terse notes from Vera wanting updates on Alex's progress. In small neat script, Alex had written to-do lists and info in the margins. These were what I'd hoped to find in Alex's belongings at his parents'. No wonder they hadn't found them. If it wasn't for the cat, no one would ever have found them. I read Alex's notes to himself about contacting auction houses and following up on leads.

The third notebook looked almost untouched but also had random folded pieces of paper poking out from its blank pages. I swear it felt like Agatha herself was beside me, whispering a million questions in my burning ear.

I unfolded the first crisp white paper.

Dear Mr. Fine,

It has come to my attention that you are looking for a previously unpublished Agatha Christie manuscript, on behalf of Vera Van Alst. I may have an item that may pique your employer's interest.

> *Sincerely,*
> *M. Merlin*
> *Merlin Rare Books and Collections*
> *New York, New York*

"Holy pay dirt, Batman," I whispered.

The cat merely swished his tale.

My mind swam in a hundred directions, and my thumbs were already tapping *M. Merlin Rare Books and Collections in New York* into my iPhone. I turned up some Merlins in the world of collections, but not the one I was hoping for. Alex had circled Vera's name on the paper, and he had written, *How could he know this? Possible fraud? Does "Merlin" have an accomplice?*

It seemed to me that Alex was suspicious right from the get-go. The following notes were about meeting in NYC to make what Alex wrote as the "exchange." It seemed likely from his notes that he was worried the meeting was a scam. But why had he gone ahead with his trip? If Alex had gone to NYC to meet with Merlin, why was the money still in my apartment?

Maybe he'd decided to leave the money at home in case

Merlin tried to trick him out of it. At least, I hoped that was the reason. The only other possibility I could think of was that Alex himself had decided to steal the money. I hated that idea.

The last note was dated the day before his death. Alex had scribbled *Bonnelly's*, the name of a boutique hotel, and *surprise Ashley*, complete with little hearts. I'd never known a man to use little hearts in a note.

Poor guy. Ashley had been surprised all right, but in a horrible, life-destroying way.

I could imagine Alex, excited to complete his task for Vera by revealing the scam, and eager to whisk his fiancée off for a romantic celebration away from their small town. It made my heart hurt. Little did he know he'd be thrown in front of a speeding train.

I felt desperate to find out more. I shook the blank notebook frantically, and a last straggler floated out. The email note to Alex from Karen Smith was also dated the day before his death. For some reason he had chosen to print it out and tuck it into his notebook.

From: Karen@thecozycorpse.com
To: Alex Fine

It was great to see you at the Cozy Corpse the other day and talk shop, LOL, pardon the pun! I just thought I would let you know that I've been contacted by a customer wanting to sell a Nero Wolfe first edition of *Black Orchids*, British printing with original cover and in mint condition. I'm 99% sure it's the one you purchased on behalf of Miss Van Alst 6 months ago. I guess I was just surprised that she would part with it after all the work she had you go through to get it. That being said, I'd certainly appreciate if you kept me in mind when selling future titles. I can only imagine the gems that collection contains.

Happy treasure hunting, hope to see you soon.

Karen Smith
www.TheCozyCorpse.com

Clearly Alex and Karen had a friendly rapport. They knew and liked each other and had even had business dealings. but this note had huge red question marks on it and a list of names under the heading: *Access to Library*.

~~Vera?~~
~~Eddie?~~
~~S Panetone?~~
~~Me~~
Brian U?

All the names were crossed off but one: Brian U.

Brian? Could that be our Brian, the gardener? I couldn't seem to recall his last name. I looked over my shoulder at my imaginary Agatha Christie; she shrugged. If she had spoken, I was sure she would have said, "I told you so."

Look for connections.

I hadn't even had Brian on my radar, and why not? My pulse was banging at my temples now. What had I missed? By this time I was pacing. I found myself at the window, staring out in puzzlement.

The sun had set by now and the stunning full moon shone down, illuminating the wide lawn, lush and well mown. The scent of the grass that had been cut that morning still lingered. Usually that was a very soothing and satisfying aroma. But that was before I'd seen the two words: Brian U. The large familiar figure on the ride-on tractor. Brian. Could he have been the man with the limp? Of course not, he didn't limp. But wait, I'd only seen him bent over the flower beds or on the lawn tractor. I didn't know whether he limped or not.

Why had I wasted time trying to implicate the innocent physio? The answer had been right in front of me all
along.

It made sense. The gardener would have known all about
Alex. Not only that, but as a staff member in the Van Alst
household, he also could easily have been aware of what
Alex was looking for. He would have keys to the house and
his own code. He was a familiar sight in the house, doing
minor repairs as well as caring for the grounds. How hard
would it be for him to get the access code to the library?
Not very, in my opinion. Vera's security system was designed
to circumvent outsiders, not staff.

There was so much to think about. Was Brian the connection with Karen Smith? Had he been selling off collectible books to the Cozy Corpse? Had Alex figured it out?
Had Alex then spoken to Karen? Perhaps he'd found other
items from Vera's collection in Karen's shop or on her online
catalog. Good-bye Alex. And later, almost good-bye Karen.
It was all falling into place. Brian must have been the person
who had picked up the box from Alex's parents. He could
have faked the call from Vera to the Fines and the Van Alst
number would have shown up on thier phone. He might even
have a red truck, although I'd only noticed a battered old
Dodge sedan. But what to do now that I had this information? I figured if I knocked on Vera's door again, that would
be the last straw for my position here. At any rate, I realized
I needed more.

First I had to confirm whether he had a limp. Vera and
the signora had both reacted strangely when I'd mentioned
that limp. They would have a lot of trouble believing that a
long-term, trusted employee was a violent criminal. I had
already made an unfair and wrong accusation against Miss
Orsini, the physio, and Eddie too, of course.

I would have to get my facts straight before I approached
anyone about this. I wasn't likely to get proof at this time of
night.

I decided to let my practical side rule. I stuck the stack of Grants and the notebooks back where I'd found them. I took a hard look at the dumbwaiter.

No one knew the money and notebooks were there. They'd be safe for another few hours. And anyway, there'd been no sign of anyone even attempting to get into my garret, if you didn't count that cat. Even the signora had been kept out by the sliding lock.

I pushed the little walnut dresser back, blocking the access to the dumbwaiter. I headed for my small (and totally unnecessary) kitchen and collected all the pots.

Next stop, my entrance. I pushed the rolltop desk in front of the door and placed my small collection of cooking pots on top of it. Someone might find a way to get in, but not without waking me up.

I really needed to get some rest. I couldn't cope with a second sleepless night. But first, I called Tiff back.

"I've been chewing my nails," she snapped.

"You won't believe this," I said, filling her in on the cat, the dumbwaiter, the loot and the notes. "But the most important thing is that I think I might really know who is behind it."

"This is like one crazy action movie. Spill."

"If anything happens to me—"

"Nothing better happen to you, because you better be calling the police."

"No police just yet."

"Oh, come on."

"No, listen. If anything happens to me, and let me finish, the name to remember is Brian. Brian with the initial U for a last name. The gardener-handyman here is called Brian, and I believe he's the man with the limp."

"Police. Is that so hard to understand?"

"Here's the thing. I don't believe that Brian is acting alone, and I do know that Officer Smiley—"

"Oh, right, Officer Stalker. I forgot about him."

"Exactly, so until we know for sure, I will rely on my uncles."

"Who are out of town?"

"Just for tonight. And I won't do anything until tomorrow. Then I'll try to flush him out."

"With the uncles as backup?"

"You got it."

"How do I know that you'll be safe tonight?"

"Because he or they can't get in here. Because he or they don't know about the money and notebooks. And because he or they don't know I suspect him or them. Plus, I've got a dead bolt on the door and pots piled in front of it. I'm all right. In fact, I might be in more danger from the dual cat situation."

I left a message for my uncles suggesting they have a word with a Brian U if anything happened to me.

And of course, I set the alarm clock.

Tomorrow would be a busy day.

CHAPTER NINETEEN

BREAKFAST WAS WARM flaky croissants with a selection of homemade preserves and the usual very good espresso. I tried strawberry, raspberry and blueberry jams along with my croissants. That's right. Two croissants two of them. The signora fluttered around nervously, adding more pots of more jams and honey too. Her cries of "Eat, eat!" seemed a little more subdued today.

Vera glowered at me from across the conservatory table.

I smiled at her and raised my coffee cup.

"Miss Bingham. I do not want a repeat of last night's outrageous accusations against Miss Orsini. Nor will I tolerate you targeting other people. Get working to find the manuscript and discover what happened to my, um, resources, or find yourself a new position."

"My apologies," I said falsely. "I didn't sleep the night before, and I think I was not thinking at all clearly. I will keep my mind on my main task. It won't happen again."

She grunted and returned to the *New York Times* crossword puzzle.

I had to assume that was a good thing.

The signora refilled my cup. I guess she agreed.

"I have an idea what happened to your, um, resources and who has them," I said.

That got her attention.

"I'll be following up on it." I grinned. "I think you will be very pleased. I'll be off to the library right after breakfast to get my last few bits of information. Why, yes, signora. I think I will have another croissant."

The conservatory had great views of the east garden from three sides. I could see Brian working diligently putting collars on a cluster of droopy peonies near the front of the house.

I waved to him, but he didn't see me.

SHORTLY AFTERWARD, ALLEGEDLY on my way to the library, I took a stroll around the property. I first went along the endless corridor and out the front door and approached Brian from that side. Before he spotted me, I watched him move on to the next garden bed, where he stopped for a minute. There was no question now that this was the man with the limp. Too bad he picked that moment to turn around and spot me. Luckily, my relatives are accomplished liars and I've learned from the masters.

"Brian," I called out. He stared and stopped moving. I smiled and strolled casually toward him. "I've been admiring the peonies. They're my favorite flower. Everyone in my family has a brown thumb. I hope that once I get settled, I can learn a bit about gardening from you." Now where had that come from?

He nodded. "Okay. Someday."

"Well, if Vera doesn't fire me first."

"She's not easy."

"She certainly is not," I said. I glanced at the peonies, pink, white and fuchsia. "They are gorgeous. Well, Vera has sent me off to the library. See you later. Don't forget, I want those lessons."

I felt his eyes on my back as I headed briskly for my parking space. I glanced around as I reached my car. Brian's battered and dusty Dodge was on one side of my Saab. I tried the passenger door to the Dodge. Brian must not have felt he had much to worry about. He didn't lock his doors. I bent down and opened the glove compartment. Sure enough, there was his vehicle registration. Brian Underwood. Brian U. The address was 43A Magnolia Lane, Harrison Falls, New York.

Just as I got into the Saab, he rounded the corner of the house and leaned against the wall. He watched me, eyes narrowed as I waved and drove away.

The library didn't open until ten. That gave me plenty of time to drive by 43A Magnolia Lane. It was a ten-minute drive to an area of rundown semis and scrubby properties. The streets all had flowery names, but the neighborhood had dropped its petals. I cruised along slowly, checking things out. Unlike the houses on either side of it, 43A was pristine and well painted. The lawn was well maintained, and the peonies were doing just fine. A red Ford pickup sat in the driveway, and I thought I spotted another car behind it. I imagined the curtains twitching in every house as I crawled by. I even thought I spotted a shadowy presence in the window of 43A.

As I pulled away, I noticed something in my rearview mirror. Damn. A cop car and a familiar face. But Officer Tyler Dekker didn't seem to be smiling.

My plan was to drop by Sal's. But I didn't want Officer Smiley to know that. I led him through every part of Harrison Falls, up and down residential streets and then toward the roundabout into the downtown area. I am quite sure that he'd begun to get bored when I rounded a corner just ahead of him and made a very sharp right turn. Next I shot down one of the few alleys in our town. I turned left and shot back up the next one, spotting the rear end of the black-and-white swinging down the first alley just as I turned right again and sped along to Uncle Mick's shop. It was closed today as the uncles were still out of town. But I had the keys. Five minutes later, with the Saab parked in full view in front of the shop, I was off in the very useful black Focus. I'd grabbed a baseball cap (Blue Ridge Diner) as insurance. We all look alike in them.

Sal agreed to meet me earlier than usual. He raised an elegant eyebrow at the baseball cap. It was clear that he didn't approve. Sal likes his women straight out of 1959.

"Necessary deception," I said.

"What can I do for you?" Sal said, once we were seated in the green leather chairs. I could feel the receptionist's puzzled glances as she watched me.

"Brian Underwood. He is Vera Van Alst's gardener and handyman. I need to know who he associates with and if there's a criminal connection. In fact, I need to know all his connections. Family. Friends. Neighbors. History. He had an injury at one time or a medical condition. I could probably find out myself if I had time, but I am in a necessary hurry. I appreciate your help. Lives are at stake."

"What do you know about this person?"

"I believe he is capable of murder."

Sal frowned. "I will see what I can find out. But you should be careful, Jordan. You told me once you wanted a quiet life of books, not your uncles' more exciting lifestyle. If this man is capable of murder, how will you keep yourself safe?"

"I have a plan. Of course, I hope I don't need it."

"Why don't you leave it to me?"

Well, because I didn't know where that would lead. Because there was a satchel of unaccounted-for money in my garret. Because I didn't mind getting some information from a less-than-pure source, but I didn't want Sal "solving" the problem. I certainly didn't want people to start disappearing. Even the people who frightened me. I had a legal plan.

"I will, for sure, if this doesn't work. Thanks, Sal."

I left shortly after, wondering if I should add "Big Fat Liar" to my résumé.

WHAT I NEEDED was proof. I seemed to be the only person who'd even seen the man with the limp. I knew he was connected with Karen, but I was more and more convinced he'd been involved in Alex's death. There was one way to get some information about that: watch images. Why hadn't I thought of that earlier? I took a detour to switch the Focus for the Saab and ditch the baseball cap until I needed it.

Next stop: the library.

But the magnificent Lance wasn't on duty. That was the bad news. The good news was that I found him lounging against his bicycle at the back door of the Van Alst mansion when I got home. By some miracle, he'd scored a couple of lattes from Café Hudson and transported them, along with his laptop, on his bike and with his mobile Internet stick in his pocket. Impressive. I wasn't so shy about letting Lance hug me.

"Need my help?" he said into the top of my head.

"How did you know?"

"Tiff called me."

We both laughed. Tiff was always looking out for her friends. We were lucky to be among them. Then I realized we'd better get inside. I wanted to get Lance's perspective on everything that I'd compiled, but I really didn't want Brian to spot him.

Lance was laboring under no such paranoia. He looked around as we walked to my door, admiring the scenery, sniffing the air, taking it all in and never spilling a drop of those lattes.

Once the door shut, I was all business.

He said, "This house is amazing. Would you call it Scottish baronial style? Can I have the tour?"

"First we need to confirm a murderer. I promise you, it will be much more exciting than a tour of the back corridors."

His eyes gleamed. "Confirm a murderer. From the minute I met you, Jordan Bingham, I knew you were trouble."

"No flirting. You're going to need that laptop." I had my own but needed Lance's skills as an online researcher and his keen eye for details and his large high-quality screen.

"And you really need to see what I've turned up on YouTube. It's going to blow you away." As we hurried up the stairs to the garret, I tried to bring him up to speed on the strange events of the past few days. Had it only been days? I ran my various theories past Lance, ending with the events involving Brian U, aka the man with the limp.

"Wow, that's a lot of information to take in." We both sat cross-legged on the wide plank floor, with the laptops on the Lucite coffee table. I took a deep breath. "Okay, I guess I'd better watch that video with you."

He said, "Prepare yourself. It's heartbreaking to watch, but not gory. You can't see Alex afterward. But it is upsetting. Are you sure?"

"I'm in."

The cat's claws caught me by surprise. Lance was very sweet about the latte I spilled down the front of his Abercrombie and Fitch button-down. What a guy. It took a while to settle down again.

When we did, the grainy video gave me the willies. A stooped man in what looked like rags stumbled up behind Alex and pushed him hard, snatching at his satchel at the same time. Alex was there one second and then gone the next while Ashley stared openmouthed. The ragged man elbowed his way past the surging crowd and out of sight. "I can't believe what people will record and post. Gruesome," Lance said.

We played every clip we could find over and over. Each time, Lance winced when the arms shot out, sending Alex sailing onto the tracks. Each time, tiny grainy people ran down the stairs and flocked to the edge of the platform, while Ashley swayed, shocked and screaming.

"That is hard to watch, but we still don't have the proof that it's Brian. I need to see that guy move."

"Give me a minute." Lance's magic fingers danced on the keyboard until he'd located a few more clips and stills of Alex Fine's horrible death. "I think I have something."

I stared at the screen as the shambling ragged man made for the stairs, clutching the satchel. Some quick-thinking person had captured that on a grainy video. A few people tried to stop him, and there was nothing weak or incapacitated in the way he fought them off. But he was clearly limping as he mounted the staircase, pausing to kick at a lone pursuer before vanishing.

"It's Brian. I know it. Download the subway footage, okay?"

"All taken care of."

My heart was thumping in my chest. "At least we have something real to show the cops, not just theories."

He said, "What do we do now? Call the police?"

"Better. We're going to take it straight to Detective Zinger over in Grandville. But first, we're going to show Vera."

"What a way to meet the terrifying Vera Van Alst," Lance said, pointing to his latte-stained shirt.

"Here, I'll get you a T-shirt." I rummaged through the bottom drawer of the walnut dresser. "I'm afraid this will have to do." I held out a *Twilight* T-shirt that said, "I like boys who sparkle" in glitter. Uncle Danny was a huge *Twilight* fan. It was not his best Christmas purchase.

Lance said, "But . . ."

I said, "No time to be a fashionista."

Lance headed to the bathroom to get cleaned up. I said, "I'll go on ahead and find Vera and the signora. They have to see this. It's almost lunchtime. They'll be in the conservatory. At the bottom of the stairs turn left. Take the corridor past the kitchen and go through the dining room. You can't miss it.

My skin was still tingling from the excitement of our find (and maybe a bit from Lance) as I headed down the stairs with the laptop with the image still on the screen.

I'd just turned into the east corridor when I heard the back door creak open. I whirled. Brian stared at me and then at the laptop screen. Could he tell what I had? Was he aware that I knew? Apparently yes. I felt a boom as he smashed my head into the wall. After a shocked second, I screamed. He snatched the laptop before it could hit the floor.

Where was Lance? Studying his handsome face in the mirror?

Brian's normally pleasant features were pinched in rage as he stared at the laptop screen. I backed down the hall away from him as fast as I could. "Brian, what are you doing?"

"I'm putting an end to your snooping."

Playing for time, I stammered, "I don't know what you're talking about." Surely someone must have heard my scream.

"You think I'm stupid? Just 'cause I didn't go to some fancy college like you? Just because Vera doesn't pay me what she pays you to chase after her useless books?" He was thundering closer. The coveralls he wore still smelled like fresh-cut grass. I'd never smell that again without shuddering. "You think you're better than me?" His hands gripped my biceps. With every word, he shook me violently. I did my best to keep backing up.

"I don't think you are stupid!" *I think you're terrifying.*

He grabbed my neck, whipped me around and started to squeeze. At the same time, he was pushing me toward the cupboard. A good place to dump a body. Little black dots swam in my eyes, getting thicker, closing in.

I caught a movement by the back door. Eddie. Was Eddie in on it after all? I was being slowly dragged by my neck. Where was Lance?

I heard Uncle Mick, my self-defense teacher, shouting in my head. Fight! Feet! Eyes! Groin! Was I screaming that out loud?

My hands clawed wildly at my attacker's eyes. He roared in pain but didn't let go of me. Letting one hand leave my neck, he groped for the knob with me struggling and scratching. As I gasped the air into my burning lungs, my vision cleared, for a second.

This is your only chance.

Brian swung the door open and tried to drag me into the closet by my throat. I gasped just enough air to function. His feet were safe in those work boots, but I drove one kitten heel into his shin and caught him off guard. He loosened his grip on me and bellowed.

Hoping there was a witness, I screamed, "You attacked Karen Smith, you killed Alex Fine!"

"Yeah, I did and now I'm going to kill you too." He snarled and lunged again. The cat that dashed in front of him was just the distraction I needed.

Using all my skills, I aimed for his eyes and missed. His hands flew to his damaged nose. I turned and ran. As I raced by the kitchen door, I heard a clang. I turned to see the signora standing over Brian with a cast iron frying pan.

"No, no, no!" she said.

Lance arrived breathing hard, because he was shaking with laughter. "Feet! Eyes! Groin!" he croaked.

Brian didn't stay down long. He was smart enough to make a break for it. He lurched toward the back door. He made good time for a man with a limp who had just been beaned with a frying pan.

"Call 911, Lance!" I rushed after Brian, even though I didn't really want to catch this maniac. But by the time I reached the door, Brian lay facedown in the pea gravel. No sound. No movement. Eddie stood over him, a shovel gripped in his fists. Vera rolled slowly forward toward the open door, brandishing a fire poker. She looked disappointed that she wouldn't have to use it.

Somewhere a cat yowled.

THE HARRISON FALLS Police were puzzled, but Detective Zinger of the Grandville force seemed satisfied in his deadpan way. Why not? It would clear up the Karen Smith case without a tap of work on his part. Once he could lay charges, that is. Of course, the Harrison Falls guys might make a solid case for attempted murder and theft. So it was a good day all round.

The main thing was that Karen Smith would be safe, I was alive and Brian Underwood was in custody and would probably be charged with Alex's murder as well, although that was yet another jurisdiction. It was all coming together.

VERA AND THE signora were both a bit glum at dinner, the signora uncharacteristically quiet and Vera dead white. Served them right for trying to shield Brian when I was asking about the man with the limp. I, on the other hand, felt elated over Brian's arrest. Hungry too.

Vera had trouble dealing with Brian's guilt. "I suppose," she said with a glower, "that he'll get bail sooner or later. I don't intend to post it for him. What a betrayal."

Betrayal? That was an understatement. I said, "If he gets bail, I'm out of this house, and I think you should be too. He has keys. He has access. He's vicious. He hates you. He hates Eddie. He hates me. Signora Panetone is the only one who might get out alive. Although after that frying pan, that's not a sure thing either."

"Eat," the signora said sadly.

"Sure thing." I was happy to accept the heaping plate of veal scaloppini in white wine sauce. It went beautifully with the linguine, and I tried not to wonder what pan she'd used. Eddie had joined us for the first time.

I don't know why I waited to tell Vera about the pile of Grants. Was there just too much Kelly in me? Did I want to hang on to the loot for just a bit longer? I was trying to come to grips with what should be done with it. The money was Vera's. But so many people had been damaged by this, that I couldn't help but think it would be fair to share it with them. What about Karen? With her terrible injury, would she ever be able to go back to the Cozy Corpse? Then there were the Fines, who had lost their only son and would always be grieving. Of course, Ashley had lost her fiancé and been attacked. Didn't these people deserve something? I was considering a Robin Hood routine: depositing serious stacks of fifties in each of their mailboxes.

But those thoughts reminded me that I needed to call Ashley and tell her that the man who'd killed Alex was now in custody. Of course, the no cell phone rule at dinner was still observed, no matter what.

AFTER DINNER I took a stroll on the grounds and finally answered the four thousand frantic texts from Tiff: *First, I'm okay. Second, I hope you have time for a chat. It may be an expensive call. Luckily, I found 50 grand in my apartment, so the call is on me. Talk in an hour. XO*

Pressing send, I laughed at the thought of Tiff pulling her hair out with curiosity.

Then I gave Ashley a call. The garden was gorgeous. It was hard to believe that all this beauty had been maintained by someone who had such a vicious character. I reminded myself that people are not always what they seem. As I expected, Ashley was very emotional when she heard the news. I gave her time to pull herself together. "Are you okay?"

"Yes. Sorry. Tell me everything again."

"The man who killed Alex and attacked Karen is Brian Underwood. He works for Vera Van Alst."

She gasped. "Was she behind everything?"

"Not at all. She's a victim too. He did it to get to her originally."

I heard her blow her nose. "Sorry, sorry. It just came as a surprise. But will they be able to prove that he did it?"

"He gave himself away in front of five witnesses today."

There was a long pause, and I imagined the expression on Ashley's battered face as she struggled to get her head around what this would mean. Finally she said in a choking voice, "I can't believe it."

"It's good news, Ashley. I think that Brian Underwood was probably the man who attacked you too, even though in the shock of the moment it was hard to get a good look at him."

"I didn't really see his face."

"And I think that we will find out more about what really happened. Police from three forces will be grilling him. He'll already be facing very serious charges in the attack on Karen Smith. Along with Alex's death, this guy is not going to see the light of day."

"Jordan, I have to get off the phone. I feel very emotional."

I couldn't quite keep the excitement out of my voice. "There may be news about the missing money too. I'll fill you in when I know more. I hope to see you soon."

"You will. I promise."

I WAS IN such a good mood that when I headed upstairs, I invited both cats back to my cabbage rose heaven. I had decided that I wouldn't deal with what to do with the money until the next morning. I was looking forward to an excellent night's sleep. I was going to need that to make the best decision about the Grants, which might not be the same as the right decision. I had just finished straightening up the walnut dresser and putting away my pot-and-pan alarm system when my iPhone buzzed across the room. I almost didn't get the call from Sal in time.

Sal didn't give his name. And I was pretty sure he wasn't phoning from any source that could be traced to him. "I tried to reach you," he said. "It kept going to message."

"Sorry. It's a rule at dinner here. And I had to make an important call. I haven't had a chance to check my messages yet. Been a crazy, crazy day."

Sal said, "So, Jordan, regarding the matter we discussed earlier. The individual involved I understand is detained and rightly so. The local cops think they'll clear up a number of crimes with this. I hear he became very violent. I hope that you weren't injured."

"Just my pride. And my bruised neck and arms."

"On that matter, if you still need the information about Brian Underwood, there is no indication that he had any business connections at all."

I figured business was code. "None?"

"Just the people he worked with. I believe those are the same connections you have. Van Alst, a Signora Panetone, and the postal worker, Eddie McRae."

"No surprise there."

"I am told that this Brian Underwood was injured in the same pileup that put your employer in a wheelchair for life. He lost his football scholarship. For some reason, your employer was covered by the right kind of insurance. Brian Underwood was not. Haven't got all the details yet. She offered him a job afterward. Felt guilty, I guess."

"So that's it. Vera and her staff were all he had?"

"And his family."

"Family?"

"Ex-wife, Martina, lives down in Albany. Remarried twenty years ago, to a Robert Snell."

I felt my throat constrict. "Snell?"

"Yes. Mean anything?"

I had to ask the question that Agatha would have expected much earlier. "Was there a child?"

"One daughter."

"Ashley," I said. "And let me guess, she took her step-father's name but later reconciled with her biological father."

"Oh, you knew that already."

"No, but I wish that I had. I am putting two and two together. Thanks, Sal. Now I need to figure out what to do about her. She knows that I was responsible for her father's arrest and yet she said nothing about the relationship."

"Why would you tell her this?"

"I feel so stupid. I didn't know she was his daughter. I never suspected her for a minute."

"I thought you had the Kelly touch."

"She completely snowed me, Sal. She has her grieving-victim routine down. I can't believe I fell for her misdirections. I bet she used an orange-in-a-sock trick to fake all those injuries. Uncle Mick told me about a guy who tried to scam his insurance that way once."

Sal said, "This seems like a very unpleasant way to earn a living."

"You should see her face, Sal. You'd never suspect her for a second. You'd never think a person would do that to herself."

"So why would she?"

"To fool anyone who was looking into it, in case they found something that implicated her. Probably in case she was suspected in the attack on Karen. She reported her attack to the police. She had an alibi: the emergency room. That put her in the clear. When I started asking questions about Karen, Ashley played me to find out what I was doing and thinking. A good plan, on her part."

Sal's voice dropped into the bass range, a sign that he was taking this very seriously. "Jordan, she is dangerous. Keep yourself safe."

"I will. I'm at the Van Alst house in my third-floor apartment. Vera has very good security." As the words were out of my mouth, I realized how foolish they were. If Brian had a key and the code, Ashley would have had them too. She knew where the garret was. She knew I was in it. "You know what? Maybe I'll spend the night at Uncle Mick's. He and Lucky should be back in this evening."

"You're vulnerable. I'll send someone over."

I hated to think how much goodwill I would owe Sal after this. "Thanks. I'll go pack now."

"Twenty minutes," Sal said. "I'm making the call."

I was tossing a few items into my orange satchel when the knock came. I had just decided that the money was safe where it was for the time being.

I left my bed and stared at my entrance door. Luckily I'd bolted it. Force of habit. *Bang, bang.*

"Dessert! You eat. Eat! Yes. Yes."

I sagged with relief. I was too knotted up to eat anything, but I knew the signora wouldn't give up. Might as well take the dessert with me. There would be a mountain of it. My uncles might find it a welcome change from violent green Jell-O or Pop-Tarts.

I unlocked the door and opened it.

"Signora," I said with a smile. The smile didn't last. "Ashley?"

My mind whirled. What was she doing here? Had I missed a call saying she was coming? And why had she pretended to be the signora? It wasn't like she had much of a sense of humor. One good thing: she didn't know that I knew who she was. No one could say this wasn't a complicated situation.

"Going somewhere?" she said, stepping past me.

"Yes, I'm going to see my uncles. Nice Signora Panetone impression. Priceless."

"Alex used to do it all the time. I guess I picked it up."

"Of course." I had to make her believe I had no idea that Brian was her father and that she herself had been an accomplice to murder and assault. "I would have loved that dessert."

She sneered. "No dessert for you."

"Make yourself comfortable, Ashley. I'm just packing a few things. Uncle Mick will be here shortly." Could I stall her until I had a good plan? Or any plan.

"Quit bluffing. We need to talk about Alex," she said, moving toward me.

"What? Bluffing about what?"

"Cut the crap. You know what I mean."

"I don't. And I have to get my stuff ready."

I backed toward the bedroom and my only chance of getting help. How long would it take for Sal's "someone" to arrive? The window was open. If I could yell loud enough, maybe he'd hear me. Who was I kidding? Whoever the someone was, he'd be sitting behind closed tinted-glass windows, bored out of his gourd. There was no hope that Vera, sequestered in her second-floor suite, would hear me shouting, but maybe the signora was still around. Or Eddie.

"Don't even think about it," she said, following me right into the bedroom.

"What is wrong with you, Ashley?"

"Didn't I tell you to cut the crap? See the gun in my hand?"

I did. It looked like a Smith & Wesson semiautomatic, but I could have been wrong. Guns are not my best thing.

"So, you've managed to get Brian locked up. You think you're pretty smart, but I am smarter. You are going to tell me where the money is."

"I don't have the money, Ashley."

"You found where Alex stashed it."

"I'm sorry to disappoint you, but if you couldn't find the money, why do you think I would be able to?"

"Because it must be here. He never went anywhere but his parents' place, my apartment and book fairs."

"It's not at his parents' place," I said. "I checked that out. I was looking for notebooks and research information, but I couldn't find anything."

"He hid it here."

"Why don't you give it your"—I stopped myself before I said "best shot." "Maybe you'll have more success than I did." My Kelly lying genes weren't enough to do the trick this time.

"You think you're so smart, but you let it slip when you talked to me earlier."

"I don't have it yet, but I hope to find it. We can share the proceeds when it turns up."

"I don't believe you."

"Ashley, I'm sorry you got your hopes up. I think he must have deposited it in a bank somewhere. Perhaps the bank card will turn up."

That was a stretch. I knew, and I hoped she didn't, that if you deposit more than ten thousand dollars, it triggers a bank report.

"He wouldn't do that," she sneered. "He wasn't stupid."

"Oh, well. He could have opened a few accounts, each of them less than—"

"Bad for you then. I'm going to shoot you somewhere very painful. Then maybe you'll talk."

I thought I spotted a slight movement behind her in the living area. Maybe Ashley was going to shoot me, but someone was going to get an earful before that happened.

I said, "You had me fooled for a while with your descriptions of Eddie as the man seen talking to Karen Smith. Did you set him up to show up at the hospital when your father tried to smother Karen? Nicely played."

She smirked.

I said, "And making sure that I knew the man who attacked you didn't have a limp; that really threw me off. It was all very clever. Still, you must have been disappointed to find out that the money was gone after Alex was killed. What a waste."

Her face twisted. The hands holding the gun shook. "He wasn't supposed to die. He wasn't supposed to struggle. He was just supposed to be knocked down and the satchel was supposed to be stolen."

"Brilliant. You could have kept Alex as your boyfriend and the money. Vera would have lost her investment. That was the whole point with your father, wasn't it? To get back at Vera."

That took her by surprise. "You know about my father?"

By this time it seemed like a good idea to let her think the whole world knew. "I'm not the only one, Ashley. As they say in the movies, you won't get away with this."

"But you're wrong, I will."

"Sorry. Too many people know."

"They'll have to prove it then. No good for you, because you might be dead if you don't tell me where the money is."

And just as dead if I did.

"Did you and Brian panic when I called from Karen's place? Did you think that I might be on to you? Is that why you decided to blacken your eyes? To throw me off the scent? Or did your father do that to you?"

"My father would never hurt me! He loves me."

"Well, you know he's going to get life. Legal fees will eat up everything, including Vera's money, which by the way, I really don't have. And as for you, it won't take much for the prosecution to demonstrate that you were the one who knew something about the book business, that you made a play for Alex when he began to work for Vera. He was shy and socially awkward, and he fell into your trap."

"That's not true! I loved him."

"Maybe, but you used him to extort money from Vera

and because you did that he is dead. You were the one with the brains and connections to make this happen. You invented Merlin and sold Alex on the idea. Your father's obsessive hatred was just the fuel. My guess is it started with Brian stealing books and you finding buyers for them. You were in a perfect position to do that. Then Brian wanted to go bigger. Really do her some damage? Or was it your idea?"

Keep her talking.

"He lost his job, his health and his sports scholarship because of her. Vera Van Alst ruined his marriage, ruined our lives. I would have been happy if she'd died. But the fact that she was greedy enough and stupid enough to pay that amount of money for a play that was a figment of my imagination, well that was just beautiful. She could have shared her insurance money with my father after the accident, but all she did was make him a garden slave. He didn't deserve that."

"Until Alex was killed."

"I said that was an accident."

"And did Karen Smith need to be eliminated because she figured out your involvement?"

"I heard her leaving you that message when I was dropping off supplies at Yummers. Saying she was worried and mentioning something of concern to your employer. That had to be about the books from Vera's collection. I knew that it was a mistake for Brian to sell them to a local dealer. I could tell by looking at Karen that she'd put it together. I called Brian and he said that he'd take care of her right away."

I shrugged. "Doesn't matter because you are going down."

"And you are going to your grave."

"Might as well be comfortable." I plunked myself down on the bed and leaned against the pillow. From the far end of the bed, the two cats watched with interest.

I hoped like hell that whoever was out in the living room had gone for help.

"If I give it to you, will you let me live? The money isn't mine, so I would be considered a co-conspirator. No one would believe my story about finding it."

"Where did you find it?"

"Will you let me live?"

"Of course I will," Ashley said with a fake smile.

"All right," I said.

She moved closer, eyes gleaming.

I waited until she got close enough for my purposes. That was close enough to see that the safety was off, not a good thing. The bronze was still under the pillow, and it was my only possible hope.

"It's just like you put your tooth for the tooth fairy," I said idiotically. "Under my pillow. You can take it all, but you have to let me go, Ashley."

She said, "You are just toying with me. I'm looking forward to getting rid of you. I am going to take that money, and I am going to watch you die."

I'd had no idea this girl was so vicious and angry. Not for the first time, I thanked my uncles for teaching me to look unafraid and think on my feet no matter how bad the situation. My knees were wobbling. I could hear the thunder of my heart. My mouth was dry.

Ashley lunged toward me, quickly. Too quickly.

Bad Cat hates sudden moves. He reached out an elegant set of claws and raked her thigh.

Shocked, Ashley shrieked and whirled.

Bad Cat licked his paw. I dove for the bronze under the pillow. With the statue in my hand, I faced her. The trouble was I lacked whatever it would take to hit a human being in the head or even the hand with a heavy metal object. Karen's injuries kept playing in my mind.

"What are you going to do with that?" she mocked. "A stupid statue against a gun?"

"This," I said, whacking that gun. It flew across the room,

hitting the floor with just enough force for it to go off. We both dove for it. I managed to butt heads with her as we tussled. I had the advantage as I still had the use of both my hands.

My ears were ringing as I struggled to my feet. I gripped the gun and pointed it at her. "Stand up and move back."

"You won't shoot me," she sneered. "You can't."

"I believe you are wrong about that," I said.

A voice came from the door to the living area. "Maybe she won't shoot you, but I can and I will."

Ashley's eyes widened as she turned to face Officer Smiley. Except he wasn't smiling now.

He said, "Just so you realize, Jordan, I wouldn't have let her shoot you."

"Good to know," I said.

"I am really sorry you got mixed up in all this. I tried to keep an eye on you when I was tracking Ashley and her father, but you sure make it hard. Anyway, when I followed her here tonight, I knew this was serious and I had to rescue you."

"You didn't rescue me, I rescued myself. You just saved me from shooting this little murderer. I'm thankful for that." I was grateful that he was holding his police-issued Glock on Ashley and especially happy that I didn't have to find out the hard way whether I would have shot Ashley.

But he wasn't done. He had a few words for Ashley. "So, Ashley. You killed my friend, a fine, decent guy that I cared about. He really loved you and you used him. Now I'm going to make sure that you go down for it. I'll be attending your trial every day, even if I have to quit my job, just so I sit and watch your face."

I was pretty sure that as a witness he wouldn't be allowed to attend the trial when others were testifying. But, of course, I only knew that bit of procedure because of my unsavory family connections. That was another thought I kept to myself.

"You can't prove it," she sputtered. Whatever you could say about her, she was no quitter.

"That's what tape is for, Ashley."

I for one hoped that as well as getting it on tape, he had called for backup. This girl was a tiger.

"As long as you called it in," I said meaningfully.

He grinned.

Ashley had started to wail. "I didn't do anything, you stupid, nosy cow."

I don't know who was more astonished, Officer Smiley or me or the guy in the dark shirt and tie with the gelled hair who appeared in the door behind Smiley. I supposed that the sound of the Smith & Wesson going off had been enough to get his attention behind the tinted window of whatever dark sedan he was driving. Of course, he wouldn't know who Smiley was. This could take another turn for the worse.

I shook my head. He frowned.

"Thanks so much, Officer Dekker. I am so glad you followed Ashley. Did you say backup is—?"

"On its way."

Sal's someone disappeared faster than a Siamese cat on a mission. I gave a sigh of relief. Sal's information had saved my life. I didn't want to have it end badly for him and whoever he'd sent to protect me.

Ashley still wasn't done.

"You can't prove that I did anything. I had nothing to do with Alex being murdered."

"We'll get you on conspiracy, theft, and obstructing a police investigation and half a dozen other offenses. We're just getting started. You were involved in the commission of a felony. That means you'll be culpable in Alex's death, Karen's attack and death threats against Miss Bingham here. Welcome to the justice system," Officer Dekker said. No smile this time.

CHAPTER TWENTY

❧

I FACED VERA across the breakfast table in the conservatory. Today's special was fragrant fresh sweet rolls. I knew
that there'd be eggs to follow and who knew what else. "I
have your money."

She lifted her gaze from the *New York Times*. "I want it
back."

"I'm sure you do, but there are terms."

She roared. "What do you mean terms? It's my money."

"There's no real proof of that."

"My word is good enough."

"Sure, it's your word in addition to my four conditions."

"I said, no terms."

"Fine. I'll turn the cash over to the police. It will get tied
up as evidence for years as this is probably going to take a
long time to wind through the courts. Of course, there's no
proof it's yours, so they may never turn it over."

"You can't do that."

"Watch me." Not only would Vera hate having her money

tied up, but for reasons of pride and self-preservation, she also wouldn't want word to get out that she'd been ripped off.

I accepted a cup of espresso from the signora, who was uncharacteristically quiet. I smiled at her and told myself never to get on her bad side.

In the end Vera agreed to make a donation to a charity of Alex's parents' choice in his memory and to provide some financial assistance to Karen.

I said, "Third, from now on, you will treat me with respect."

She almost choked on my fourth and final condition.

TWO WEEKS LATER, the grand dining room was all done up for a festive occasion, something that had been missing in the Van Alst house for too many years. But no longer. The table was set for thirteen, and the dinner party was in full swing. Vera Van Alst was fulfilling condition number four, reluctantly, but so what. We had a lot to celebrate. The many things that some of our guests had to mourn were set aside for the evening.

The ornate Royal Crown Derby china gleamed in the softly glowing light from four large silver candelabras set with high beeswax tapers. I'd managed to hook up a small music system, which was now playing some soft background music, although conversation was drowning it out. I was feeling very party-like in my emerald-green vintage Christian Dior party dress with its deep and dramatic neckline and swirly skirt.

As part of condition number four (host a dinner and be pleasant and hospitable for the duration of the event), Vera was doing her best not to glower. I had presented her with a silk blouse in royal blue. It went with the china and flattered her skin tones. She'd seemed pleased. Cyndi from Scissors on Wheels! had styled her hair, and I had bullied her into wearing lipstick. I'd placed Uncle Mick next to her at the far end. I figured those were dollar signs and not stars in his eyes. Vera, like so many women before her, was smitten. Maybe it was the ginger eyebrows or the gold chain nestled in the chest hair. Whatever, Vera had ignored the eggplant, mint and hot pepper salad and the roast veggie and farro salad. I can attest that both were fabulous. Eddie sat across from Mick, watching him like I might watch a tarantula. I'd put him there to be near Vera. I hadn't predicted that the Irish charm would work on her. Eddie wasn't used to being at the table, and now he was too heartsick to eat.

I felt bad about that, especially as I'd learned late in the game that his only reason for talking to Karen Smith at the book fair had been to find a special gift for Vera. Unrequited love. What can I say?

Speaking of Karen, she was finally well enough to go out. In fact we'd delayed the dinner until she could join us. She was still pale and rail thin, but even so, practically delirious to be invited to dinner at the Van Alst house. She also seemed tickled to be seated next to Detective Zinger, who was ostensibly there to question some witnesses and had been encouraged to stay to dinner. We wanted to avoid the appearance of a conflict.

The Fines were not completely comfortable with Vera, although they had come to accept that she wasn't responsible for Alex's death, or completely unfeeling about it. The donation in Alex's memory had done the trick. I'd placed Officer Tyler Dekker in between them. That had been a good seating choice.

Earlier I'd even considered inviting George and Jeannette Beckwith. I felt a bit guilty about suspecting them of complicity with "Merlin." But when I'd mentioned this to Karen, she reminded me that even if he was not guilty, George could be a serious jerk.

Signora Panetone swooped around the room in her glory. She had reluctantly agreed to us hiring some help to serve, but she'd made every mouthful herself. A lot of food would be eaten. The main course was game birds with a creamy garlicky polenta. Uncle Lucky stared at it with suspicion. What kind of can had this come from? He'd barely recovered from the risotto with saffron and mussels. Seated next to him, Miss Orsini, who was almost as quiet as Lucky, leaned over and whispered an explanation. I'd only invited the physiotherapist because I felt guilty about my false accusation, but it was already paying off in Uncle Lucky's continuing education.

Walter was parked next to Lucky, glancing meaningfully at his red dog bowl. The signora had already fed him at least once, but dogs are always optimistic that there will be more. Both cats stared daggers at him from their entitled perch on the priceless sideboard.

Karen leaned across the table and said to Uncle Lucky, "You don't know how grateful I am that you are willing to keep Walter. The doctor has said it might take months for me to fully recover, and I was so afraid I would have to send him to a shelter. This is a huge weight off my mind."

Uncle Lucky flinched at the word "shelter." Walter stared bug-eyed. Lucky uncle and lucky dog.

A hiss was clearly heard from the sideboard. Can't please everyone.

I was shoulder to shoulder (and knee to knee) with Lance, a payoff itself. It wasn't how I'd devised the seating, but someone had switched my hand-lettered place cards. And across from me I had a fine view of the baby blues and blushing cheeks of Officer Tyler "Smiley" Dekker and the Fines doting on him. Mrs. Fine was saying, "We hope you will be able to join us for Christmas dinner this year. We would like that so much."

At the end of the table, to my right, in my usual place, was the empty chair for our symbolic guest, Agatha Christie, the Queen of Crime.

Once the *torta di miele* and custard were served and

twelve small glasses of Limoncello filled, I stood. "I'd like to make a toast to Agatha Christie, without whose guidance and ideas Brian Underwood and Ashley Snell would have gotten away with murder. I never thought I'd be wrapped up in a mystery like Poirot and Miss Marple."

Everyone rose, even Vera. Glasses were raised.

"To Agatha!"

"Eat!" the signora thundered.

And of course, we did.

RECImPES

—◄•►—

Signora Panetone's Mushroom Risotto

1 onion, finely chopped
2 tablespoons chopped fresh Italian parsley
1 clove garlic, finely chopped
2 tablespoons butter
⅛ cup dried porcini mushrooms, soaked in warm water
    for a half hour, drained and liquid reserved
1½ cups Arborio rice (or other short-grain Italian rice)
3½ to 4 cups boiling hot chicken stock (can use vegetable
    stock)
½ pound mushrooms, sliced
2–3 tablespoons fresh Parmesan, grated

Sauté the onion, parsley and garlic in one tablespoon of butter until soft (and onion is translucent).

Dry the porcini, then chop porcini and add to the other ingredients. Add rice and stir. Do not allow it to brown!

Add the stock slowly, by half cups. Stir and allow the rice to absorb the liquid. Keep stirring. Risotto is all about the stirring. Luckily, it's good exercise. When the rice is half-cooked (around ten minutes) add the reserved liquid and the sliced mushrooms. Stir for another ten minutes or until rice is soft and the mushrooms are tender. Do not overcook or your rice will be mushy.

Remove from heat and add the rest of the butter and the cheese.

Let it stand for about five minutes and serve.

SIGNORA PANETONE'S TRADITIONAL TUSCAN TOMATO AND BREAD SALAD (PANZANELLA)

2 large ripe tomatoes, cut into bite-sized pieces
1 small red onion, finely diced
1 clove garlic, very finely minced
1 cup fresh basil leaves, shredded (or rolled and sliced)
½ cup extra-virgin olive oil, plus more as needed
3 tablespoons red wine vinegar, plus more as needed
Salt and freshly ground black pepper, to taste
About eight slices thick country-style Italian bread or
    sourdough bread torn into bite-sized pieces. Bread
    should not be fresh! If it's too dry, soak it in water, and
    then squeeze dry.

In a bowl, combine the tomatoes, onion, garlic and basil. Drizzle with the half cup of olive oil and three tablespoons of vinegar, season with salt and pepper and toss well.

Place half of the bread in a wide, shallow bowl. Spoon half of the tomato mixture over the bread. Layer the remaining bread on top and then the remaining tomato mixture. Cover and refrigerate for at least one hour or until serving time. Just before serving, toss the salad and adjust the seasonings with salt and pepper. At this point the bread should have absorbed the water from the tomatoes. You can add a little bit of olive oil if necessary and toss well. Serve immediately.

Sometimes the signora likes to break with tradition and toss in some slices of buffalo mozzarella or other soft cheese or else one small cucumber, peeled and diced. Even though it is not part of the signora's family tradition, many people do add cukes, and she does like to change it up.

SIGNORA PANETONE'S CREAMY POLENTA
WITH GARLIC AND CHEESE

1 cup coarse yellow cornmeal, stone ground is best
3 cups chicken or vegetable broth
½ to 1 clove garlic, finely minced
¾ to 1 cup milk or cream (depending on your diet)
2 to 3 tablespoons freshly grated Parmesan cheese
Salt and pepper to taste
Butter or olive oil

In a bowl, mix cornmeal with one cup of cold broth and blend well. Bring remaining two cups to a boil add the mixture to it, slowly, stirring well as you go. Boil for three minutes (don't forget to stir), then add garlic and salt and pepper.

Reduce heat to medium low and cook until mixture pulls away from the sides of the pot. Stir in milk or cream. Cook until soft and creamy (10—20 minutes). Stir every now and then. Stir in cheese and adjust seasoning.

Serve like mashed potatoes, adding butter if you want or drizzle with very good extra-virgin olive oil.

Answering tricky reference questions is more than enough excitement for library director Lindsey Norris. That is, until another murder is committed in her cozy hometown of Briar Creek, Connecticut, and the question of who did it must be answered before someone else is checked out—for good.

FROM *NEW YORK TIMES* BESTSELLING AUTHOR

JENN MCKINLAY

DUE OR DIE

-A Library Lover's Mystery-

Carrie Rushton, the president of the Friends of the Library, has been accused of murdering her husband. The evidence is stacking up against Carrie, but neither Lindsey nor the Briar Creek crafternoon club is buying it.

When a nor'easter buries the small coastal town, the police are too busy digging out the locals to investigate the murder. With the help of her crafternoon friends and an abandoned puppy they name Heathcliff, Lindsey has to solve the question of who murdered Mr. Rushton before the killer closes the book on Carrie...

facebook.com/TheCrimeSceneBooks
penguin.com

M1148T0712